Readers love
JOHN INMAN

Ginger Snaps

"If you like light and fluffy with an HEA, you'll love the books in this series. I highly recommend you pick up this series if you haven't already."

—Love Bytes

"For those who need a dose of sweet humour that is effortlessly timed then this is the book for you."

—Gay Book Reviews

Laugh Cry Repeat

"*Laugh Cry Repeat* is a powerful story, a novel hard to forget for the themes it speaks of…"

—Scattered Thoughts and Rogue Words

"This story captivated me… A perfect finish and happy ever after."

—Open Skye Book Reviews

The Hike

"*The Hike* is one of my favorite stories of the year so far."

—Joyfully Jay

"Once again, John Inman assures his spot as a topnotch horror writer who uses a deft hand to weave in just enough romance to ease the tension and keep the reader on the edge of their seat."

—The Novel Approach

By JOHN INMAN

Acting Up
Chasing the Swallows
A Hard Winter Rain
Head-on
The Hike
Hobbled
Jasper's Mountain
Laugh Cry Repeat
Love Wanted
Loving Hector
My Busboy
My Dragon, My Knight
Nightfall
Paulie
Payback
The Poodle Apocalypse
Scrudge & Barley, Inc.
Shy
Spirit
Sunset Lake
Two Pet Dicks
Words

THE BELLADONNA ARMS
Serenading Stanley
Work in Progress
Coming Back
Ben and Shiloh
Ginger Snaps

Published by DREAMSPINNER PRESS
www.dreamspinnerpress.com

JOHN INMAN
NIGHTFALL

DREAMSPINNER
PRESS

Published by
DREAMSPINNER PRESS

5032 Capital Circle SW, Suite 2, PMB# 279, Tallahassee, FL 32305-7886 USA
www.dreamspinnerpress.com

Nightfall
© 2018 John Inman.

Cover Art
© 2018 Tiferet Design.
http://www.tiferetdesign.com/
Cover content is for illustrative purposes only and any person depicted on the cover is a model.

Trade Paperback ISBN: 978-1-64080-643-6
Digital ISBN: 978-1-64080-642-9
Library of Congress Control Number: 2018934231
Trade Paperback published September 2018
v. 1.0

Printed in the United States of America
∞
This paper meets the requirements of
ANSI/NISO Z39.48-1992 (Permanence of Paper).

CHAPTER ONE

On June 24 at 1400 hours Greenwich Mean Time, all aircraft flying above 26,000 feet were diverted to lower elevations due to a sudden bombardment of high-energy charged particles into the uppermost tiers of the atmosphere. These high-energy charged particles, brought about by disruptions on the surface of the sun, created dangerous levels of cancer-inducing radiation that could penetrate the fuselage of a plane as easily as microwaves piercing a TV dinner.

This was not the first time a solar storm had caused commercial and military flights to be rerouted, nor the first time satellite reception worldwide was disrupted, consequently requiring extensive recalibration to correct the damage incurred by such an event. Little mention was made of this in the news or in scientific circles, since after all, while rare, a solar storm is not an unheard of occurrence. And who, after all, did it truly inconvenience other than several thousand airline passengers? A few pilots and air-traffic controllers perhaps, a handful of satellite maintenance personnel.

Consequently, this was not the first time scientists would blithely ignore the potential for destruction generated by such a storm in space.

It was, however, the first time they would come to regret that decision.

The full moon hung low in the summer sky, bloated, pale, and somehow oddly tinged with pink. It shone through the shifting treetops like a watchful, bulging eye staring down the world below. It radiated evil intent, that damnable moon, and Ned Bowden, for one, was tired of it hanging over his head. It was like the red-rimmed eye of a hawk, that moon, poised to attack at the least sign of movement. And Ned was the poor, puny bunny rabbit trembling in the weeds, cowering among the shadows, waiting for the stab of talons and the first terrifying sensation of flight as those piercing claws dragged him skyward, kicking and screaming, toward a slow, devouring, blood-drenched death.

On the other hand, Ned was standing in a forested canyon, and the moon provided the only light by which to navigate, so he kept telling himself he should be thankful for its guidance. Otherwise he would be tripping over logs, banging his head on low-hanging branches, or tumbling down embankments as he followed a nearly invisible path through the trees—as he followed a path toward the only spark of happiness his miserable little life was offering at the moment.

That spark of happiness was named Joe. Joe Chase.

As the path began to climb again and Ned eventually crested a hill, he whirled toward a sound on the dusty trail behind him. Was it the echo of his own footsteps, or was it something else? Someone stalking him perhaps? A *predator*?

Shuddering, Ned pushed that thought away as quickly as he could.

He gazed around. From here he could see the shimmering San Diego skyline, winking at him through the pines. He stood motionless, a little breathless from the climb, the dead pine needles still crunching under his feet as he nervously shifted his weight. He leaned forward and tipped his head to the side, listening.

But for the distant hum of late-night traffic, Balboa Park was as still as death. Not a promising simile by any stretch of the imagination.

The screech of a howler monkey split the darkness, and Ned jumped. Then he laughed. Just past the trees and across the Cabrillo Freeway, which threaded a path through the valley below, sprawled the San Diego Zoo and its one hundred acres of imprisoned wildlife. On a night such as this, when the dew-moistened air lay still upon the earth, their cries could be heard for miles around. The screeching laughter of hyenas, the howl of dingoes, the piercing roar and wail of the big cats—all carnivorous beasts who would never see their homelands again, feel the spring of natural grass beneath their paws, or experience the joy of stalking their own twitching dinners. Poor things.

And again Ned laughed. He laughed because only moments before he had been thinking *he* might become some creature's twitching dinner.

Joe was right when he teased Ned about being a city boy. Ned *was* a city boy, through and through. Even a late-night stroll across Balboa Park in the moonlight to meet his best friend was enough to leave him a quivering pile of jangled nerves. Bunny rabbit indeed.

Ned stood on the shadowy path, barely able to see his hand in front of his face. Behind him, through the trees, still shone the diamond sparks of the city skyline. In the other direction hovered that beautiful, scaryass moon.

He froze, as off in the trees to his left, he heard the crunch of footsteps again. His heart did a somersault because this time they most certainly were *not* his own. Maybe it was some homeless person. Maybe it was some *homicidal* homeless person. Yikes.

"Joe?" Ned whispered—a tremulous hiss. "Is that you?"

No answer. Standing as stiff as a fence post, he waited a minute longer. Still no answer.

As silently as he could, Ned turned and resumed his walk, as much to continue his forward progress as to evade those encroaching footsteps. It wouldn't be the first time Ned Bowden had found himself running from shadows. It wouldn't be the first time he felt niggling fingers of fear creeping up his spine.

Something about the darkness had begun to bother Ned lately. He couldn't pinpoint exactly what it was. He hadn't mentioned it to Joe, of course, or anyone else for that matter. Good grief, Ned was twenty-eight. The last thing he wanted Joe to think was that he was afraid of the dark.

Even if he was.

Ned had other things in his life bothering him too, but those were happier things. Astonishing things. Those were things he could barely tolerate to think about because they filled him with such a rush of joyous hope. It was an uphill battle keeping them tamped down enough to prevent himself from grinning like a sap and breaking into song every five minutes. Ned didn't need that. People thought he was crazy enough.

Ned followed the hiking trail down another slope, this time toward the deep canyon that cut the park in half from one end to the other. Eventually, he burst through the trees and stepped out onto the footbridge spanning the canyon and the freeway below. A few scattered cars were whizzing by underneath, as if scurrying past with their tails tucked beneath their legs, knowing they would catch it when they got home for staying out so late.

Ned almost giggled at the thought.

The footbridge was walled and roofed with heavy mesh wiring, totally enclosing the structure to prevent sad people from jumping off.

Every time Ned stepped out onto the bridge he cast a gentle prayer skyward, thanking the person who had decided to do that. Because frankly, before the astonishing, happier things began to dwell in Ned's damaged little brain, he thought he might have been one of those sad people who would be tempted to take a swan dive into the traffic below.

Happily, his days of thinking such thoughts were now past. Ned touched the scar hidden among the waves of blond hair at the side of his head and gave it a squeamish prod. The scar had been there for years, but still he treated it as if it were new, as if it had only recently been carved there, as if he could still feel the scabs and stitches of his long recovery from it. Nowadays, of course, it was simply an old wound, one that had reluctantly released Ned from its pain long before. Why he treated the scar as if it still carried the potential to hurt him, Ned wasn't quite sure. Respect, maybe. And a touch of trepidation, possibly, since who knew when the damaged nerve endings might decide to roar back to screaming life like a sleeping volcano shaking itself awake if Ned didn't treat them with the proper humility.

Still, that was doubtful, wasn't it? The injury had occurred so long ago. Back when he was sixteen. Back when he was still in high school, a dozen years ago.

The memory of his injury, like the scar itself, Ned also treated with respect and a touch of superstitious fear. And shame, of course. Always shame. He never talked about it. Even Joe didn't know the story behind the scar. Not only did Ned never mention it, he tried never to think about it either.

Sometimes he even succeeded. For a while.

Ned glanced at his wristwatch and saw that he was early, so he dallied on the footbridge. He leaned his forehead against the cool wire mesh and stared down at the cars zooming past below. Standing there made him feel like one of the animals in the zoo, peering out through the bars of its cage. Longing to be a part of the world outside. The world it used to know. The world it used to *own*.

Ned had once felt caged in that world as well, although he had to admit he was enjoying his freedom more and more since he took the tiny ground-floor studio apartment on Kalmia Street and struck up a friendship with his next-door neighbor, Joe. Well, actually, he hadn't struck up the friendship. Joe had. And that, Ned only recently decided, was the most astonishing item of all on that long list of wondrous things Ned found himself contemplating so much these days.

With his forehead pressed to the cool mesh, and his gentle, prodding fingertip still idly stroking the scar at the side of his head, Ned closed his eyes and listened to the bombarding sounds of life flooding over him. The whoosh and roar of traffic. The keening wail of another dingo somewhere off in the distance. The hushed rush of his own blood sluicing through his veins. The lazy patter of his heartbeat thumping beneath his ribs. The rattle of the wire mesh surrounding him. The way it thrummed against his skin when a big truck zoomed past below. The sound of the night breeze merrily rustling pine boughs at either end of the bridge, like cheerleaders waving their pompoms high above their heads.

And oddly enough, the sound of the darkness. It was so deep, so *profound*, it could almost be heard as well. With that thought, Ned bit down hard on his fear and forced a smile. His smile widened when he remembered a short conversation uttered only hours before.

"Are you sure you want to meet me after work and walk me home?"

"Sure, Joe. Why not. I like our walks."

"Well then, where shall we meet? On the little footbridge in the trees, in the spooky, monster-riddled darkness of the woods, or up above on Cabrillo Bridge, where the streetlights will keep you safe from all the boogeymen hoping to gobble you up because you're just so damned tasty."

Ned had rolled his eyes, hoping he looked brave. "There are no boogeymen, and I'm not that tasty. I'll meet you on the path. Down by the little footbridge."

Joe had given him a teasing wink with one of his beautiful hazel eyes. "Well, if you're sure. Wouldn't want you to be scared now."

"Ass," Ned had muttered, blushing, while Joe howled with laughter.

So here Ned was, waiting for his friend on the shadowy little footbridge like he said he would. And while he waited, he watched the cars slide past below like antelope fleeing a predator that was hot on their heels, coming to snatch them into oblivion.

Ned would have felt braver on the big bridge up above, in the safety of the streetlights and the traffic, but there were always people there. These moments when he met Joe after work on the silent paths meandering through the trees and hillsides in Balboa Park were more intimate. They had each other to themselves.

Here on the dusty trails in the darkness under the trees, Ned didn't have to share Joe with anyone.

That thought filled Ned with such a rush of longing, he actually clutched at his heart and squeezed his eyes shut so he could savor the feeling.

Then, slowly, he opened his eyes again. Lifting his head, he studied that fat, creepy moon up above. It hung there like a big fat BOSU ball slathered with cream cheese. The Cabrillo Bridge loomed overhead too, massive, its masonry a century old, cracked in places, flooded with lights, dwarfing the shadowy little footbridge below. Dwarfing Ned as well.

Just as Ned felt dwarfed when he stood in Joe's shadow. After all, Joe was six two. Ned was a squirt next to him, barely topping out at five seven. To see Joe's smile, Ned always had to tilt his head back and look up. Not that he minded. Nope. He didn't mind at all. And sometimes when they laughed together, Joe would reach out and stroke a warm hand through the hair on Ned's arms or brush the nape of Ned's neck with tickling fingertips. Ned didn't mind that either.

He glanced at his watch again. Should he wait here for Joe, or should he climb the next hill toward the back fence that bordered the zoo, where Joe would slip through at the end of his shift?

San Diego's Balboa Park was only a hundred acres smaller than the 1,300 acres of Central Park in New York City. Ned knew this because he had googled it with the computer at the public library. And like Central Park, Balboa Park was tucked neatly into the very heart of a great city. The apartment complex where Ned and Joe lived side by side stood at the western edge of the park. Back before Joe had entered his life, Ned had spent long hours standing at his apartment window on the first floor, observing the trees and the strolling passersby, feeling lonely, feeling as if he didn't belong to the world he was forever gazing out upon.

But Joe had changed all that. Joe was his friend now. And Ned still couldn't believe how much Joe's friendship had changed his life.

Sometimes Ned wondered if maybe Joe was a little damaged himself. He didn't have a scar on his head like Ned, but maybe Joe's damage was deeper, hidden down inside where it couldn't be seen. Why else would he have sought out a friendship with Ned? Joe was handsome and strong and tall and kind—brave too, since the darkness didn't scare him at all—and Ned was forever puzzling over what Joe might have seen in Ned that made him want to be friends. Not that Ned was complaining.

Apart from the day the scar was etched on his head, the day Joe reached out to Ned in friendship was the single most seminal event of Ned's life. And Ned damn well knew it. There were days when he thought Joe knew it too, and *that* thought made Ned happy. He *wanted* Joe to know how much it meant to him they were friends. Even if Ned *did* live in terror that Joe would find out the other thoughts that had gradually burrowed into Ned's brain. The more personal thoughts.

The *sexy* thoughts.

Ned stood with his forehead still pressed to the wire cage surrounding the footbridge. He squeezed his eyes shut to better allow the clean night air to cool his senses. After all, those *sexy* thoughts always brought heat with them. Heat that sometimes avalanched over Ned like a flurry of embers, drenching him from head to toe with searing splashes of fire. He could feel his ears burning even now as he stood in the darkness with his heart thundering in his chest and his fingers woven through the wire mesh—the mesh that kept the sad people safe.

With that thought, he stepped back and rubbed his forehead to erase the lines the brittle strands had left on his skin. The sudden infusion of heat through his body began to dissipate too as Ned tried as hard as he could to push those other thoughts—those *sexy* thoughts—away. He listened again to the night sounds around him. The cooing of a pigeon somewhere. Or was it an owl? The chitter of a squirrel, maybe chattering in its sleep. The gentle stirring of the treetops. The rustle and creak of pine branches shifting in the wind. The occasional patter of pinecones, jarred loose and tumbling to the ground with a teeny thud.

When the fear of darkness started to creep back in, Ned began to whistle a tuneless little song. Tuneless because since the day his scar was carved in the side of his head, his whistling had been atonal. As had his singing. Somehow he could no longer carry a tune to save his life. But Ned didn't care. He whistled anyway.

And in the distance, he heard someone whistling back!

Suddenly he forgot the darkness completely. Along with his fears. In fact, those fears seemed pretty silly now. Silly and immature. Ned's face twisted into a grin. He leaned his back into the wire mesh, letting it cradle him while he waited for the sound of familiar footsteps on the path ahead, leading down from the back of the zoo. While he waited for the whistling to approach even closer. The melody of it was far more pleasing to the ear than his own had been, because Joe managed to whistle on key.

Before Joe appeared through the darkness, Ned barked out a merry laugh that rolled off into the trees around him. It was joined by another laugh coming down the hill. A laugh and a familiar voice.

"Good Lord, Ned!" the voice bawled out. "Standing in the middle of the park laughing by yourself in the moonlight? People will say you're nuts!"

"Maybe I *am* nuts!" Ned barked back. "So what?"

Any second now, that bodiless voice would burst from the shadows onto the moonlit trail ahead, and there he'd be. Smiling, happy, handsome. Joe. Ned's favorite person in the whole wide world.

Even Ned's fingers tingled with anticipation as he brushed at his clothes, trying to make himself presentable.

JOE CHASE felt at home in the dark. He loved the smell of the towering pine trees and the sweet aroma of honeysuckle that flavored the night air. He smiled inside at the throb of katydids in the undergrowth and the way they clammed up when he drew near, as if they were holding their breath, waiting for him to pass before resuming their cheerful racket.

Joe wished he could remove his shoes and socks and walk barefoot down the darkened path, enjoying the feel of cool dirt and cushiony pine needles between his toes, but he knew he couldn't. People were stupid. They dropped bottles and trash along the park trails. If he walked here in the dark without shoes, he'd probably slice his feet to ribbons and end up with lockjaw.

As quickly as that thought reared up, he just as hurriedly pushed it away. Tonight was not the night for being peevish or morose. He was about to meet up with Ned, and meeting up with Ned always made him happy.

Joe stumbled to a stop in a patch of darkness so deep he couldn't see a thing. He stood there in the shadows, enjoying the sensation of being invisible, and a smile stretched his mouth wide. He had been smiling a lot lately when he thought of Ned. It was a smile of wonder as much as happiness. It was a smile of slowly dawning surprise too. Surprise at Ned. Surprise at himself. And most of all, surprise at the way the two of them got along.

The last thing Joe Chase thought he would ever seek out was a friend. He had spent his life avoiding friendships. It wasn't that he hated people. He just didn't enjoy their company. Or at least he hadn't enjoyed their company until Ned came along.

Joe had seen Ned around the apartment building, of course. Heck, they lived right next door to each other. Sometimes one would be coming in while the other was going out, and they would casually speak, since there was really no graceful way not to.

Joe knew Ned was shy. Joe wasn't shy, but he could recognize it in someone else. No, Joe's self-imposed seclusion from the human species wasn't brought on by shyness. It was brought on by the fact that he simply didn't *need* people. He had acquired his self-reliance through long years of loveless but dutifully caring foster homes when he was a kid and through a few tumultuous years of being bullied in school. The bullying came his way because he was different, and Joe understood that. It didn't mean he had to like it, though. And with a little help from a favorable chromosome or two in his DNA strand that gave him muscle definition and some serious length of bone by the time he was fourteen, he learned he didn't *have* to like it. As soon as the other kids knew bullying Joe Chase was asking for a black eye and maybe a few missing teeth, they didn't bother him anymore. And that was the way Joe liked it.

It was the way he *still* liked it. At least it had been until the day Ned Bowden stepped into his life. Astonishingly, it was on that very day that Ned began to fill an empty niche in Joe's psyche. There had been a vacant spot inside him all along, it seemed—a spot that needed caulking; a spot that Joe had never known was there. Had never *imagined* was there. Until Ned came along.

Yet it didn't take Joe long to realize that simply patching the empty holes in his life with Ned's friendship wasn't enough. He knew the time was quickly approaching when he would have to do something more. If for no other reason than to give himself a little peace of mind. Still, had he read all the signals wrong? Would he be making a cataclysmic mistake? If he took the actions he wanted to take, would it be the end of their friendship altogether?

God, he was so tired of worrying about it. As momentous as the idea was, he still tried now and then to push it from his mind.

Sometimes he succeeded; sometimes he didn't. Tonight he sort of did. At least for a while.

Joe's back was stiff from working a long shift, so he stopped and gave it a good stretch. Flinging his arms wide, he managed to squeeze out a yawn while he was at it, although he wasn't sleepy. As soon as his long frame was limber enough, he set off down the trail again, his step springy, his eager smile still in place because he knew Ned was waiting for him in the darkness up ahead.

Sweet, loyal Ned.

It was that final, happy thought of Ned waiting for him that brought the whistling tune to Joe's lips. That and the other tune he could hear being butchered somewhere down among the night-shrouded trees. It was Ned, of course, and the tune he whistled was so thoroughly botched it might have been anything from "Turkey in the Straw" to a medley of Lady Gaga's greatest hits.

Ned was a lot of things, but musical wasn't one of them. And at *that* thought Joe suddenly laughed out loud.

He burst from the trees and spotted the footbridge up ahead—and the young man standing on it.

Oddly, at that moment, Joe's heart hammered a little more quickly, a little more loudly. Never before had he questioned the fact that the sight of a mere friend should produce such a biological reaction. After all, Joe wasn't used to having friends. This was a learning experience for him. And besides, Ned wasn't just a friend. He was far more than that. Or soon would be if Joe had anything to say about it.

So when his heartbeat ratchetted up a notch, Joe didn't think anything about it. Not much, anyway. He simply sprang from the shadowy trail into the moonlight and rushed up to Ned standing on the bridge. Ned jumped, of course. In fact he almost looked like he was having a heart attack. Then just as quickly, laughing, they fell into each other's arms in a friendly hug. After a couple of beats found them still hugging, Joe began to feel a little awkward and reluctantly eased himself out of Ned's arms.

"Hi," Joe said. He could feel his smile creasing the skin around his eyes.

"Hi back," Ned said, his own smile exposing every moonlit tooth in his head.

Joe stood a head taller than Ned. Still standing close, they turned toward the mesh and stared down at the cars zipping by below. When a big semi roared past, the wind of it blasted over them. Ned's T-shirt billowed up around his stomach, exposing his belly button for a brief, wondrous moment that Joe captured with his startled eyes. He suspected he would drag that mental snapshot out later when he was alone in his apartment. And heaven knows what he would do with it then.

"How was work?" Ned asked in a quiet voice, and when he did, he turned to Joe with an eager light in his eyes. Joe's breath caught because he really liked it when Ned's soft gaze drifted his way. He liked it in the daytime, he liked it at night, he liked it always.

Joe thought Ned was the handsomest guy he'd ever seen, even with hair that always seemed to be in need of a cut. Ned kept it long, of course, because of the scar, and Joe understood that. Made perfect sense. And that thick mop of blond hair certainly didn't detract from Ned's looks. If anything, it multiplied it.

Ned's eyes were a gentle, pale blue. Surrounded by long, light-colored lashes, those baby blue eyes could lock on and nail a person in place. Joe, at least. Ned had such a sparse growth of blond beard that he had once admitted to Joe he only shaved on Sundays. Sometimes, along about Saturday or so, Joe had noticed that if the sunlight caught Ned just right, a sort of a nimbus formed around Ned's face where the light sifted through the baby hairs, almost like the halo that circled Jesus's head in an illustrated Bible Joe once had foisted on him when he was a kid. An aura. An iridescence. At moments like that, Ned seemed to glow from within.

And when he did, it took most of Joe's willpower not to reach out and stroke that lustrous shimmer of light from Ned's downy cheek.

He and Ned did not talk about *adult* stuff. Sex. Love. Those were subjects they never touched upon with each other, and Joe had begun to wonder why. Other guys did. With some other guys, that was *all* they talked about. God knows the thoughts were there, at least in Joe's head. And he thought maybe they were now and then in Ned's head too. He saw the way Ned looked at him, how his gaze mellowed as if the very sight of Joe brought him contentment. How touches sometimes lingered. How tiny intakes of breath occurred at the unexpected stroke of a hand along an arm. The way Joe sometimes pushed Ned's hair out of his eyes without asking, and the way they occasionally grew still at the exact same moment, as though the same intriguing thoughts had entered each other's heads simultaneously, pulling them together.

Buried among all the other dawning emotions, Joe felt protective of Ned, and he was aware Ned looked up to him. No one had ever done that before. No one had ever needed Joe at all. No one but Ned. Somehow that made all the other feelings even more profound.

Joe suspected the other tenants of the apartment building where they lived gossiped about them, since they were together so much, but he didn't care. In fact, if the neighbors had read the thoughts that had been creeping into Joe's head almost from the day he and Ned met, the gossip mill would have gone crazy.

Joe was torn from his musings by the scream of an airliner swooping low over the park, powering down and lining up for a landing at Lindburgh Field to dump its cargo of tourists. San Diego was a great tourist destination. There were strangers everywhere, every single day of the year, slathered in sunblock, toting cameras, gaping at the sights.

JOE COULD not know, of course, that the jetliner overhead was not dropping tourists bound for San Diego at all. It was, in fact, a Lufthansa Airbus A380 en route from East Meadow, NY, to Beijing, rerouted to San Diego due to atmospheric conditions, and carrying 514 passengers, each and every one of them as mad as a hornet that their schedules were being disrupted.

Nor would Joe have cared about the angry passengers, for his priorities, like his gaze, were focused elsewhere at the moment. They were focused on the man standing beside him.

"HOW WAS work?" Ned asked again.

"Work was good," Joe said, shaking himself back to the present, shelving all his inner ponderings, as he always did when Ned was around. "We planted the miniature palms inside the gorilla enclosure I told you about. Remember?"

Ned nodded. "What did they do with the gorillas?"

Joe shrugged. "Shunted them into an adjacent enclosure. Not that they would have bothered us. We just didn't want to scare them with all the bustle and noise."

"I like gorillas."

Joe grinned. "So do I."

Joe's grin softened to a lazy smile when Ned laid his hand on his shoulder and pointed to the sky. "Look," Ned said. "Am I crazy, or is the moon sort of pink?"

Joe edged a little closer to Ned because he really liked the way Ned's hand felt resting on his shoulder. He gazed upward to where Ned was pointing.

"I'll be!" he exclaimed, staring at the moon through the surrounding mesh. "It *is* pink."

"What does it mean?" Ned asked.

Joe shrugged, turning his eyes back to Ned. "Beats me. Smog, maybe? Some sort of mutant space crap in the atmosphere? Could be anything, I guess."

Ned was still looking skyward. "It's kind of pretty," he said. As he spoke, his hand slid along the expanse of Joe's broad shoulder blade, outlining the edge of it with his fingertips, almost as if doing so helped him think.

Joe studied Ned's face for a moment before trailing his eyes back up to the moon. "You're right," he said. "It is pretty." As soon as those three little words were out of his mouth, he reached up to his shoulder and stroked the back of Ned's hand. Ned eased his hand away and stood there awkwardly, turning away from that weirdass pink moon to gaze up into Joe's face. Such an astonishing expression of innocence lit his face that Joe all but gasped at how beautiful it was.

How beautiful *Ned* was.

So being braver tonight, and being on the verge of major epiphanies and damn well knowing it, Joe reached around Ned's waist and pulled him close.

He felt Ned tense for a moment before he relaxed against Joe's side. They stared down at the passing vehicles scooting by beneath their feet.

"I'm glad you met me," Joe said, and when Ned let his head fall to Joe's chest, Joe felt his heart speed up again. "It's a long lonely walk on the nights you don't come."

"I like meeting you," Ned said, his lips moving against the khaki shirt with The San Diego Zoo above the breast pocket and another patch above that reading simply Joe. Still standing close, Ned snaked an arm around Joe's waist too. They stood there in the moonlight for the longest time, watching the traffic go by. Joe enjoyed the sensation of being close, holding on. He hoped Ned enjoyed it too.

When Joe tilted his head down and dug his chin into Ned's hair, he felt a sudden hunger that made his dick shift inside his pants. He closed his eyes at the sensation.

After a few heartbeats of silence, Ned lifted his head to gaze into Joe's eyes. "You tensed up," he whispered softly.

"Backache," Joe lied, wondering what Ned would think if he knew the *real* reason he'd tensed up. *Sorry, kid. Couldn't help myself. Had a boner.*

Ned nodded as if he understood, which of course he didn't, thank God. "You work too hard," he said.

They stood silently arm in arm. As if the same thought struck Ned at the same time as Joe, they both tilted their heads up to gaze once more at the rose-tinted moon. In a lull of traffic below, which also cast them suddenly into darkness, the silence of the sleepy night flooded over them. The sweet scent of pine and honeysuckle tinged the air like some giant was out there with a big can of Glade, squirting it around.

Joe chuckled at that ridiculous thought and gave Ned a nudge with his elbow. "Walk me home," he said, and Ned nodded shyly.

SIDE BY side, their arms bumping together now and then in a comfortable sort of way, they left the footbridge and entered the shaded uphill path leading into the trees.

With Ned at his side, Joe enjoyed the darkness and the shadows far more than he had when he was alone. Ned relaxed too, as if any night fears he might have felt before were now swept away in Joe's presence.

Halfway home, at a rough spot in the trail, Joe took Ned's hand, offering him support. Even when the trail leveled out again, he didn't relinquish it.

Still holding hands, they talked quietly of inconsequential things.

"How was *your* work?" Joe asked. Ned worked in a deli, serving customers, building sandwiches, sliding endless chunks of meat through an electric slicer, then cleaning the slicer, over and over and over again.

"It was exciting," Ned said. "Any day I leave work with all ten fingers still attached is exciting."

The trail was so deeply hidden in shadow at this point that the only connection Joe felt to the world at all was the warmth of Ned's hand in his and the crunch of pebbles beneath his feet. That and Ned's sweet, mellow voice wafting through the darkness toward him.

"That's good," Joe said. "Wouldn't want you losing any body parts."

"No indeed," Ned agreed. "I might need them someday." Joe knew Ned was smiling because he could hear it in his voice. He really liked hearing a smile in Ned's voice. But was that last comment about body parts Ned's way of teasing Joe about the cloud of sexual energy that had been hovering around them for a couple of months now? Or was that sexual energy only in Joe's imagination? Maybe Ned didn't feel it at all. Maybe he was just kidding. Innocently. Heterosexually. *Butchly.*

And wouldn't *that* be a fucking bummer.

Another airliner roared past overhead, swooping low toward the city skyline and the airport just beyond. They both looked up. "It's long past midnight," Joe said. "Usually incoming flights have stopped by now. I think it's an ordinance or something that they can't land after a certain hour."

"Well, they're landing now," Ned said.

Joe nodded. "So they are."

They resumed their walk. Joe thought about his job as groundskeeper at the San Diego Zoo. It was a job requiring night hours because the zoo honchos didn't want maintenance people or landscapers with shovels and hoes and sweating like pigs distracting the paying customers. Theoretically, a trip to the zoo should be like a visit to Disneyland. You never saw anybody scrubbing toilets or planting begonias there either. It was all done at night.

The only thing Joe didn't like about his job was that it cut into his time with Ned, who, naturally, worked days. Most of their time together was spent doing exactly what they were doing now. Walking home side by side after Ned met him on the trails after work. It was Joe's favorite hour of the day.

He knew Ned had been having money problems, and he broached the subject now because sometimes Ned let things slip past without noticing. "Did you pay your rent at the apartment?"

Ned's fingers tightened around his. "Yes, Daddy, I did. You don't have to ask me every month. I only forgot a couple of times."

"I know, Ned. Sorry. I'm like an old hen. Pecking away all the time."

What Joe *didn't* say was that one of his greatest fears was that Ned would be evicted from the building. God knows where he would end up living then. And worse than that, God knows if they would even see each other again. That was a possibility Joe simply didn't have the heart to face. Not now. Not ever.

"I like hens," Ned said. There was a smile in his voice again. "They taste good with dumplings."

"Asshole," Joe said, grinning too.

"Yes, even assholes are yummy," Ned said. "Or so I've heard. Of course, not with dumplings."

"Eww, I guess not."

A moment later they were both howling with laughter.

Still chuckling, Joe stopped and grabbed Ned, pulling him into an embrace. "One of these days your jokes are going to get you in trouble. Someone is liable to take you up on one of your little double entendres, and then what will you do?"

Ned gazed up at Joe with merry, teasing lines carved all over his face. His eyes were dancing in the moonlight. "Lie back and enjoy it?"

Joe stood there, his long arms wrapped around Ned, holding him close. It was either a wrestling hold or a romantic embrace. He wasn't entirely sure which, and he wasn't entirely sure he wanted to know. Joe hated himself for always balking at stepping over the line with Ned. After all, there was nothing he wanted to do more. But did Ned want the same thing, or was Ned just being Ned? Funny, innocent, a little off-kilter.

And so beautiful standing there cradled in his arms.

What Joe *did* know was that he had never been more tempted to kiss the man. But once again, he didn't. The risk was too great. If it wasn't something Ned wanted, it would break Joe's heart and probably ruin their friendship to boot.

So once again Joe pulled back, afraid of taking that last step, terrified of tumbling headfirst into what, he had no doubt, could be something wonderful. Or something absolutely disastrous.

Still afraid of doing the wrong thing, he said, "Best be getting home, I guess."

"Yeah, I guess," Ned muttered.

They walked on. They weren't holding hands any longer. Joe wasn't sure when he had let Ned's hand slip away, and he wasn't sure how to reclaim it without looking like a needy putz. A needy *gay* putz.

And even if he did, he wasn't sure what Ned would think about it. And that worried him greatly.

NED LOOKED up at the sky again. The planes were coming in one right after the other now, dropping down through the flight path like lemmings sailing over a cliff. He had never seen the air traffic so busy this late at night. Even so, while gazing skyward, he took the opportunity to take a peek at Joe's face in the moonlight. His dark hair. The clean line of his jaw, shadowy with beard since he hadn't shaved since morning. He was so handsome, standing there looking up at the sky, the tendons in his neck taut. When Joe licked his lips, a tiny shudder ran through Ned.

He loved that Joe was so hands-on in his friendship, always touching, sometimes hugging. But every time Joe put his hands on Ned, he felt his self-control crumble a little more. He told himself he would never make the first move with Joe, and he had held himself to that. But it wasn't easy. It wasn't easy, and it most certainly wasn't what he wanted.

Even now, Ned edged closer to Joe, and when their hands touched, he took it upon himself to fake a stumble. He casually slid his fingers through Joe's as if he needed the support to keep from falling. Jesus, he was pathetic.

But at least he was *successfully* pathetic. After all, he was holding Joe's hand again. And that had been the plan all along. Was he sneaky, or what?

They were crossing a glade now. The trees had fallen back, and the trails and valleys had ended. They were in a part of the park where the bocce courts were located. The lawn had been trimmed recently, and the smell of freshly cut grass hung heavy on the night air. The grass was wet with dew already, and the cuttings stuck to the toes of their shoes. Up ahead, at the edge of the park, they could see the lights of their apartment building. Ned's heart sank. That meant their walk together was almost over.

"Look!" Joe suddenly cried, stabbing a finger at the western sky. "The birds!"

Joe startled Ned so that Ned slid in the dew-soaked grass and would have fallen for real if he hadn't still been holding Joe's hand.

"Wow!" Ned exclaimed, staring where Joe was pointing. "What the hell is making them do that?"

Directly in the path of the latest incoming airliner, a great flock of birds had risen into the night sky. The wheeling birds were so thick they looked like a solid mass. It was too far away to see what kind of birds they were, but limned in the light from the city skyline they could be seen blocking out everything in their path. It was like a great black cloud billowing up from the earth.

The airliner tilted to the left. Its turbines roared as they worked to lift the airliner back into the sky. In a desperate attempt to abort the landing, the airliner tipped away from the vast cloud of birds and veered off toward the coastline and the safe, empty skies above the calm Pacific.

Ned and Joe stood rooted like statues as the plane veered south. The swarm of birds continued to billow and swoop among the spires and towers of the downtown skyline. The flock was so thick it blocked out the tops of buildings and erased long swaths of starlight from the sky.

Hearing a second roar of turbine engines, Ned spun around and spotted another airliner angling away from the flight path, following the first plane out toward the water. They would circle around, Ned supposed, while waiting for the birds to leave. Waiting for the air to clear of avian life so they could line up for another approach to Lindburgh Field.

Again, under his breath, Ned whispered, "Wow. I've never seen so many birds in my life. And I've never seen the planes do what they're doing either."

"Neither have I," Joe echoed.

He turned to Ned, and with a resigned look in his eyes, said, "I guess we'd better get home. You have to go to work early."

Ned nodded, feeling as empty as Joe looked. "I know."

At some point during the excitement with the birds, Joe's hand had slipped out of Ned's grasp again. This time, Ned didn't have the courage to reclaim it.

They walked on in silence, Ned heartsick that their time together was ending.

LATER, IN his bedroom all by himself, Joe didn't think back to the birds or the planes. He had all but forgotten them, in fact. Instead, he relived that one spectacular moment on the footbridge when the wind had lifted Ned's T-shirt, exposing his belly button. It was a silly thing to have captured his imagination, but there was no denying it had. Joe milked the memory for all it was worth, and then he dragged out other recollections too. He had a collection of them. The line of Ned's hip as he retrieved something from the ground. In a splash of sunlight, a vein pulsing in the little triangular hollow at the base of Ned's throat. A glimpse of a pale collarbone peeking through a shirt collar. The promising bulge under the fly of Ned's blue jeans. The spray of blond hair across the arch of a foot when Ned ran barefoot through the apartment, kidding around.

So beautiful. Everything about him was so beautiful.

As his collection of memories played out on a continuous loop inside his head, one right after the other, Joe touched himself beneath the covers in his lonely bed. He squeezed his eyes shut when that lingering touch became hungrier, when his fingers no longer stroked, but clutched, when his cock no longer stiffened, but sang. At the moment of release, when his juices splattered across his chest, Joe bit his lip to keep from crying out.

Later, he felt lonelier than he had before. It was that loneliness that carried him into sleep. But even in sleep he could not escape his longings. For Ned always waited for him there.

And in his dreams, Ned was just as hungry as Joe.

JOE OPENED his eyes to the craziest morning he could ever remember. Through his bedroom window, the sky was red! Not the orangey blush of an early summer day, but the deep, deep red of fresh, steaming blood. A crimson miasma drenched the atmosphere and inflamed the sky from one horizon to the other. Joe pressed his cheek to the window pane and strained to peer eastward, seeking the familiar sight of the fiery sun cresting Mount Miguel, climbing its daily path heavenward, en route to bathing the coast in its glorious golden light just as it always did in Southern California.

But the sun wasn't there. It was lost somewhere behind that vast infusion of bloodred haze that coated everything, including the very air. When Joe thrust the grubby curtains aside, dust motes shimmered pink, dancing around in the reddish fog that penetrated even his own little bedroom. Joe went so far as to shake his alarm clock, thinking it had stopped, thinking it was still dawn. But he was wrong. It was after nine, just as the stupid clock said.

He stood naked at his window, once again staring out. He remembered his lonely orgasm the night before and had to squeeze his eyes shut for a second to keep his cock from lengthening again at his thoughts of Ned.

Joe gazed out at the street that bordered the park on one side and his own apartment building on the other. Cars were moving along it as usual. The only difference was that some had their headlights on, since the day was so muddied by that scarlet murk. From his vantage point, he could see a couple of people standing in their front yards, staring upward behind shielding hands, contemplating the strange red sky just like Joe.

Grabbing a pair of jeans off a chair, Joe awkwardly climbed into them while stumbling across his studio apartment. He tapped lightly on the wall inside the tiny hallway that led to his bathroom. Laying his ear to the plaster, he listened for Ned's answering knock, but it didn't come. Ned had already gone to work.

Suddenly Joe was worried. Ned could be so easily freaked. Had that weird red sky frightened him? Had he rushed off to work terrified anyway, not wanting to disturb Joe's sleep, because Ned always worried about things like that? Did Ned—like Joe—figure whatever that red sky meant, it was connected somehow to the pinkish haze that had lain over the moon last night? Did Ned simply decide it was one of those odd quirks of nature that sometimes surprise everyone? Or had he raced down the street to the deli where he worked, scared out of his mind, his beautiful blue eyes flitting nervously about while his heart thumped in terror?

Joe grabbed his cell phone, but just as quickly tossed it on the bed. No. He wouldn't call the deli; he'd go down there himself. If Ned was okay, Joe could have breakfast, and maybe they could sneak in a little conversation between Ned's duties. His boss was pretty cool, never minding when Joe stopped by to visit. He also seemed to genuinely like Ned and always tried to take care of him. For that reason, Ned's boss was one of Joe's favorite people and always would be.

Joe quickly finished dressing. He stood in his bathroom long enough to brush his teeth and try to do something with his mop of brown hair short of actually shampooing the sleep out of it. When he was as groomed as he was likely to get, Joe grabbed his phone again, snatched up a few bucks from the dresser, and headed out the door.

Since the deli was only six blocks away, he decided to walk. Well, jog. After all, he was in a hurry. He really was that worried about Ned.

It was strange seeing his neighborhood cast in vermilion tones instead of the usual California banana yellows and sunlit greens, with crystal spears of brilliant white light bouncing off high-rise windows. Even out here on the street, when Joe aimed his eyes eastward over the trees in the park looking for the sun, there was nothing there. Not even a hint of the rising sun penetrated the bloodshot sky. In fact, the rosy haze was so thick Joe couldn't see the mountains either. It was as if a ketchupy fog had settled over the city, over the state, maybe even the world, painting the air adobe red, leaving nothing as it used to be.

Leaving nothing looking—*right*. This was science fiction stuff, Joe decided. Something you'd see in a movie. Something that simply couldn't *be*.

He quickened his pace. The few pedestrians he met appeared as confused as he was. Some of them were clearly frightened by the monster-movie haze that had been pulled over the city like a red cloak. But still, life goes on. People have to work; they have to shop; they have to do the things they always have to do. Even in fear, the mundane survives. Even in moments of deepest terror, the desire to floss one's teeth probably pops up now and then.

Joe quickened his pace. His need to know that Ned was all right was almost a physical pain inside him now. It was a nagging ache. The only way he could cure the ache was to see Ned with his own eyes, safe and sound and innocently handsome. Just as he always was.

Just the way Joe loved him.

At that thought, Joe stumbled to a stop. It was as if the L-word passing so unexpectedly through his brain had short-circuited all motor functions it crossed along the way.

Love. Yep. That was a show-stopper all right. And perfectly true, Joe suddenly realized, standing there like a dunce in the middle of the sidewalk. He *did* love Ned. Joe didn't just have the hots for Ned. He was head over heels in love with the guy.

And just what the hell was he going to do about *that*? Joe had never talked with Ned about being gay or *not* being gay. He had never questioned the deep friendship they shared. Had never spoken to anyone else about it either. But somehow Joe knew there was more than friendship constantly hammering away at the two of them these days. Not only inside his own heart, but inside Ned's heart as well. Wasn't there?

Joe stood on the sidewalk as headlights zoomed past in what should have been broad daylight but wasn't. Instead, the sky rolled red and sunless across his head. While the world fell to shit around him, Joe found himself wondering if Ned might conceivably love him back.

And at that astonishingly untimely thought, Joe actually laughed at himself. With the planet gone to hell in a handbasket, here he was fretting about romance. Talk about having your priorities screwed up.

NED WAS on weekly bacon duty this morning. Today was the day he stood at the grill and continuously fried up mounds of the stuff, enough to last the deli for a week. After he fried it up, he would stuff it in plastic bags, each bag holding about five pounds, then toss them into the big walk-in refrigerator to be hauled out when needed. By the end of the day his clothes, his skin, even his hair, would be coated with bacon grease. It was annoying, but he was used to it. He even liked it. On the days when he worked the bacon, he didn't have to deal with customers. Ned didn't like dealing with customers. He always thought they were laughing at him. Joe told him they weren't, but he could never convince Ned. God knows Joe had tried often enough.

Ned grinned while methodically flipping away at a carpet of bacon on the sizzling grill. Thoughts of Joe always made him grin. Either that or they made him frown. The frowny thoughts weren't really sad, of course, they were just *contemplative*. He could never tell in which direction thoughts of Joe would take him. He just knew he liked thinking them.

As he worked, he occasionally wiped the greasy sweat from his brow and the back of his neck with an old towel. Mixed in among his thoughts of Joe, he also thought about the eerie red sky that had hovered over his head while he walked to work that morning. He had almost been afraid to leave the apartment. Had even considered waking Joe up to see what he thought about it. But in the end he had swallowed his fear and let Joe sleep. The guy worked so hard. He needed his rest.

Spooked, but determined to be brave for Joe's sake, Ned had walked to work all by himself, just like a proper adult.

Ned's boss, Mr. Wong, gave Ned an idle pat on the back as he hustled past on the way to the ovens in the corner where biscuits were baking for the breakfast crowd. "Good boy," Mr. Wong mumbled, as he always did when he patted Ned on the back for no earthlier reason than the fact that he was a good guy. Ned knew he would never find a nicer boss, and he was grateful. Ned had limitations, and to find a boss who was willing to overlook them was a godsend. Ned wasn't smart like Joe. He wasn't as good at dealing with people as Joe was either. But still both Joe and Mr. Wong liked him, so he supposed he must be doing something right.

Mr. Wong was a wiry little guy in his high forties who smiled all the time, bowed in respect to everyone he met, and who had eight kids of graduated height who were always popping into the deli for free stuff, which Mr. Wong didn't seem to mind doling out at all. Ned had never seen Mrs. Wong, but he could picture her in his mind, standing at a kitchen sink somewhere in San Diego's tiny Chinatown district, where he knew the Wongs lived. He pictured her forever leaning over the stove in her immaculate kitchen with a kid on her hip, whipping up a mess of pot stickers or stirring fried rice in a wok. Despite never having met Mrs. Wong, Ned liked her as much as he liked Mr. Wong. Ned was magnanimous that way. If he liked one person in a family, he liked them all.

Still flipping endless rashers of bacon, he peered through the greasy kitchen air and out the back door leading to the alley where the garbage cans sat. The day was still red out there. In fact, it looked like maybe it was even redder than it had been earlier. The sun didn't appear to be close to poking a hole through the bloody haze that coated the sky, and that was odd in itself. It gave Ned the creeps is what it did, and Ned found himself hoping Joe would pop in for breakfast. Sometimes he did. At least when he could afford it. Ned hoped today would be one of those mornings when he could.

While Ned worked, and while he kept a hopeful eye peeled for Joe coming through the deli's front door, he allowed his mind a little time off so it could wander here and there at random. A lot of times, those random thoughts steered him toward the scar on his head and the history behind it, but not today. Today he concentrated on last night's stroll with Joe through Balboa Park while that funny pink moon floated high above their heads.

He remembered the feel of Joe's gentle hand at the back of his neck, the gentle probe of his fingers on his skin. He remembered the warmth of Joe's khaki zoo shirt pressed against his cheek when Joe playfully squeezed him into a hug. Joe's shirt had smelled faintly of sweat and loam and some sort of plant life—maybe the miniature palm trees Joe said he had planted at work—and underneath it all there was the homey, welcoming scent of Joe himself, a scent Ned couldn't imagine tiring of.

Ned also remembered how he never wanted those hugs to end. He could have happily melted into Joe's broad chest and snuggled there, wrapped in Joe's strong arms, content for the rest of his life.

He remembered wanting other things to happen between him and Joe too, but this was no time to think about those. They were better left pondered when Ned lay naked and alone in his bed, not while he was flipping forty pounds of bacon and trying not to drown in his own sweat or gag on the stench of grease. Yet even naked and alone in his bed, those were thoughts he tried not to let in. Not usually anyway. Not on a regular basis. But sometimes thoughts of Joe simply couldn't be stopped. No matter how hard he tried.

Ned often laughed at himself when he let himself get too carried away in the endless ways he found to think about Joe Chase. But not today. Today it seemed important to know that Joe had been there for him last night, as Ned knew Joe would be there for him today. And tomorrow. And the day after that.

Joe was his friend. And at the moment, being friends was enough. Almost.

Once again, Ned's eyes were drawn to the door leading out to the alley and to the crimson canopy covering the city. The air was cooler now, he noticed. Even with the heat of the grill billowing up around him, he could feel a cool breeze wafting in through the open door. It felt nice.

He readjusted his grease-drenched paper hat, which he was convinced made him look like a bozo. Then he flipped a few more rows of bacon. Others, once they acquired the right crispness and color, he scooped up on the belly of his fat spatula and dumped into the bags the deli stored them in.

Still Ned waited and hoped for Joe to show up. And while he waited and hoped and sweated, he happily freed his mind, letting it wander back to him and Joe walking among the trees the night before. And the way Joe had hugged him there on the footbridge.

And how in the middle of that hug, Ned had breathed in the wonderful scent of Joe's shirt.

JOE POKED his head in the deli door and looked around. A few customers sat at the little plastic tables and chairs lined up along the windows overlooking the street. Every one of those people had their eyes trained on the sky. They looked worried, although it didn't seem to hinder their ability to pound down the food. Behind the deli counter stood Mr. Wong, along with one of the Wong children who was helping his father today. At the moment, he was slicing pastrami and stacking it in neat piles to be wrapped in waxed paper later.

Mr. Wong lit up like a sunrise (like a *normal* sunrise) at the sight of Joe peering in off the street. He beckoned Joe inside with a broad smile and pointed toward the kitchen in the back.

"Neddie back there! You go talk to him. You hungry?"

Joe's budget was a little tight today, so he shook his head no and patted his stomach like he'd just eaten, which he hadn't.

Mr. Wong wasn't born yesterday. "You growing boy. You eat anyway. I bring you something. Now go talk to Neddie. And wear this. I don't want honky hairs in my food." And with that, Mr. Wong howled with laughter while sticking a paper hat on Joe's head just like the one Ned wore when he cooked. Only Joe's hat didn't reek of bacon grease. Not yet anyway.

Before Joe could hustle off to the back, Mr. Wong slipped from behind the counter and stood next to Joe, gazing out at the red morning.

"Not normal," he said with a troubled expression. His voice was low, as if he didn't want to upset the customers, who weren't paying attention to what they were saying anyway.

"No," Joe agreed, standing at his side and, in deference, keeping his voice low too. "There's nothing normal about it."

"What you think happen?"

Joe thought about it. "I think nature fucked up."

Mr. Wong, who was about two heads shorter than Joe, gazed up into Joe's eyes and lit up with another beaming smile. "That's what I think too."

"You know what they say," Joe said.

"What *who* say?"

"People."

"No, Mr. Joe. What do people say?"

Joe frowned, still staring at the crimson sky. "They say, 'Red sky at morning, sailors take warning.'"

Mr. Wong stared through the crimson shimmer on the plate glass window. He didn't look happy. "You think we should be taking warning, Mr. Joe?"

"I think it wouldn't hurt," Joe answered, and he said it with such conviction, he surprised himself.

"That what I think too," Mr. Wong replied. He gave the blood-tinted heavens a last uneasy glower, then reached his arm up high and gave Joe a friendly pat on the back. "Go talk to your friend. Neddie a little freaked-out. He's been watching for you, I think. You go. I'll bring you a sandwich on the house. You no eat, you shrink down to my size. Only Chinese people are cute when they're little like me."

Joe grinned. "I've noticed that. Thank you, sir."

Mr. Wong gave a little pout, like he'd just been insulted. "I no sir. I friend. Now you go see *your* friend. And tell Neddie if he burns the bacon, I'll chop him up for stir-fry." With a wink, he pushed Joe toward the back.

"But you don't sell stir-fry," Joe threw back over his shoulder. Teasing.

"Then I'll add it to menu. Red sky special. Neddie chow mein. One day only. After all, 'waste not want not.' Old Chinese proverb."

"No, it isn't. It's an old *English* proverb."

"It Chinese now."

Still beaming, Mr. Wong scurried behind the counter and started building Joe a sandwich, slapping it together with this and that like a croupier dealing out cards. While he worked, Joe maneuvered his way to the door leading into the kitchen. He wasn't through the door more than two seconds when the delicious reek of crisp, hot bacon sent his salivary glands into overdrive. A couple of other glands—ones related to sex and desire by the feel of them—perked up as well when Ned brightened at the sight of him. A beautiful smile tore a trench across Ned's sweat-shined face, and even with the silly paper hat perched on his head, Joe thought he had never seen a handsomer man in his life.

"You came!" Ned exclaimed.

A blush warmed Joe's cheeks. "I did. Couldn't seem to stay away, in fact."

"Did you come for breakfast?"

"According to Mr. Wong, I did. Actually I came to see if you were okay. So are you?"

Ned gave an exaggerated shrug, arms flung wide, flapping his greasy spatula around in midair. "I am now!" Then he quickly turned back to the grill to flip more bacon before it burned.

Hearing the enthusiasm in Ned's answer made Joe's blush deepen to the same color as the sky outside the deli window. He knew this from spotting his reflection in the stainless-steel ice machine standing in the corner. Trying to ignore his own goofy face staring back at him, he grabbed Ned by the hips from behind and gazed over his shoulder at the broad marbled carpet of bacon slices, bubbling and browning on the grill.

"Smells great," Joe said.

"Who? Me?"

Joe snorted a laugh and gripped Ned's hips a little tighter. "Yes. You *and* the bacon. In fact, you both smell pretty much the same."

Ned groaned. "I'm sure we do." He gave the sizzling bacon a quick perusal to make sure nothing was burning, then angled his way around to face Joe without forcing Joe's hands to leave his hips.

"I was hoping you'd come."

"I was hoping you were hoping I'd come."

It clearly took Ned a second to untangle that sentence. Once he did, he laughed, making fun of himself.

Joe had an almost uncontrollable urge to lean forward and lay his lips over that gorgeous smile. For better or worse, he didn't get a chance, because a moment later, Mr. Wong's eldest, a twelve-year-old named Bobby, came dashing into the kitchen with Joe's sandwich wrapped in a napkin.

Joe quickly released Ned and took a step back. Bobby smiled as if he knew he had caught the two at an awkward moment, but awkward or not, it didn't seem to bother him much. He simply handed Joe the sandwich and eased the spatula out of Ned's hands.

"Neddie, Pop said for you to take a break and talk to Joe while he eats his sandwich. I'm supposed to relieve you."

"Goodie," Ned said, beaming.

Bobby gazed down at the seething blanket of bacon bubbling in front of him and blanched. "Yeah, I thought you'd like that."

"Come on," Ned said, grabbing Joe's sleeve and tugging him toward the back door. "Let's sit outside."

Happily, Joe let himself be hauled away, leaving Bobby staring morosely at the steaming grill and mumbling something to himself about child-labor laws.

In the alley, they perched on side-by-side garbage-can lids and wiggled their asses around until they were comfortable. Joe unwrapped his sandwich, which turned out to be roast beef on rye, and since it was already cut diagonally, offered half to Ned.

"It's not bacon, is it?" Ned asked, looking suspicious.

Joe smirked. "What? You got something against bacon?"

Ned pulled the greasy paper hat off his head and tucked it in his shirt pocket. "Today I do."

"Well, don't worry. It's roast beef."

"Oh, okay, then," Ned said and took it. With one hand he fed himself the sandwich, and with his other hand he ruffled his blond hair until it stood straight up off his head like a field of wheat. Joe smiled to himself. Ned really hated that paper hat.

They sat quietly for a couple of minutes, chomping away at the roast beef and gazing around at the vermilion morning. Where the sky would have been blue on an ordinary day, it was now a dusty rose. Where the scattered passing clouds would have been fluffy and white, they were now fluffy and puce, as deeply tinted as splotches of red wine. They reminded Joe of blood-soaked balls of cotton. Against the paler rose sky behind, the clouds were really quite lovely. Colorwise.

And the most unnatural thing Joe could imagine.

"It's getting worse," Ned said around a mouthful of roast beef. "Redder, I mean. Those clouds are starting to look like chunks of raw liver."

While Ned gazed straight up at the sky, Joe allowed himself a moment to study the topography of Ned's neck. The way his Adam's apple slid up and down when he talked. The way the baby blond hairs on his throat glowed faintly pink in the light. And farther down, where the vee in his work shirt exposed an expanse of golden skin that seemed as mesmerizing to Joe as that science fiction sky hanging over their heads.

Unable to keep his hands away, Joe leaned over and straightened Ned's collar where it had been pinched up under the straps of the apron he wore to protect his clothes from the grease splattering off the grill.

Ned's gaze trailed away from the sky and focused on Joe. There was a silent thank-you in Ned's eyes, and Joe just as silently nodded "you're welcome."

"I knew you'd come," Ned said quietly.

"I was worried about you."

"I'm glad," Ned answered and took another bite of his sandwich. Chewing, he added, "It's nice to be worried about."

A comfortable silence settled over them as the wail of a siren rose in the distance. It sounded like an ambulance. Since they lived in the heart of the city, it wasn't an unfamiliar sound. But somehow, on a morning like this, when the world seemed to have slipped a cog or two and taken a turn toward the Daliesque, that piercing wail took on a more ominous meaning. For Ned, at least. Joe could see it in his eyes.

Joe reached over and patted Ned's knee. "It's just a siren. It doesn't mean anything. We hear them all the time."

Ned gnawed off another bite of sandwich. The fear that had briefly touched his eyes disappeared. A calming word from Joe was all it took. A calming word from Joe was all it *ever* took. And Joe knew it.

Through the alley door, they heard Bobby wail even louder than the siren. "Fucking grease!"

And from deeper in the deli, they heard Mr. Wong cry out, just as loud and just as angry. "Number one son watch mouth, or he'll be cooking bacon till he's thirty! I'll send Neddie to college instead!"

Joe and Ned howled with laughter at that, while Bobby mumbled something about Charlie Chan movies they didn't quite catch. Whatever it was, it didn't sound complimentary.

Ned turned to Joe. He had about two bites left on his sandwich while Joe's was already gone. "Can I meet you after work again tonight?"

Joe tore his eyes from Ned's eager face and studied the sky for the umpteenth time that morning. "Maybe you shouldn't," he said. "Look at where the sun should be, but isn't. If the moon gets covered up like that by whatever this red stuff is, it'll be pitch-black out on the trails. You'll break your neck."

"I won't break my neck. I know those trails by heart."

"Meet me on the big bridge instead. There are streetlights up there."

"No," Ned said. Stubborn. "I'll meet you on the little bridge down below. Just like last night."

"What if you get lost?"

"What am I? Six?"

Joe laughed. "Arguing with you is like arguing with a fire hydrant."

Ned shot an elbow into his ribs. "Yeah, but I'm cuter."

The innocent way Ned said it stopped Joe like a brick wall. He sat there staring into his friend's pale blue eyes. "Yes," he finally said, his voice barely loud enough to hear. "You are."

As if on cue, they both blushed. A minute later they were laughing at each other again.

NED'S GIGGLING fit eased up when he stuffed the last bite of his sandwich into his mouth. He knew Joe went to work about the same time Ned finished his shift at the deli. Their days off were different too. The hours they were free to be in each other's company were limited. He wasn't about to let Joe walk home from work alone, no matter what Joe said. It was one battle Ned had never lost, and he didn't intend to start losing it now.

"Regular time," he said. "On the footbridge. Be there or be square."

"Corny," Joe said, rolling his eyes. "But okay. You win." There was a tiny scowl on his face. "The footbridge it is."

Ned wondered if Joe was as reluctant on the inside as he appeared to be on the outside. He hoped not.

"Good," Ned said, forcing a smile. At the same time, he pushed away any lingering doubts he might have about Joe actually wanting to meet him after work at all. He tried not to ask himself if Joe was just being nice, or if their nighttime walks together meant as much to Joe as they did to him. Or was that even empirically possible?

"I like our walks," Ned said. He tried to sound casual when he said it, but his eyes never left Joe's face while he uttered the words. He knew he was fishing, but he couldn't seem to stop himself.

When Joe's hazel eyes found their way to Ned's and his lips softened into a smile, Ned received the answer he had hoped for. When Joe said, "I like them too," Ned believed Joe had spoken the truth. He had never once seen a lie in Joe's eyes, and he didn't see one there now.

When Joe scooted a little closer on the garbage can and reached around to lay an arm over Ned's shoulder, Ned felt a quiver shudder through him. Joe leaned in and whispered, "I like everything about you, Ned. Don't ever doubt it for a minute." Joe had seen the insecurity on his face, Ned thought, and he was doing what he could to make it go away.

They sat in silence for a minute while Ned enjoyed Joe's gentle fingers massaging the back of his neck. Ned sensed that Joe wanted to say something else, and he leaned closer, snuggling under Joe's arm. He gazed up into the crimson clouds as if by looking away, he could give Joe the courage to speak. It worked.

"I want you to trust me," Joe said. He had tilted his head even closer, and when he spoke the words, his lips softly brushed Ned's ear. The shudder that had rumbled through Ned before was nothing like the shudder that rumbled through him now.

"I do trust you," Ned all but gasped. "I always have."

This time it was Joe's turn to say, "Good. I also...."

Ned tore his eyes from the sky and twisted his head around to study Joe's face. They were so close, Ned could feel Joe's breath flowing across his cheek. When Joe's eyes clamped on to his, Ned found the nerve to ask, "You also what?"

But Joe wouldn't answer. He merely shook his head as if it wasn't important. "Nothing."

"You were going to say something."

Their eyes were still riveted together. "I'll say it," Joe said. "I promise. Just not right now."

"Oh. Okay."

Joe smiled, and Ned smiled along with him, while deep in his heart Ned knew, like Joe, there were things he didn't want to say right now either, but one day he would. He'd have to, or he'd explode.

Bobby poked his head through the kitchen door. He was holding the spatula like an ax. He didn't say anything. He simply stood there glaring. At Ned. At Joe. At the greasy spatula in his hand. There were three Band-Aids on his forearm that hadn't been there before. Grease burns obviously.

"Poor kid," Joe finally said, nudging Ned. "I think you'd better get back to work. Your replacement seems to be a trifle cooked himself."

Ned grunted and eased himself off the garbage can.

At that moment, a horrific rumbling noise bounced across the heavens over their heads. It sounded like thunder, but there had been no lightning. The rumbling quieted, then started up again with a loud *clap* that made Bobby, Ned, and Joe all jump like they'd been poked with pins.

Cowering, Ned stared up into the crimson sky. From inside the deli, he heard Mr. Wong exclaiming to anyone who would listen.

"World gone to shit! What the hell happening now? *And why nobody flipping bacon?*" As Ned reached for Joe's hand to steady himself—and maybe give himself some much-needed courage—an icy wind blew down the alley. It crashed into them like a winter gale, lifting their hair and flattening their clothes. It was without a doubt the last thing in the world anyone would expect to feel on a summer San Diego morning.

"Christ, it's freezing!" Joe cried as the wind bit into his cheeks and the goose bumps rose on his arms. Ned saw them there as plain as day, and looking down, he saw his own goose bumps popping up too. He shivered against the cold, and Joe pulled him into a protective embrace.

With his face half-buried in Joe's chest, Ned watched as Joe beckoned Bobby to him too. The boy rushed forward, eagerly accepting the safe harbor Joe offered, his eyes wide with confusion and maybe even fear.

As that freezing wind blew over them—over the city—the three stood huddled together, waiting for the blast to end.

In the deli doorway stood Mr. Wong, his eyes as big as saucers.

"Summer over," Mr. Wong said, nervously eyeballing the sky.

With that, he yanked the three boys through the door and slammed it shut behind them, blocking out the frigid air.

Ned imagined a stunned silence falling over the city. It took him a minute to realize his heart was pounding like a jackhammer. There was nothing imaginary about *that*.

Bobby tore off his silly paper hat and flung it to the floor. Thrusting the greasy spatula in Ned's hand, he said, "Here. I'm going home."

Mr. Wong, still looking stupefied, let him go. Without comment, he wandered back to the front of the deli. There, he stood at the plate glass window, peering out, watching the pedestrians, most of them dressed in summer tees and shorts. They were rushing to and fro like ants, heads down, their arms folded over their chests against the icy wind, their faces expressing shock, bewilderment, confusion. Cars had pulled over to the side of the street while drivers looked around, trying to figure out what was going on. The customers who had been seated at the little plastic tables were no longer there. Idly, Ned wondered where and when they'd gone.

A moment later, the neon lights inside the deli flickered, went out, and then just as quickly flickered back to life. At the same time, the gauzy red haze deepened. Rose-hued darkness settled more heavily over the city. Ambient light dimmed. Vision diminished, and noises dulled. A distant siren sounded thin and reedy, as if the air had suddenly lost the ability to carry sound waves properly. The gusting frigid wind died down, and the temperature began to creep up again.

Stunned and frightened by everything that was happening, Ned sought out Joe's hand and clung to it like a lifeline. Joe edged nearer and held Ned close.

Standing safe in Joe's arms, Ned listened to the power crank back up to full force. That ever-present background hum of electricity one usually never notices until it stops started up again. Traffic lights flashed back to life and started to blink out on the street once more. Cars began to move, pulling hesitantly away from curbs, lining up once more in an orderly fashion like herded sheep, resuming their original paths to wherever they had been headed before the world stopped making sense.

At that precise moment, a delayed epiphany came out of left field and smacked Ned upside the head. He freely admitted to himself for the second time in as many hours that he wasn't just smitten with

Joe. It wasn't a crush. He was flat-out stark raving nuts about the guy. Period.

Great timing too. With the world falling apart around him, what the hell was he supposed to do about falling in love *now*?

CHAPTER TWO

SOLAR FLARES erupting across the surface of the sun began to increase in size. In concert, coronal mass ejections, or CMEs, emitted massive clouds of magnetic particles into the solar system. These particles funneled into near-Earth space where they reacted with oxygen and nitrogen, further weakening the sun's ability to radiate light. The skies over every corner of the planet deepened to a ruby red.

Power grids tried to compensate for the encroaching darkness. The ones in more heavily populated areas were the hardest hit. Fearing the grids were being taxed to their limits, electrical output was powered downward across the US and throughout many of the more technically advanced countries. But almost immediately, despite warnings from the scientific community, most power grids were quickly rebooted to their original output for fear of public outcry.

At the same time, ambient light began to fade even more across the day- and nighttime skies. The moon dimmed. Stars disappeared one by one until only Polaris remained visible. Migratory patterns of birds worldwide were affected when they lost their ability to read the stars, rendering their internal GPS useless.

After a tumultuous drop of fifty-three degrees that only lasted a minute or two, temperatures across the planet leveled out to an average of twenty-eight degrees below normal.

Since the powers that be did not expect a solar storm to create any of these events, neither they nor the scientific community quite knew what to do about them. For lack of a better plan, they continued to monitor and recalibrate and argue. Endlessly. They continually postponed a decision on what actions should be taken. Instead, they simply waited. Waited for the solar storm to stop. Waited for nature to readjust.

After all, it was just a glitch. An anomaly. One of nature's little quirks, people said. The solar system had decided to play a few head games on the feeble-minded dolts below. The universe was keeping *humanity on its toes. No need to panic. It would all straighten itself out in the end.*

True concern, as so often happens, was slow in coming. Too slow. Even scientists—people who should have known better—did not feel it yet.

Later, they would ask themselves why. But by then, of course, it would be too late.

JOE WAITED all day for a phone call from his supervisor at the zoo telling him to take the night off. He wasn't sure why he expected it. It's not like the planet had ground to a halt over the fact that the sun had disappeared, the sky had turned red, and the temperature in Southern California had leveled out to almost thirty degrees cooler than what it should have been for that time of year.

It wasn't as if the zoo had actually closed up shop for the day. That would have been truly historic, since the San Diego Zoo had rarely closed its gates since they first opened almost a century before. The last closure was due to high winds that threatened to uproot tall eucalyptus trees on the zoo grounds, with the added threat that those collapsing trees might conceivably flatten a few paying customers when they fell. Bad for publicity, that.

Joe snickered. No, it was unlikely the zoo would close now. And he was right. No phone call came. So at 4:00 p.m., like always, Joe donned his dungaree pants and the khaki shirt with his name and the little zoo emblem over the breast pocket and set off walking to work. He could have driven, but then he would have deprived himself of the joy of having Ned walk him home later. That he would not do.

Stepping outside, Joe was amazed to feel how much the temperature had dropped since that initial blast of frigid air at the deli earlier. With sunset approaching, the air wasn't just nippier, it was downright cold, or it felt that way to him. Of course, Joe was a San Diegan. To San Diegans, if the thermometer falls below sixty, it's considered polar, and everyone breaks out earmuffs and parkas.

Joe barely got past his front stoop before he did an about-face and raced back into his apartment to grab a jacket. If it was this cold now, what would it be like at two in the morning when he got off work?

The sky was a deeper red than it had been this morning. As the day progressed, visibility had lessened to the point that it was almost impossible to see anything more than two or three blocks away. Funny how you didn't miss the crystal clear California air until it was swept away in some sort of global cataclysm.

Joe shook his head ruefully. It was downright disappointing. Annoying really. You'd think nature would be more organized than this.

He stood on Sixth Avenue, staring down the hill toward the downtown skyscrapers, which he couldn't see through the bloodied air at all. Drivers were once again using their headlights, but Joe doubted it was helping them much. This wasn't like natural darkness. This was more of a red fog, a vapor, a miasma. It swallowed the very *possibility* of light, leaving the world obscured, lost in a dull crimson gloom that appeared to deepen with every hour that passed.

Drivers were scuttling home from work, their eyes more on the skies above than the road ahead. Joe scrambled across Sixth Avenue, weaving a treacherous path through distracted rush-hour traffic, then jumped gratefully over the curb onto the grassy lawns of Balboa Park, glad to have made it without getting himself run over.

Slightly shaken, he set off across the grass. Up ahead he would duck beneath the trees and enter the same hidden trails he and Ned would follow later on their return trip home. But before he reached the trails, Joe understood that nature had shifted somehow. The world had changed. Things were not the way they had always been.

It began with the stillness of the air. There was no breeze. None whatsoever. It wasn't the usual lull of a windless day; it was more profound than that. It was as if the very air around him had grown stagnant, listless, too pumped full of the strange red haze to nudge itself awake. Like a fat leech, engorged with blood, unable to even squirm, the air lay inert across the city. It was so lifeless, so *dense*, Joe felt he was not simply walking but wading through it, fighting it, forcing his way forward. It was as if the air had become as thick as soup, when in reality it was only the absence of light that made it seem that way. Or was it?

It was creepy. Joe knew that much. He also knew Ned would be frightened by it. Ned didn't have a cell phone, so Joe considered calling the deli's landline, right now, to insist Ned not meet him after work. Yeah, right. He could talk himself blue and Ned wouldn't change his mind. Ned would come to meet him whether Joe wanted him to or not. Ned was stubborn. He wanted what he wanted. And what he wanted was to meet Joe.

With that thought, Joe eked out a smile. No, he wouldn't call Ned. He would let Ned connect with him on the trails after work, like Ned wanted. Because that was what Joe wanted too. No matter how crazy the world had become, no matter how many ways the planet might find to flip itself on its head, the two of them, Ned and Joe, would still want to spend time together. It would take more than a red sky to change that. In fact, *nothing* could change it. And that was exactly the way Joe liked it.

Stepping away from the park's grassy lawn, with its doggy enclosures and bocce courts, Joe walked into the murk of one of the shadowed paths. Those paths wove here and there among the densely packed pines that carpeted sloping canyon walls throughout the park. With the light as dim as it was, being on the trail now, even in daylight, was almost like being on the trail at night. The red haze was diffused by the trees, making it even darker beneath them. The ambient light on this particular path, made even dimmer by the sprawling branches overhead, was almost nonexistent. Not quite, but almost. Still, like Ned, Joe had grown up in San Diego. He knew Balboa Park like the back of his hand. Like the gentle curve of Ned's ear. Like the grateful smile Ned gave him when Joe had pleased him in some little way. In other words, there wasn't a trail in Balboa Park that Joe didn't have memorized from the get-go. Still, it was strange, moving through this weirdass darkness during daylight hours. His feet knew the path; it was his eyes and his mind that balked at the strangeness of it all.

Usually when Joe walked to work, he would meet joggers on the trail. Pretty girls with their ponytails bouncing at the backs of their heads, or fit young guys in shorts, with sweaty torsos, eyeing their Garmins and trying to beat their own personal records as they raced up and down the hilly paths, barely glancing Joe's way as they passed. Too wrapped up in themselves to notice anyone else.

Ned always laughed at the joggers. He thought it was funny the way they continually tried to outrun their own mortality, while Joe thought maybe they were simply having fun.

A keening, high-pitched wail tore through the canyon. It ricocheted over Joe's head and screamed off into the trees. It came from the zoo up ahead. A snow leopard. Joe recognized its cry. Usually they only wailed like that at night. Maybe the red sky had confused it. Maybe this infernal red haze was as disconcerting to the animals as it was to the people.

God knew the birds were having fits. They were damn near as noisy as the snow leopard. Joe could see them now through an opening in the branches above his head, swooping and soaring and screeching just above the treetops, a dozen different breeds all mixed in together, their varied voices a cacophony. Doves, sparrows, crows, seagulls, even a pelican or two were swooping back and forth over the park. Joe had seen them from his apartment window. They had been in the sky for hours, endlessly circling. It was almost as if they were afraid to set down. As if their only hope of surviving was to keep circling, keep moving, keep squawking and bitching and railing about their plight. Joe wondered if it was simple confusion that kept the birds in flight. What with the red gloom blocking their points of reference, maybe they could not find their nests, not tell directions.

But not all flying entities were circling in confusion.

For the first time, Joe noticed that incoming flights to the airport had stopped altogether. There were no airliners lined up in the sky over the city, waiting to land. This was unheard of. Ordinarily there was an endless queue of jets dropping toward Lindbergh Field from dawn to early evening, one right after the other, their great engines powering down as they methodically sank from the heavens and lined up with the runways. It made Joe wonder what was happening in the rest of the world. He knew the skies were red everywhere. He had seen it on the news, but that was before TV reception became so bad he couldn't see anything at all. Back in his apartment, he had finally switched the television off in disgust and simply sat around staring through the window, waiting for it to be time to go to work. It had been during those empty hours of the afternoon when he had missed Ned the most. And he still missed him now.

A thought suddenly stopped Joe in his tracks. Maybe tonight he would ask Ned to stay with him in the apartment. Because of the red sky, he would say. Because it was scary, and he didn't want Ned to be alone.

That wouldn't be the real reason, of course.

Joe stood on the shadowy path and stared up through the still trees at the endlessly circling birds, their strident voices screaming in frustration.

His heart started pounding at the thought of spending the night with Ned. It would be the first time they shared a bed.

Joe squeezed his eyes shut while butterflies flittered around inside his stomach. By the time he blinked his eyes open, he was determined. He would insist Ned spend the night with him, and for the first time, he would tell Ned how he really felt about him.

Joe swallowed hard. *After that, who knows what will happen.*

AFTER WORK, Ned kicked off his shoes, opened a can of split-pea soup, his favorite, dumped it in a bowl, and sat in his lonely apartment waiting for it to nuke in the microwave. He had stopped at the market on the way home to buy candles since he was afraid the power might go out, what with everything going on. With Joe at the zoo, Ned didn't relish the idea of being home alone if the lights went out after sunset, so the candles would help.

After he ate, he took a long shower to wash away the bacon grease that coated him from head to toe. As always, he had to wash his hair three times in steaming hot water to get it out. By the time he stepped from the shower and dried off, he felt like he'd been boiled alive. Studying his naked reflection in the bathroom mirror, he could see that even his shoulders and chest were flushed pink from the hot water.

It had been a long day, and he was tired. His mind a blank, he stared at himself, at his lean frame, pale skin, and blond pubes, and that little patch of fluffy hair that circled his belly button. His cock hung flaccid. The uncut head, hidden in its sheath of flesh, brushed against the cool porcelain of the bathroom sink. He was tempted to peel that sheath back and take his dick for a spin, but he didn't. He was tired of touching himself. He was tired of thinking of Joe when he did. He was tired of spilling his seed by his own hand. He wanted more. For a long time now, he had wanted… more.

He brought his hand up and swept it through his wet hair, lightly stroking the scar at the side of his head. Leaned in closer to the mirror and looked at it. The scar too was pink from the hot water. It looked like it had back in the days when the wound was fresh, when it still burned his skin like a branding iron.

That's sort of what it was, after all. A brand. He had been branded for being the way he was. The way he *still* was. Ned sighed, fighting the guilty thoughts running through his head he had been *conditioned* to think. No matter how hard he tried, he couldn't push them aside altogether, no more than he could avoid the temptation to touch the scar that evoked them. Would he ever be able to leave the memories behind?

Ned turned away from the mirror and tugged on a ratty old pair of pajamas that he liked to lounge around in after work.

Ned's early evenings were all spent doing the same things. He would read or watch TV—when it worked, and today for some reason it didn't. He would continually glance at the clock, waiting for the hour hand to tell him it was time to meet Joe in the park. Those were two of the major components of his life: the hours at work and the hours of waiting. Yet it wasn't really so bad. He did get to see Joe every day. That was the third part. That was the part that mattered. That was all he really cared about. Seeing Joe. Being with Joe. Watching—and wanting—Joe.

Ned sat in the battered old recliner he had bought at the Salvation Army store down the street (in fact, Joe had helped him carry it home). Sitting there, his feet up, his eyes aimed blankly at the ceiling, he was less than surprised to feel a tear slide down his cheek. This was the time the tears always came. These last few hours when he waited for Joe to get off work. Before he braved the darkness—and now this weird coppery dusk—and went to meet Joe in the park. In truth, even before the spooky haze came along to drool its red misery over the planet, the shadowy trails in Balboa Park had scared the hell out of Ned. But fear was a small price to pay for the privilege of being with Joe again. Hearing Joe's laughter. Seeing Joe's smile. And sometimes, when he was lucky, feeling Joe's arms snake around him and pull him close in an innocent hug.

Blinking away the tears and trying not to wonder what Joe would think if he knew how those innocent hugs *really* affected him, Ned turned to the window and stared out at the gathering darkness. The crazy wheeling birds still screamed in the sky. They had been up there all day. Ever since that weird rush of cold air blasted through the city when he and Joe were sitting out in the alley behind the deli. That snap of freezing air had been the strangest thing Ned had ever experienced. It hadn't lasted long, but even now, the air was cooler than it should be. A lot cooler. Ned would have to wear a coat when he went to meet Joe. Maybe he'd even take an extra coat, in case Joe had forgotten his.

Absently, Ned touched the scar at the side of his head again. Stroked it as one would to calm an anxious pet. But when the texture of it began to incite those painful memories, he forced his hand down and shook his head. Then, as if he couldn't bear the silence for another minute, he softly said, "Joe," whispering it like a spell against the emptiness he felt inside.

With that one little word echoing faintly in his head, Ned managed a trembling smile and closed his eyes. Soon, with the alarm clock set for midnight so he wouldn't be late for his rendezvous with Joe, he dozed off.

Joe met him there in his dreams, as he always did. And when Ned awoke, he was hungry for his friend all over again. He lay there sprawled out in his ratty recliner, struggling to ignore his hard-on. Dreams of Joe *always* left him with a hard-on. He tried to hum a tune to take his mind off it.

At that moment a loud crash startled him so that he leaped right out of the chair, boner and all.

Spinning around, seeking the source of the sound with wide frightened eyes, he spotted a smear of dirt on the living room window that hadn't been there before. He stepped toward it and, with shaking fingers, touched the pane. Was it his imagination, or was the glass still vibrating?

He pressed his forehead to the window and tried to look down at the ground outside, but it was too dark to see anything.

Still barefoot and wearing his pajamas, Ned opened his front door and peeked outside. Taking a deep breath to calm himself, he stepped out onto his tiny front landing. Unable to see anything from where he stood, he descended the single step and walked onto the lawn so he could tiptoe toward his besmeared window. The night air was freezing. He hissed in surprise when his bare feet hit the cold, dewy grass.

Leaning over the short hedge that lined the front of the building, he peered down into the shadows below his window and saw a turtledove lying in the dirt. The dove's feathers were ruffled, its neck twisted into an impossible angle. It had flown into the glass, confused by the strange murkiness, maybe, drawn to the light inside. When it struck the window, it must have broken its neck. The dove was dead.

Ned emitted a quiet groan. Poor bird. He lifted his gaze to the sky and saw… nothing. Peering at the heavens was like staring at the ceiling of a pitch-black room. What stars were there, or at least had always *been* there, were lost behind the haze-filled darkness. The rising moon, no doubt paler than usual but still visible, he hoped, was hidden by the office building on the adjacent lot. He gazed along the front of his own building, first left, then right. As usual, at this late hour, his was the only apartment window lit.

Yet even through the blinding darkness, Ned could hear the birds overhead, endlessly circling somewhere up there in the lightless night where his eyes couldn't descry them. He could make out the muted roar of thousands of beating wings and the cries of an endless eddy of lost creatures, crying out in frustration, excitement, or anger—whatever the hell it was.

Ned shivered. As much from fear as from the cold. His feet were starting to feel like ice. After a final pitying glance at the poor dead dove, he hurried through the wet grass toward his front door. Before he reached it, another crash made him jump. A second bird had flown into his window! It tumbled to the ground, wings flapping, squawking up a storm. This collision was louder than the first. The bird was bigger. It sounded like a seagull. It was a wonder it hadn't broken the glass!

Ned leaned over the hedge again and spotted the white bird flopping around on the bare dirt between the hedge and the foundation of the building. Suddenly, as if shot from a cannon, the bird catapulted itself into the air, barely missing Ned's head. It soared off into the dark with a furious cry. By the time it was gone, Ned's heart was pounding like a tom-tom, and he was clutching his chest like he was about to faint. Christ, it had really given him a scare! Well, at least the seagull wasn't hurt. Not too badly at any rate.

Ned stood in the freezing air, wondering what would happen next. But there was only the continuous screeching and muffled wingbeats of the birds wheeling overhead. And the cold. He gave himself a shake and rushed back inside before something else *did* happen. Once through his front door, the first thing he did was turn out his living room lamps so no more birds would be drawn to the light. He quickly closed his door behind him to block out the cold. Then he flicked the dead bolt to lock out the night.

He squinted through the darkness to the clock on the bookshelf. It was almost time to leave. Humming a tuneless melody to calm his frazzled nerves, he began pulling on his clothes in the dark, snatching them off the bed where he'd laid them out earlier. Grabbing an extra coat for Joe (he remembered!), he then rushed back through the front door and diligently locked up behind himself. Still a little rattled and on unsteady legs, he took off at a brisk clip for the park.

Boy, the air was really cold now. And the darkness was as deep as Ned had ever seen it. It swallowed everything. Thank God for streetlights, although even they seemed to shimmer weakly over his head, barely offering any light at all. There wouldn't be any streetlights in the park, though. It was a good thing he had the trails memorized. A crease furrowed his forehead when he thought of feeling his way through the trees in the dark, but he dredged up thoughts of Joe again, and that gave him the courage to swallow his fear and keep going. In his eagerness to see Joe, he walked faster.

Traffic had died down. After all, it would soon be one in the morning. If it hadn't been for the shrieking birds, circling somewhere in the gloom above his head, the night would have been as still as death.

And with that uneasy thought of mortality, Ned wondered about the poor dead bird that had crashed into his living room window. Did it have young ones sitting in a nest somewhere, starving, waiting in vain for food that would never come? He hoped not. The thought bothered him, so he shot a heartfelt prayer skyward to a God he wasn't sure he believed in, pleading for it not to be so.

After that short, fleeting prayer, Ned turned his thoughts back to Joe. Desperate to see him now and already tired of being alone in this damned darkness, he left the openness of the park's great sloping lawn and stepped onto the first pitch-black trail leading down through the canyon.

Total darkness swallowed him up in a heartbeat. Hurrying dead center along the pathway to avoid the menacing shadows that reached out for him on either side, hiding God knows what, Ned hugged the extra jacket to his chest, as much to keep himself warm as to keep it safe for Joe.

It was only then, once he left the streetlights and the scattered ricocheting headlights of passing automobiles far behind, that Ned realized the moon had completely disappeared. It had to be up there somewhere, but not even a vestige of its glow could be seen. The red fog enveloping the planet had swallowed it completely, leaving those parts of the city that were bereft of artificial light, such as this spot he was now on, steeped in cheerless, impenetrable shadow. Standing only yards into the trail, tucked under the overhanging pines, Ned held his hand up to his face, flexed his fingers, and saw… zilch. Always before, he could navigate by the light of moon and stars, or by the distant glitter of the city skyline, but with them gone, he was blind. It was like being rudderless and lost on a vast, wallowing sea of black.

A shiver shot up his spine, and for the first time Ned wondered why he hadn't brought a flashlight. Jesus, he could be so stupid sometimes. Should he go back and get it? No. What if Joe got off work even a few minutes early and rushed down the trail to meet him, only to find Ned wasn't there waiting for him?

That thought brought courage and determination to Ned. Although the shadows were relentless and terrifying, he straightened his shoulders and plodded on. He moved deeper into the trees, placing every footstep carefully on the invisible path. The park's trails were so familiar he somehow knew where he was by the bumps in the ground beneath his feet and the tilt of the hillsides he traveled across. Even the passing scents of honeysuckle and loam were like a road map for Ned. He thought back to all those many nights he had passed this way bathed in moonlight. Concentrating on not letting himself get lost now that the moonlight was gone helped control his fear of the dark. He was able to tamp it down into a place deep inside himself where he could keep it at bay, at least for a while. With that fear out of the way, he could concentrate on more important things—like a smiling Joe Chase waiting for him somewhere up ahead.

For the first time since he'd left the apartment, Ned managed his own feeble smile. The darkness still frightened him, of course. But the promise of Joe made the fright bearable. Joe was worth a little fear. Joe was worth whatever it took.

Sucking in a quiet breath of determination, Ned plodded on. Like a whisper, he passed over the lightless, rutted path, moving deeper and deeper into the trees. Into the darkness. Here, the air was tainted with the stench of at least one pissed-off skunk. Ned hoped to God he wouldn't run into it.

As he drew farther into the shadows, mixed in with the screaming of the ever-circling birds, he began to hear the cries of other beasts. Furious wailings, maniacal screams, and howls. Barks, yowls, yips. Horror movie stuff. They sent goose bumps skittering along the back of Ned's neck.

What frightened him even more was the knowledge that the sounds came from the zoo! *What was happening there? Why were the animals making all that racket? What in the world had angered them so?*

Suddenly scared more for Joe than for himself, Ned increased his pace along the invisible path. He hurried, his hands splayed out in front of him in case a low-hanging branch should suddenly reach down to whack him in the face. The eerie, mind-numbing darkness no longer frightened him.

It was Joe he feared for now. Only Joe.

More unnerved by the howls and cries than the blinding dark, he slapped his hands over his ears and plodded on.

IT HAD been the most bizarre night at work Joe could ever remember.

On any other night of the year, he was a groundsman. A gardener. That's all he did. That's all the powers that be expected of him. He tended the foliage that decorated the zoo grounds: replanting, pruning, fertilizing, keeping the proper moisture levels in San Diego's desert soil to best nourish each individual species of flora. After all, some of the zoo's ferns and trees and flowering plants were just as rare and precious as the animals on display. And like the animals, they needed constant care and knowledgeable tending. What Joe did not know about their needs, the botanists who supervised the work did.

The last few nights, as Joe had mentioned to Ned, the grounds crew had spent their shifts planting young palm trees in and around the gorilla enclosures.

Tonight they were supposed to begin pruning the foliage and cleaning the dead leaves out of the pools in the Amazon enclosure. They used cherry pickers to reach the pools with their long rakes and shears and cleaning nets because the crocodiles and caimans that inhabited the enclosure were always hungry and not exactly friendly. To a croc, apparently, a gardener was a perfectly acceptable side dish to the usual fare the keepers tossed his way.

But instead of Joe and his workmates being trucked to the Amazon arena as expected, they found themselves doing work they never imagined would fall to them.

Joe had known something was wrong as soon as he clocked in. There were animal tenders present in the botanical shed whom the groundskeepers usually never saw. The tenders always worked during the daylight hours, not at night when the zoo was closed. Also present was the director of the San Diego Zoo's overall operation, Mr. Daily. The head honcho himself. And Joe couldn't help but notice he looked fairly anxious.

As if all that wasn't bizarre enough, the behavior of the animals was even stranger.

Before Joe entered the zoo grounds, he had heard them. Every beast and bird present seemed to be crying out in frustration. The lions fought in their enclosure, their angry growls a terrifying thing to hear. Elephants trumpeted furiously and rocked their great bodies against the iron fences that penned them in, systematically seeking weaknesses in the structure. The fences groaned and sang their own song of anguish, popping and snapping as rusted rivets twisted in their sockets. By the sound they were making, Joe was amazed the fences were holding at all.

Gators and crocs in the reptile pools were grumbling and bellowing, twisting and thrashing in the water, fighting each other, tearing at the plants in their enclosures, and furiously slashing their great tails against the moat walls. In the paddock by the moving sidewalks leading up the hill from one of the many canyons that peppered the zoo grounds, antelopes and okapi were stampeding in an endless circle, mimicking the birds in the sky. Their frantic, thunderous hoofbeats raised a thick cloud of dust that blended with the red haze and limited vision even more than it already was.

Toucans railed in their aviaries, banging their huge beaks against the wire mesh, creating an incredible racket all on their own. Their great mouths agape in fury, hippos in the pond were charging at the underwater Plexiglas wall that separated the beasts from the viewing public, as if attempting to crash their way through. Keepers were already there, trying to turn them with long poles, perplexed that the massive creatures should suddenly be venting their fury on the glass wall when always before they had ignored it completely. A young hippo, born only six months earlier, had already fallen victim to the onslaught, inadvertently crushed to death by its own mother in the turmoil.

Zoo-wide, in enclosure after enclosure, the animals were flinging themselves at their cage walls or attacking each other in a murderous rage. The big cats were the worst, fighting and clawing. Several young cubs had been accidentally destroyed, and one of the two mature black panthers had fallen victim to the fury. She now lay dead in the cage, her bloodied body being devoured by the creature that killed her, her mate of many years.

Even the silverback gorilla, who had been so placid and patient the night before when Joe and the grounds crew worked in his enclosure planting the young palms, was running around uprooting the foliage and pounding his chest in threat displays, while the females cowered inside a man-made cave with their young clutched protectively to their breasts.

Joe couldn't believe what was happening. The whole zoo was going crazy. Between the cacophonous birds in their cages and the howling creatures penned on the ground, the noise was almost unbearable.

Ordinarily at night, the animals were left to enjoy the seclusion of darkness, just one more way the zoo had found to afford them a stress-free existence—as stress free as a life of captivity can be, at least. But tonight the floodlights were lit, illuminating the zoo's entire hundred-acre compound and every single creature residing inside it. Still, the red haze that had fallen over the city had weakened the effect of the floodlights considerably. What should have been a blazing, shadowless blanket of white light, exposing the enclosures and the beasts within in sharp relief, was reduced to a murky, vermilion pall, which if anything appeared to infuriate the animals even more than the brightest lights.

Because of all this wanton destruction perpetrated by the animals themselves, and since the animal tenders couldn't be expected to work twenty-four-hour shifts, the grounds crew had been called in to help stem the fury. They hoped to do this by simply feeding the creatures. It was really no more complicated than that. Yet it was still a massive chore. The grounds crew's usual agenda of tending the 700,000 exotic plants on the zoo grounds was for this one night put on hold while they fed extra rations to the 3,500 animals, representing 650 species and subspecies, held captive on the premises. All in the hope of stopping them from killing each other, or for the creatures held in solitary confinement, to prevent them from beating themselves to death on their cage walls.

A few of the usual tenders were there as well, voluntarily pulling a double shift. They looked exhausted and worried sick about the animals in their charge. Joe knew the zoo's high muckety-mucks must be desperate, or they would never have allowed a bunch of gardeners to tend the very expensive beasts in their care.

Joe stood staring into a hand wagon filled with large chunks of bone and gristle. Horse meat, he figured, although he wasn't sure. It seemed he had drawn the big cats to feed. He wasn't too thrilled about it either, thinking he'd have been far happier feeding the fucking ducks. Hard to get mauled to death by a duck. He was especially concerned since the big cats had worked themselves into such a savage frenzy, roaring and charging the fences, attacking each other in that strange murderous madness that had been brought about by the red haze. Joe couldn't imagine why it would infuriate them so, but it clearly did.

Happily, the task of feeding the rampaging carnivores was not assigned to Joe alone. The head keeper of the cats, a zoologist with a master's degree and about two decades' worth of experience tending these beautiful but extremely dangerous creatures, was there to walk Joe through it and make sure Joe didn't inadvertently feed himself to the cats as well. Or so his new boss had told him with a wink. Joe's response had been a sardonic "Har, har." But he wasn't smiling when he said it.

Most of Joe's night shift was spent standing around nervously waiting while the experts coaxed and coerced the big cats into their secondary enclosures so the extra rations could be introduced to their primary cages. The San Diego Zoo boasted dozens of the great predators. Lions, tigers, black panthers, jaguars, snow and clouded leopards, pumas, lynx, ocelots, bobcats. The list was endless. And on this night, each and every one of the beasts had worked itself into a lethal, raging fury.

Once the enclosures were cleared, the keepers turned to Joe and a couple of his cronies from the grounds crew for the grunt work. With shovels, pitchforks, and bare hands, they transferred the huge cuts of meat from the hand wagon into the cages. While they worked, the big cats leered at them through the wire mesh of their temporary holding cells, eyes wild with anger, great fangs exposed, claws working. Time and again they flung themselves at the wire trying to get at the workers. Their aggressive displays were so heart-stoppingly insane, even the seasoned animal handlers were unnerved. His shift had barely begun before Joe knew he would never look at these creatures the same way again. In fact, he was pretty sure they would scare the crap out of him for the rest of his frigging life. He also developed an immediate appreciation for the plants in his care. At least the plants didn't try to eat him.

The zoologist supervising the work looked extremely relieved when Joe and his cohorts finally finished feeding the four Bengal tigers in his care. He backed away from their vast enclosure, sweating bullets, watching in amazement as the four creatures fought and slashed at each other, trying to claim their fair share of the meat.

"This is fucking nuts," Joe heard the man mumble as he turned away, shaking his head in disbelief.

"Totally," Joe echoed in response as he wheeled the hand wagon toward the next enclosure and what were probably the most dangerous predators of all. The leopards.

It was a long, nerve-racking night. All that kept Joe sane was thinking about Ned, sweet Ned, waiting for him on the trail at the end of his shift.

He couldn't have known that Ned was facing problems of his own.

NED COULD hear his pulse thumping inside his head. He was at that point on the trail when it began to dip into the largest canyon—down, down, down to where the roar from the Cabrillo Freeway could begin to be heard. Down to where the little footbridge stretched across the four lanes of traffic below. He loved the footbridge. He would feel safe there. Safer than where he stood now, at least, because this darkness was really starting to freak him out. He couldn't see the slashing strobe of the freeway traffic's passing headlights yet, but the distant hum of automobiles whizzing along somewhere up ahead began to restore his confidence. Frankly, it was the first smidgeon of confidence he had felt since he stepped out of his apartment.

The trail was so much darker than he had expected. Ned had never seen it like this. Light was absolutely nonexistent. Even overhead, there was no moon, no stars, nothing. A hand held smack in front of his face was an empty void hovering over a deeper, denser void. He could squeeze his eyes shut and see exactly what he saw when they were opened wide. Nothing.

After hurrying across Balboa Park's broad, sloping lawns, illuminated by ambient light from streetlamps and passing traffic back along Sixth Avenue, Ned groped along now on the pitch-black trail, as blind as he had ever been in his life. He had finally overcome his fear of the bellowing zoo animals up ahead and once more held his arms stretched out in front of him to ward off anything that might suddenly block his way. He knew where he was on the trail, but still the darkness left him leery of his instincts. With every step, he imagined himself walking into a tree or tripping over a root or tumbling over a cliff, or simply wandering off in the wrong direction and losing himself among the pines.

Or even more frightening, plowing without warning into another human being approaching along the trail from the opposite direction. A human being, shall we say, with maybe less than harmless intentions.

It wasn't only the dark and his imagination and the distant cries of the zoo animals that spooked him. It was the sounds he kept hearing nearby. Furtive sounds. The rustle and crunch of pattering footsteps somewhere out there in the surrounding trees. The sounds were so soft and so many, he couldn't begin to determine from which direction they came. Wherever they were, or whatever was making them, Ned knew they were keeping pace with him. When he walked, they followed along. When he stopped, they fell silent, as if waiting for him to start up again. And when they did grow still like that, it left the woods absolutely soundless but for the thumping of his own heart and the clamoring of the beasts in the distance.

Oddly, the small creatures that *usually* accompanied him on these walks—the scurrying squirrels and feral cats, the night birds flapping and cheeping in the bushes, the crickets and the humming insects—were no longer present. Or if they were, they were just as frightened as Ned and so had chosen to cower motionless and silent in the shadows, waiting perhaps, for nothing more than this ungodly night to pass.

During one of those frozen moments when Ned stood listening with every fiber of his being for a sound he probably didn't want to hear, he actually heard it. It was the brittle snap of a twig, off to his left, out among the trees.

At the same time, something settled against the side of his foot. He nudged it with his toe and felt it shift. It was a long piece of wood. Part of a fallen branch perhaps.

When he heard another twig snap somewhere off to his right, as if whatever was out there was maneuvering to sneak up on him from another direction, Ned slowly bent and hefted the branch in his hands. It was maybe three feet long and heavy enough to be used as a cudgel if the need arose. Just the fact that Ned was now standing there in impenetrable darkness gauging the weight of a cudgel in his hand scared him even more.

He stood rooted to the trail, club in hand, turning first one way, then the other. He looked forward, then back, then tried to peer into the trees at either side of the path. Of course, it was all a big waste of energy. It was so dark he couldn't see a fucking thing in *any* direction.

He cursed himself again for not bringing a flashlight.

Gulping hard to swallow his fear, he once again began to work his way downhill along the trail. It was steep here, leading down toward the freeway and the little mesh-covered bridge. Once there, he would have light from the cars below and the safety of the wire surrounding him. Danger would only be able to come at him from ahead or behind, not from either side or above. He could defend himself. Maybe.

As soon as he was moving again, the sound of footsteps in the trees started up once more. Those sounds came from every direction now. Clearly, whatever stalked him wasn't alone. There was more than one of them out there, lurking in the shadows. Ned stopped at the snap of a twig that sounded closer than the others. His heart shot up into his throat, and he gripped the cudgel like a baseball bat, squinting this way and that into the darkness. He worked his fingers around the rough wood, holding on for dear life. A rivulet of icy sweat slid down his rib cage, making him almost gasp. He had tied the extra jacket he carried for Joe around his waist, knotted by the sleeves, to free up his hands. He imagined the jacket offering a little added protection for whatever might come flying out of the shadows to rip his guts out.

That thought was so far over the top, even Ned couldn't stand it.

His anger swelled, and he screamed into the trees, "Go away! Leave me alone!"

And that's when he heard it. A growl. No, not one growl. *Two.* One off in the trees to his right and another to his left. A heartbeat later, he heard yet another growl stuttering out of the darkness somewhere back along the trail he had just traveled. It sounded close. *Too* close.

Jesus, how many of them are there?

His first thought was to flee, just run like a rabbit and never look back. But he knew if he tried to run full tilt down this sloping dirt trail in pitch blackness he would never be able to stay on his feet. And once he stumbled and crashed to the ground, they'd be on him. Whatever the fuck they were. Then they really would rip his guts out, just like on those PBS wildlife shows where a herd of wolves brought down a moose. Ned, like the poor moose, might be able to fight them off for a minute or two, but then by sheer numbers, the wolves would overpower him. Slowly, with excruciating deliberation, they would settle in and systematically tear him to pieces.

Ned swung the cudgel hard enough to hear it whistle through the air. The rustle and snap of branches coming from two or three different directions told him whatever was out there was still drawing closer.

There wasn't much doubt about it now. As in that PBS special, Ned was the prey, and he was being stalked.

Suddenly through the blackness at the side of the trail, he saw two red spots of light. Eyes. Then from back along the trail behind him, another set of eyes. They disappeared for a second as the beasts, whatever they were, blinked. Then they were back again, along with two more pinpoints of dim red light that appeared on the trail just ahead of him. It was that last pair of eyes that told him he was surrounded. And *that* realization made his heart give a fearful lurch.

To Ned's own surprise, with fear came a bubbling up of anger. He gritted his teeth and hunched in on himself, holding the bat in readiness for the assault that he knew was about to come.

Somewhere in the analytical part of his brain, Ned wondered how those eyes had absorbed enough ambient light from this impenetrable darkness to create a reflection. But in a more practical part of his mind where his furious desire to survive had apparently lain dormant until this very moment, he just wanted to get the battle over with.

"Come on, then, motherfuckers!" he screamed. "Take your best shot!"

As if goaded into action, they did exactly that.

From four different directions they moved in. Dogs. For that's what they were, Ned suddenly realized. Plain old frigging dogs. A couple of them weren't even that big. Terriers, maybe, by the sound of them. Ned couldn't be sure. But even if a couple of them weren't exactly big enough to snatch his life away, there were still two others Ned had to worry about. By the deep thunder of their growls and snarls, he knew those two weren't small at all. And it was from them that the greatest danger would come.

The utter lack of light seemed to heighten Ned's other senses. He could smell the dogs now. It was a sickly, sour smell. Unwashed. Feces and wet fur. They were probably feral like the cats that lived in the canyons. In their stench, he thought he discerned a wary anger. A *hunger*. As if they had it all planned out. As if they would bring him down, rip him to pieces, and divvy him up like four homeless guys splitting a Big Mac.

Ned's reflexes too were suddenly sharper than he could ever remember them being. It was like he had sonar. As if even in utter darkness, he could feel the animals approach. As if he would be able to sense when they came within reach of his club. And when they did, he would swing it with all the force he could muster and knock their blocks off.

The first dog to attack came from beneath the trees to his right. The scatter of pine needles beneath its scurrying paws gave away its location, and as soon as Ned heard that sound, he roared at the top of his voice and swung the cudgel low across the ground in front of him, right where he knew the attacking beast had to be. And sure enough, it was.

He felt the reverberation in his arms when the club struck the animal's legs. A howl of pain erupted, and no sooner had it risen up than Ned swung the club again, this time chopping it straight down toward the ground like an ax.

His second blow struck the animal's torso. Whatever it was, it felt big. Like German shepherd big. He thought he heard the crack of ribs; he *knew* he heard a great expulsion of air and a second whimper of pain.

At the rustle of weeds behind him, Ned whirled and once again swept the club through the air in a wide, sweeping arc. This time, by sheer luck, he struck another creature, this one lower to the ground. One of the smaller dogs. By the feel and give of the blow, and by what sounded like the clatter of teeth, he thought he had banged it across the head. It collapsed to the ground as the club swept into it again with a dull *thonking* sound, and this time there was no whimper of pain. There was no movement at all. Ned knew he had either killed it or knocked it senseless, and either option pleased him just fine. The little fucking mutt.

He was about to give a victorious shout, when strong jaws clamped around the back of his shoe. He tried to kick the creature away but couldn't. The teeth had latched into his tennis shoe like a vise. He whirled around, trying to strike at the beast with the club, but he couldn't get the right angle. This wasn't one of the small dogs. Its low, thundering growl sounded ferocious. And big. Another German shepherd maybe. Or a Rottweiler. He felt a vicious tug and knew it was trying to drag him into the bushes at the edge of the trail.

Ned got one good swing in, striking the dog in the side, but the jaws only clamped down harder onto the back of his shoe. Still awkwardly swinging his club, Ned tried to shake it off, hopping around on one foot now, screaming in fury at the top of his lungs.

Just when he knew he was losing his balance, when he knew the dog was about to pull him down to the ground, another furious roar exploded from the trail ahead of him. This time it was a human roar. A moment later, a blinding spear of light stabbed through the darkness and settled over him.

It was the beam of a flashlight! And Joe was the one aiming it.

"Beat it, you stupid mongrels. Get the hell out of here!" Joe bellowed like a foghorn, furious and fearless. He waded into Ned's battle without an instant of hesitation.

As much from the shock of finding Joe suddenly there to protect him as by the tugging of the dog at his heel, Ned finally lost his balance and toppled over, striking the ground hard. Winded by the fall, he quickly rolled over onto his back, thinking the dog would come for him, clamp those ferocious teeth onto his throat and shake him like a rat until he was dead. But whatever the dog's plan was, it didn't get the chance to set them in motion.

In the erratic beam of light shooting off in every direction at once, Ned watched as Joe loomed over him long enough to bring the heavy flashlight down on the dog's head. Releasing his hold on Ned's shoe at last, the creature snarled once, then tore off into the trees, escaping into the darkness. With their fury suddenly startled out of them and their leader heading for the hills like a coward, the other dogs followed suit, all but the small one Ned had killed with his club.

Joe centered his light on the creature lying dead on the path, then aimed the torch at Ned. "Did you do that?" he asked, coughing up a nervous laugh from all the adrenaline coursing through his system.

"It scared me," Ned explained, and then he dredged up a wary grin too. Still lying flat on his back, he tossed the cudgel aside and grabbed the hand Joe was holding out. With Joe's help he hoisted himself off the ground with a grunt.

Still breathless, still trembling with an overdose of adrenaline just like Joe, Ned simply said, "You came."

Joe stared at him in the light from the flashlight, which was pointed at the ground now so it wouldn't blind them. Ned watched in awe as Joe's smile disappeared and his fingers tightened around Ned's hand.

"I'll always come for you," Joe said quietly.

Ned knew beyond a shadow of a doubt that was true. Whatever happened, Joe would always be there for him.

Ned gave Joe's hand a yank and launched himself into Joe's arms. Joe accepted him, his strong arms folding around him as if there was no other place Joe would rather he be.

Ned dredged up a shaky laugh. Then, when his fear of the darkness and the dogs threatened to creep back in, he squeezed his eyes shut before the tears could well up for Joe to see.

He pressed his face to Joe's chest and whispered, "Thank you."

Joe cupped his fingers around the back of Ned's neck and pressed his lips into his hair.

That was the only answer Ned needed.

"ARE YOU hurt?" Joe asked, his arms wrapped tight around Ned's small frame, his chin settled firmly in Ned's hair. "Are you bitten?"

With his face still resting on Joe's chest, Ned shook his head. "No. Not a scratch."

"You were lucky."

"Thanks to you," Ned said. "How did you know I was in trouble?"

"I heard you yell."

Joe breathed in the scent of Ned's hair. It smelled like strawberry shampoo, with maybe a tiny dash of terror mixed in to give it a little zing.

"I was on the other side of the footbridge," Joe said. "After I heard you yell, I heard the dogs. They sounded just like the animals at the zoo. They've all gone wacky tonight. I guess that's why the dogs attacked you."

"It's the red sky," Ned said. "It's driving the animals nuts. You can't see them, but the birds are still wheeling around up there too. I don't think they've landed all day. They must be exhausted."

Joe tightened his hold on Ned because he felt so good in his arms. Ned's trembling had stopped, or at least most of it had. "Don't worry," he said. "They'll have to come down sooner or later. They can't fly around forever."

"But what's making them do it, Joe?"

Joe shook his head, and Ned's hair tickled his chin. "I don't know, buddy. I don't have a clue." He tucked a finger under Ned's chin, tilted his head up, and studied Ned's face in the nimbus of the flashlight's beam. Even with the flashlight aimed at the ground, it shed enough light to see the remains of panic still rattling around in Ned's eyes. Nevertheless, Joe was pretty sure he had never seen anything as beautiful as Ned's face at that very moment. He shuddered with sheer exuberance at having Ned standing there in his arms.

Ned misunderstood the shudder. He stepped back and unwrapped the extra jacket from around his waist. "You're cold," he said. "I brought you another coat. Put it on. It's warmer than the one you're wearing."

"Thanks!" Joe exclaimed, taking the coat gratefully. The air was colder than he had expected it to be. An extra coat would help a lot.

Once he had it zipped up snug to his throat, he reached out and laid a hand to Ned's cheek. "Thank you," he said.

Ned nodded. His eyes were big and round, and he looked embarrassed. Clearly hoping to change the subject, he asked, "So the animals at the zoo were acting up too?"

Joe smiled, knowing Ned must have already heard them. Hell, Joe could hear them *now*. He reached up to brush the curtain of pale hair away from Ned's eyes. "Crazy as bedbugs." Without asking permission, he pulled Ned back into another embrace.

In return, Ned wound his arms around Joe's waist. His hands came up to splay wide across Joe's back. Joe loved the way they felt.

Staring down once again into Ned's upturned gaze—he still looked a little shell-shocked, Joe thought—Joe threw caution to the wind and leaned in to plant a gentle kiss on Ned's forehead. Ned closed his eyes. The corners of his mouth turned up in a faint little smile.

"You've had a rough night," Joe said, his lips still grazing Ned's forehead. "You shouldn't be alone. When we get home, I want you to spend the night with me at the apartment. Will you do that?"

Following a gentle exhalation of breath, as if Ned had been surprised by the question—but perhaps not as surprised as he should have been—Ned stammered, "Y-yes. Whatever you want."

The way Ned answered without hesitation caused Joe to smile.

"I can sleep on my couch if you want," Joe ventured. "You should have the bed. You must be exhausted."

Ned tilted his head back. His expression was open and sweet and fearless. "I'll only take the bed if you're in it with me." Joe smiled again, pleased and contented. "I suppose that can be arranged."

Joe stepped back, the move mirrored by Ned as if by a prearranged signal, and Joe took Ned's hand and led him up the trail in the direction of home. They followed the beam of the flashlight as it bounced around in front of them. Now and then Joe sent the spear of light shooting off into the trees to illuminate every questionable shadow he spotted along the way.

"Are you really tired?" Joe asked quietly. The darkness and the hush of the old trees beneath a lightless sky was enough to dampen *anybody's* conversation.

"No," Ned answered, his voice as breathless as Joe's. "I'm not tired. I've never been more awake in my life."

Joe tightened his grip on Ned's fingers, and Ned stepped closer to Joe as if once again offering himself up for Joe's protection. Maybe that wasn't what Ned was thinking at all, of course, but Joe didn't care. His heart swelled at the idea anyway. He *wanted* to be Ned's protector. He *wanted* Ned close.

Having Ned next to him on the trail was one thing, but the prospect of having Ned next to him in his bed for the rest of the night was almost more than Joe could bear to contemplate. Already his heart was hammering like a bass drum, and it was taking every ounce of willpower he possessed not to touch his cock as it lengthened in his pants.

For the first time since the world fell apart, Joe was thankful for the dark.

His thankfulness evaporated immediately when Ned roughly grabbed his arm and yanked him to a stop.

"Listen!" he hissed, and Joe obediently froze.

Somewhere on the trail up ahead, he heard cursing. Grunts and groans. Male voices. Then came the unmistakable sound of a fist striking flesh. There was a fight going on. Two guys. Maybe more. It was hard to tell the way the noises sifted through the trees and the way the unnatural darkness muted sound. There could be five or six guys duking it out up there for all Joe could tell.

"You think people are going crazy too?" Ned asked in a breathless whisper. He didn't sound as if the idea pleased him.

Joe didn't like the idea much either. "I hope not," he whispered back. "Seems to me people are crazy enough on a *regular* basis. They don't need to be any *more* nuts."

Joe switched off the flashlight and tugged Ned close, still speaking softly. "Come with me into the trees. We'll go around to avoid them."

Only inches away in the shadows, but absolutely invisible to the naked eye, he could hear Ned swallow. Ned clutched at the hem of his coat, gathering a fistful of it to hold on to. "No argument here," Ned whispered back. "Lead the way."

Keeping Ned close, clutching a clump of Ned's jacket sleeve so they couldn't wander away from each other in the dark, Joe ushered Ned off the path and ducked into the pitch-black shadows beneath the pines.

They circled far around, groping along from one tree to the next, carefully planting their feet so they wouldn't make a sound. The pillow of pine needles on the ground helped. Also, there wasn't a lot of undergrowth to have to claw their way through. For both those things, Joe was intensely grateful.

Minutes later, the sounds of fighting seemed to come from behind them rather than in front. Joe could see glimpses of streetlights now, so he knew the woodsy part of the park was coming to an end. They would be on the open lawns soon, and from there they could make a dash for their apartment building. Joe didn't know what those people were fighting about, and he wanted to keep it that way. Ned had suffered one close call already tonight, what with the attacking dogs. That was pretty much all the excitement he needed. Joe didn't think either one of them could stand much more.

Besides, he wanted to get Ned home and into his bed in one piece. That was tantamount to everything else. It didn't matter what happened once he got him there. Anything, everything, nothing. He just wanted Ned safely in his arms.

Next to him, he felt Ned breathe a sigh of relief. "I don't think they'll bother us now. I can see our building."

"Me too," Joe said, spotting the dim glow of a streetlight up ahead. He sputtered up a weird little laugh, which was sort of like opening a sluice gate to run off a few extra gallons of adrenaline.

Ned giggled beside him. "You sounded scared back there."

"I *was* scared. Weren't you?"

Ned still hadn't finished giggling. "Shit, yeah. I'm a nervous wreck."

Taking a firmer grip on Ned's hand, Joe tugged him out of the trees, and side by side, laughing like loons now from relief more than anything else, they took off running across the dewy grass toward the lights up ahead. They swerved around the bocce courts and the horseshoe field like the boogeyman was after them.

Breathing hard, they flew across Sixth Avenue, where there wasn't a single car coming in either direction. A second or two later they flung themselves into the yard of their apartment building. They hurried past Ned's apartment with its darkened windows, one of which still had a pigeon's feather stuck to the glass, and flew up the stoop to Joe's front door.

With a trembling hand, Joe extracted his key from his front pocket and rattled it into the lock.

"Come inside," he said, a sappy grin still lighting his face. "Let's get out of the cold."

"And away from the crazies," Ned added, looking bright-eyed and rosy-cheeked from either the cold night air or the remnants of fear, Joe wasn't sure which.

A moment later, they stood together in Joe's living room. Still clinging to Ned, Joe extracted one hand from Ned's and turned to lock his front door, sealing them inside, safe and sound. When that chore was out of the way, he flicked on the lights.

Only then did they step back and study each other with shy, eager eyes.

"WANNA BEER?" Joe asked, casting his gaze around his own apartment as if he had never seen it before. He was afraid to settle his eyes on Ned for fear Ned would see the hunger in them.

"Sure." Ned smiled. He ran his fingers through his pale hair and looked down in surprise when they came away wet. In their time outside, dew had settled over both of them. Their shoulders sparkled with droplets of moisture, their hair shone damp on their heads. Add to that a goodly amount of nervous sweat from having been attacked by a pack of crazyass dogs, and Ned felt like he needed a bath.

"Can I take a shower? I feel kind of funky."

Joe was relieved. He needed a shower too after working all night. The last thing he wanted to do was crawl into bed with Ned while smelling like a goat, even if all they did was sleep. "Sure. You shower first, then I'll go. We'll have our beers after. Throw your wet clothes out the bathroom door, and I'll hang them up in the kitchen to dry." He saw a flash of concern cross Ned's face, and he grinned. "Don't worry. I won't leave you naked. I'll lay out something for you to wear."

Ned's face turned as red as a brick, but all he said was, "Okay. I won't be long."

He ducked into the bathroom. He was no sooner gone than Joe yelled through the closed door, "Clean towels are under the sink!"

"Thanks!" Ned yelled back, and with that out of the way, Joe peeled his own damp clothes off and tossed them in a hamper. He donned a ratty pair of lounging pants and a T-shirt and padded around the apartment barefoot while waiting for Ned to finish.

Remembering what he'd said, he dug through his dresser in the bedroom and found an old pair of pj's he had purchased long ago but never worn. They were still in the original packaging. He tore them out of the plastic and tried to shake the store wrinkles out of them, which didn't work very well. They had been wrapped up so long, the wrinkles were pretty much impervious.

He held the pj's at arm's length and frowned. They even looked too big for *him*. Ned would probably disappear inside them entirely. Well, hopefully not entirely. Joe prayed there would be a smidgeon or two of Ned left for him to ogle. At that thought, he grinned to himself. *God, I've got it bad.*

He could hear the shower running, so he tapped lightly at the bathroom door. When he didn't get an answer, he peeked in. The bathroom was misty with steam. Through the opaque shower curtain, he could see a vague outline of Ned's naked body twisting under the stream of hot water. Joe's heart practically skidded to a stop. After all, the mere sight of Ned's belly button the night before had activated his slut genes. The sight of Ned standing naked in his shower catapulted him onto another hormonal plane altogether.

Not wanting to be caught snooping, Joe quickly hung the pajamas over the towel rod and quietly closed the door.

At the last minute, after he'd tossed an industrial-sized bag of potato chips onto the coffee table in case Ned was hungry, Joe hurried into the bedroom to change the sheets. He had barely finished when Ned stepped through the bathroom door.

His blond hair was still damp, only this time from the shower, not dew, and as Joe suspected, he looked like he was swimming in the pj's Joe had given him. His hands were lost in the sleeves, his bare feet buried in the clumps of leg fabric that puddled on the floor. The tail of the pajama shirt fell to six inches above his knees. Ned was using a free hand to hold the pants up.

He was the cutest thing Joe had ever seen.

Ned looked less than happy. Once again his face was as red as a brick, and Joe didn't think it was from the hot shower.

"Maybe naked would be better," Ned said while some sort of internal battle between laughing at himself and dying of embarrassment showed on his face.

Joe shot him a lascivious wink. "Then by all means, naked it is."

Ned looked down at himself and the twenty or thirty yards of extra pajama fabric pooled around his body. A doubtful grin won his internal battle. "Well, maybe not."

Joe made a big show of looking hurt and disappointed, snapping his fingers in disgust and pouting like a six-year-old. "Well, darn," he grumbled. And at the expression of horror on Ned's face, Joe burst out with a howl of laughter.

Taking pity on the poor guy, Joe ducked into the bedroom and snatched the belt out of his bathrobe. He passed it to Ned. "Here. Tie your pants on with this so you won't have to hold them up all night. I won't be a minute."

With that, Joe slipped into the bathroom and stepped under his own steaming shower. He was grinning like a sap, his head still filled with the image of Ned standing there embarrassed while Joe's pj's hung all over him.

Joe ducked his head under the spray and laughed at himself. *God, I really, really do have it bad.*

NED WATCHED Joe leave the room.

When he was alone, he glanced around Joe's apartment. He had been here before but had certainly never stayed all night. He contemplated what wonders he might experience by morning, if any. Or was Joe's invitation to spend the night nothing more than an innocent attempt to keep Ned safe and unafraid after what had happened to him out on the trail?

He spotted the humongous bag of chips on the coffee table. He also noticed that Joe's bed looked neater than it had when he stepped through the door. From the floor of the closet, spilling through the not-quite-closed door, he saw a tangle of sheets and realized Joe had changed the bedding while Ned was in the shower. Ned considered slipping over to his apartment to grab his own pajamas, which weren't a gazillion times too big for him, but decided against it. Ned sort of liked having his naked body swathed with clothing that belonged to Joe, even if it did make him look like a twit.

Dutifully, he knotted the belt around his waist and tucked a few rolls of material from the pajama pants around it until they were short enough he could see his feet. It left a bulge around his waist and made him look like a turnip, but at least he wouldn't trip on the pant legs and break his neck.

He heard the shower running and tried not to imagine Joe's naked body slathered with soap suds while rivulets of steaming water sluiced down his strong legs. Ned had partaken of Joe's mouthwash while he was in there, so he knew his breath was okay. Still it would have been nice to have a toothbrush.

He gave his head a long shake to dry his hair and, finally tired of standing, dropped onto Joe's couch and waited for him to return. He didn't want to dig around through Joe's fridge for a beer. Joe might think he was being pushy. But as quickly as the thought came, it was derailed by the certainty that Joe wouldn't think any such thing.

Ned dried his hands on his pajama legs. They were clammy again, not from fear this time, but from—well, okay. Maybe it *was* fear. Fear of his own lack of control once he and Joe were in that bed together. If only he knew whether Joe wanted the same things he did. If only Joe would come right out and tell him exactly what he expected from Ned.

Ned touched the scar at the side of his head. It was quiet at the moment. It wasn't singing its sometime song of pain. But still it was there. And just by being there it reminded Ned why it had been inflicted to begin with. It also reminded Ned that because of that scar, he had not really acted on his "special desires," as he called them, since he was sixteen years old. He had been living a lie for more than a decade! But lately he had known a change was coming. He couldn't live that way much longer. Not since the day he met Joe, in fact.

Ned clasped his hands together, making one big fist. After a minute, pain from the tension in his fingers began to awaken. It was a trick he had learned to draw his thoughts away from himself, to make the bad memories go away. Tonight, though, it didn't seem to work. He relaxed his fists and let his mind run free. It was a guilty indulgence usually reserved for those nights when he lay alone in his bed. Those nights when the burning desires simply couldn't be ignored. God, he hated those nights. Hated them and loved them. He loved them because on those nights he could finally let his imagination run wild, filling his brain with thoughts of Joe. Always Joe.

He sighed and gazed around at the apartment. Joe was a better housekeeper than he was. His apartment was spotless. Ned's apartment was kind of a mess.

Ned wiggled around, getting comfortable on Joe's couch. He rested his hands on his knees and stared at them. His heart was dancing a jig, and his imagination was executing somersaults inside his head as he wondered what Joe was doing on the other side of that bathroom door. And how he was looking while he did it. And how he might feel—how he might *taste*—if Ned should somehow step into the shower with him and drop to his knees at Joe's feet.

That thought came with such a rush of desire, Ned had to squeeze his eyes shut to fight against it.

Ned froze when the sound of the shower stopped. The shower curtain rattled as Joe stepped out of the tub. Joe was softly humming to himself, and that made Ned feel a little better. It was good to know that Ned was the only one having a nervous breakdown here. It was good to know that Ned was the only one envisioning things he shouldn't.

His gaze skittered back to Joe's bed. It was a bigger bed than his own. Ned had a single, Joe a double. It took up a lot of space in the little studio apartment, and Ned found it hard to tear his eyes away from it. Soon the two of them would be in that bed. Together.

Christ knows where that will lead.

Once again, Ned squeezed his eyes shut and waited. And while he waited, he stroked the scar at the side of his head with a trembling finger. He pictured Joe standing naked at the side of the tub, toweling his body dry. Ned squeezed his eyes shut tighter, trying not to imagine how Joe would look, how Joe would smell all soapy and clean. He sighed and reached for a chip.

BACK IN his ratty lounging pants and threadbare T-shirt, Joe switched off the light on his way out the bathroom door, shot Ned a wink, then headed straight for the fridge to pluck two beers off the shelf. He twisted the caps off and tossed them in the sink, then carried the bottles across the apartment to hand one to Ned before plopping down on the couch at Ned's side. He propped his bare feet on the coffee table, and Ned followed suit. Joe lifted the bag of chips off the table and tucked it between them so they wouldn't have to stretch to grab a bite.

He took a long sip of beer and turned to Ned. It wasn't easy thinking of Ned sitting there beside him naked under those ridiculous pajamas, but Joe did his best. He tried to focus his thoughts on Ned's face. He figured he wouldn't get in too much trouble that way. "You've had a hell of a night," he said with a *tsk*. "Are you really okay?"

Ned tugged at his shirt, neatly arranging the folds of the damn thing around him as if reading Joe's mind about his being naked underneath. He cast Joe an awkward glance; then his lower eyelids flicked upward a fraction, which Joe knew was a sure sign that Ned was about to say something serious.

"My night might have had a really different ending if you hadn't come along when you did. That big dog was about to pull me down."

Joe's face sobered. "I hate to think what might have happened if it had."

Ned nodded and plucked a chip from the bag. In the midst of crunching it to mush, he said, "You and me both."

"He had hold of your foot," Joe said. "Did it break the skin? Let me see." And without asking, he set his beer aside and bent over to pull Ned's pajama cuffs away from his ankle. He slipped a hand under Ned's leg and lifted it off the table so he could see the heel. While his fingers slipped through the soft hair on Ned's calf, Joe studied Ned's skin for a wound but didn't find anything. Just the feel of Ned's leg hair on the palm of his hand made his breath catch.

"Looks okay," he managed to say in a throaty voice.

Ned flexed his toes and stared at Joe's hand cradling his leg. When he spoke, his voice was just as breathless as Joe's. "Told you."

He hated doing it, but Joe released Ned's foot and replaced it gently on the table. He sat back, tossing the bag of chips on the table so he could sit closer to Ned. He suspected they were close enough when their shoulders and legs touched and there was barely enough room to insert a potato chip between them.

Joe retrieved his beer. Hoping for levity, he said around a smirk, "I *had* to rescue your puny ass. You're the only friend I've got."

He turned his head to see how Ned accepted that statement. He found Ned staring at him with a wide, sweet gaze. Ned took a moment to lick his lips, as if it would give him just a split second more to think about what to say. "You're my only friend too," he finally answered.

"That's not true," Joe said. "Mr. Wong's your friend."

Ned snorted. "Mr. Wong's not my friend. He's my boss. He just happens to be a nice one." A comfortable silence settled between them. They sipped their beers and nibbled on a few chips while Joe tried not to concentrate too hard on the feel of Ned's lean thigh pressed up against his own. The air around them was redolent of the scents of soap and shampoo. They were both as clean as a couple of whistles.

Ned's nearest hand was resting on his own leg now, as if he didn't know where else to put it. Swallowing away a burst of fear, Joe laid his hand over it and gave it a squeeze. "Anyway, I'm glad you're safe, and I'm glad you're staying over."

"Me too," Ned whispered, while a crooked smile curved his lips.

Ned had said those two little words so quietly Joe had to lean in closer to hear them. All the time he was leaning in, he never lifted his hand from Ned's. In fact, he let his thumb slide down to caress the web of flesh between Ned's thumb and index finger. The blond hairs on the back of Ned's hand all but sparked against the palm of his hand, like a surge of electricity. Joe thought maybe he had never done anything so erotic in all his life as the simple act of resting his hand over Ned's.

Ned sat quietly, his pale blue eyes riveted on their two hands nestled together. While Joe sifted through his brain for something halfway intelligent to say, Ned turned to stare at the living room window. Only then did Joe realize Ned had pulled the drapes shut while Joe was showering. In the nighttime skies beyond the walls of his tiny apartment, Joe could hear the raucous, desperate cries of all the birds still circling endlessly overhead. Ned was right when he said the poor things must be exhausted.

But it was another sound that truly captured Joe's attention. It was the tiny intake of breath Ned gave just before he opened his mouth to speak.

Joe turned to him in time to see his lips move as he said, "I'm glad you asked me to stay with you, Joe. Those dogs really rattled me."

There was such emotion in that simple statement that Joe could only offer a nod in response. Rather than answer, he clutched Ned's hand a little tighter while weaving their fingers together until they were firmly connected. After taking a moment to appreciate Ned's fine-boned hand in his, Joe offered, "You're safe now. You don't have to be scared anymore."

"I know. I'm not."

A hiccup in the power grid made the lights dim, but it only lasted a second. The fridge in the kitchen fell oddly silent before the motor kicked back on with a whirr. Joe almost smiled when Ned tensed and tucked his fingertips into the palm of Joe's hand as if making himself ready for whatever might happen next. Farther down, Ned's toes edged closer until they touched the side of Joe's foot. In turn, Joe moved his foot closer too.

They sat there listening while the fridge cranked back up to full power. It was Ned who finally broke the silence. "What do you think is going to happen, Joe?"

Joe shifted nearer until he had four points of connection with Ned: hands, feet, legs, shoulders. And still they weren't nearly as close as Joe wanted them to be.

"You mean with the red stuff or with us?" Joe asked.

Ned blushed. "I mean the red stuff."

Joe tried not to be disappointed by the answer. He would far rather be talking about the two of them. But he had to try to calm the disquiet in Ned's eyes. The thought of Ned still being frightened made Joe ache inside. In fact, he couldn't let it happen. He *wouldn't*.

"I think it will turn out fine," Joe said. He wasn't quite sure he believed that at all, but for Ned's sake he had to say it. The words were barely out when, with a moment of further reflection, he decided he honestly *did* believe it. Or at least he *wanted* to. "Whatever is happening in space—like a sun storm and sunspots and all that stuff scientists talk about—I think it's just a monkey wrench God threw in the works to keep us on our toes. We were getting a little too rambunctious, maybe. He had to cool our jets a little."

Ned grinned. "Are your jets cooled?"

Far from it. Joe's gaze settled on their clasped hands, then slid down to their bare feet propped against each other on the table. Those two contact points of Ned's skin touching his were sending an endless hormonal surge through Joe's body, and most of it seemed to be centered on his crotch. For the last few minutes, he had been holding his beer in his lap for no other reason than to hide the erection that had snuck up on him about five minutes before, although hiding it was the last thing he wanted to do.

Spotting a familiar line of red flesh under Ned's hair, Joe twisted around to face him. He reached up and gently separated the hair to better see the scar at the side of Ned's scalp. Ned flinched. His gaze burrowed into Joe's, but he sat obediently still, trembling like a nervous pet being caressed by an unfamiliar hand. Ned didn't pull away when Joe stirred through his hair, exposing that which Ned was obviously most embarrassed about. Joe had been watching Ned treat that scar like it was something to be ashamed of since they first met. Until this moment, for Ned's sake, Joe had never acted as if he'd noticed. Had never acted as if he had the least interest in knowing how the scar came to be there.

Now, for the first time, without warning or apology, Joe laid a careful fingertip atop the scar, testing the puckered flesh, absorbing the rigid texture of it. Ned's eyes narrowed as if he was fighting the urge to flinch while Joe dragged his finger over the rippled wound. With Ned's eyes dead center on his own, Joe got the sense that Ned was offering the weakest part of himself to Joe, to be done with as Joe deemed fit. Joe was stunned by the emotion he read in Ned's gaze. The total, unrelenting trust.

"You've never told me how you got this," Joe whispered. "Do you want to talk about it?"

"No," Ned whispered back. "Not yet."

"Do you mind me touching it?"

"No, Joe. I don't mind. I—I like the way your finger feels on my skin."

Joe smiled and laid his hand flat to the side of Ned's head. For a second or two, Ned leaned his head into the caress.

"Do you like that too?" Joe asked softly.

Ned slowly blinked, as if in contentment. "You know I do."

Joe set his beer bottle aside and with beer-chilled fingers brushed Ned's hair back away from his eyes. It wasn't wet anymore. Ned's hair was dry and fluffy and soft. With his heart hammering in his chest, Joe leaned in and pressed a kiss to Ned's scar. The moment his lips touched it, Ned shivered and closed his eyes.

"Ned?" Joe breathed, still caressing Ned's ear, the side of Ned's head, his lips still brushing Ned's scar.

"Hmm?"

"Do you know why I asked you to spend the night?"

Ned opened his eyes. He cleared his throat as if he had almost forgotten how to talk. "Because I was scared, and you didn't want me to be alone?"

Joe smiled a sad little smile, which Ned stared at with widening eyes. "No, Ned. I asked you to stay with me because *I* was scared and because *I* didn't want to be alone."

Ned offered a tiny frown. "I've never seen you scared of anything."

"I'm scared of one thing," Joe said.

"What's that?"

Joe pulled back to study Ned's face. He slid his thumb over Ned's lips as an uncontrollable urge to gauge their softness took him over. He gave Ned's chin a gentle squeeze between his thumb and forefinger. It took every ounce of willpower he possessed not to lay his lips to Ned's mouth. But he still didn't know if he was welcome there. And how the hell would he ever know if he didn't just come right out and ask?

"I'm afraid of *you*," Joe said, his gaze once again settling onto Ned's pale blue eyes. Joe wasn't sure, but he thought he could feel their two hearts thumping in tandem. The time had come to say what he'd waited so long to say. Ned was sitting there. He was being receptive. There would never be a better time.

Please God, let Ned be ready to listen. And please God, let him want the same thing I want.

JOE'S FACE was so handsome and perfect hovering over his it almost pulled the breath from Ned's body. He raised his hand and laid it flat on Joe's cheek. The stubble of a sprouting beard scraped at the tender skin on the palm of his hand. Joe's beard was dark and bristly while Ned's was pale and soft as cotton. The prickle of Joe's unshaven jaw sent a shudder of desire rumbling through him so strong, Ned had to hold his breath for a moment to deal with it. Once he had processed that piece of wonderment, Ned began to sift through the words Joe had spoken.

Some of the things Joe said had dug their way into Ned's heart and made him happier than he could ever remember being. Was it possible that Joe really did think about him in the same way Ned thought about Joe?

"Please don't be afraid of me," Ned said impulsively. He stared up into Joe's eyes, feeling the warm fragrant brush of Joe's clean breath blowing across his face. "Whatever you want, I want it too."

"Are you sure?" Joe asked. "Are you really sure about that? Do you even know what it is I want?"

Ned smiled without fear. The absolute certainty of that smile lay there on his face, spread wide, offering more of himself to Joe than he had ever offered to anyone. By the understanding burning at the back of Joe's eyes, he thought maybe Joe knew it. At least he hoped he did.

"You never have to be afraid of me," Ned said, pushing a little harder. He laid his hand on Joe's broad chest and immediately felt the tremor of Joe's heart thundering inside. "And I think maybe I don't have to be afraid of me anymore either."

He watched as Joe chewed on his bottom lip with his neat white teeth. His eyes slipped away from Ned's face and traveled over the apartment—to the door, the window, farther away to the mirror he could see in the bathroom that was still steamed up from their showers. Apparently Joe couldn't find what he was searching for anywhere else, so in the end his hazel eyes wandered back to Ned. Ned thought they were the widest, most wondrous eyes he had ever seen. He loved being their focus. He loved the way they infused him with heat.

"Do you really want me to tell you how I feel?" Joe asked. There was a quaver in his voice, like he was suffering from stage fright. And for all Ned knew, maybe he was.

"You *have* to tell me, Joe. I don't think I can live now if you don't."

Joe grinned. "You're always so melodramatic."

"Am I?" Ned asked, but there was no humor in the question. It was simply a sincere desire to understand.

Once again, Joe's eyes peeled away to travel the apartment, seeking—*what*, Ned wondered. Courage? Permission? A way to escape?

Still, Joe hesitated to say what he was really thinking.

Ned twisted around on the sofa and leaned in, laying his forehead against Joe's chest. A sigh came all the way up from the pit of his stomach when Joe's arms automatically wrapped themselves tight around him, holding him in place.

"Ask me, Joe," Ned whispered, his lips brushing the threadbare fabric of Joe's T-shirt. It was little more than a rag, the poor thing. It felt terribly fragile, as if one more wash would make it disintegrate into dust. Still, Ned loved its softness against his skin. "Ask me before I lose the courage to listen."

Joe paused, his hand at the nape of Ned's neck. Ned could sense him thinking. Finally he spoke. "Like I told you before, Ned. I'm afraid. I'm afraid I'm… wrong about you."

Ned pressed his face harder into Joe's chest. Joe couldn't really see him there, and that was the way Ned liked it. It gave him the courage to place a sly kiss on the shirt fabric. It gave him the courage to taste it on his lips without Joe really knowing.

Suddenly he didn't want to hide anymore. The cowardice Ned had lived with for so many years seemed to simply slip away. He was ready to face the truth now. The truth about himself. The truth about Joe. The truth about the two of them together.

He tilted his head up and studied Joe's face. "You can't be wrong about me, Joe, because whatever you want me to be, that's what I want to be too."

Joe's eyes were the saddest Ned had ever seen. "I'm not just afraid of you, Ned. I'm afraid for me too. I don't want you to break my heart," Joe sighed. "I guess that's really what it boils down to."

"Breaking a heart would imply… feelings," Ned carefully answered.

"Yes," Joe said, his eyes troubled, his mouth tense. "Feelings." There was a faint tremble in Joe's chin that captured Ned's attention.

Ned's eyes began to burn. His vision blurred behind rising tears. "Feelings for me, Joe?"

And Joe nodded. "Yes. Feelings for you."

Ned's breath caught, and before he could analyze how he felt, he said, "I feel them for you too. I think I always have."

They sat motionless on Joe's couch, each eyeing the other. Not wary, just entranced. Slowly, Ned's mouth twisted into a smile.

JOE COULDN'T believe he had finally said the words. He felt like… well, he wasn't really sure *how* he felt. But he did know Ned had sat there patiently, letting him say what he wanted to say. And then Ned had spoken the very same words back to him. Like Joe had always imagined he might. And wonder of wonders, Ned was *still* sitting there, he was *still* holding on to Joe, gazing up at him now through sparkling eyes with that strange little smile on his face. He didn't look upset, or shocked, or even hardly surprised. Just happily content to be where he was. In Joe's arms.

In Joe's heart.

Joe opened his mouth to say something else—he wasn't sure what—but before he could figure out what it should be, Ned laid his fingers over Joe's lips, silencing him.

Ned's pale eyelashes were wet with tears. His eyes were bright and shiny and so focused on Joe's face that Joe thought he could feel the heat of them burning into his skin. Ned's hands came up behind Joe and rested on his back.

Joe cupped Ned's face and tilted his head up. The movement caused a tear to spill down Ned's cheek. Joe carefully laid his lips to it and kissed it away. Ned shuddered. Then Joe was shuddering too.

"It's been so long, I'm practically new at this," Ned whispered. "Making love. Being with somebody."

"Me too," Joe whispered back. "Don't be afraid."

At that, Ned finally laughed. "I'm a million things right now, but afraid isn't one of them."

"Good." Joe smiled, and without warning, his kiss slid inward across Ned's tear-soaked cheek and came to rest on Ned's lips. With the faintest startled gasp, Joe felt Ned's mouth accept the kiss.

It was their first real kiss. Joe was scared to death. Ned was too, Joe thought, even though he said he wasn't. But neither let their fear stop them. The kiss went on and on as they sat there on Joe's beat-up couch and clung to each other.

The kiss only ended when Ned tugged at Joe's T-shirt, trying to lift it over Joe's head.

A moment later, on wobbly legs, Joe led Ned to the bed, flicking off lights along the way.

They quickly shed their clothes in a flurry of activity that left them naked and trembling, staring at each other in the narrow oblong of illumination from the streetlight outside.

Joe gasped when Ned stepped forward and slipped naked into his arms for the very first time.

Lost in the wondrous heat of Ned's satin flesh, Joe tumbled backward onto the bed, dragging Ned down along with him.

In a rush of laughter and soul-searing joy, they twisted around in opposite directions on the bed and tasted each other for the very first time.

And later, when their juices spilled and they cried out loud, each in the arms of the other, Joe felt himself melt into the flesh of the man he held. The man he *clung* to and emptied himself into.

Ned's seed was the sweetest Joe had ever tasted. The receiving of it was the single most unforgettable act of Joe's twenty-nine years on the planet. He knew how special it was, even while his own body still convulsed with release. Even as they drank from each other with equal hunger, equal desperation. In the midst of it all, Joe understood one inescapable fact.

The memory of this night would be with him forever.

Afterward, Joe lay silently in the dark, still caressing the man who lay exhausted in his arms. Gratified, and still a little amazed, he thought back to everything that had happened. At every single moment of the time they had spent naked in each other's arms making love.

"Joe!" Ned had gasped, just as his back arched and his seed exploded from his body. "Joe!"

Joe smiled now and pressed his face to Ned's warm belly, inhaling Ned's scent. He closed his eyes, wishing none of this would ever end. And when Ned's arms slid around him to hold him close, Joe gave the faintest whimper of contentment.

It was the last sound either of them made before sleep found them. But even sleep couldn't hold them for long. As the night began to die and resurrect itself as morning—if the world still had a morning left to offer—they drank from each other again. Lying together later, secure in the cocoon of Ned's gentle embrace, Joe knew beyond a shadow of a doubt that in this one single night, his life had changed.

He wrapped Ned reverently in his arms and held him snug to his chest. Ned's smile brushed the skin at the base of his throat, and his eyelashes tickled Joe's neck. Ned planted a kiss there with gentle, worshipping lips. It was just a little kiss. Almost an afterthought after everything else that had happened between them.

But the words Ned began to speak in the darkness were not an afterthought at all. They clearly came from his heart.

As Joe listened, he nested his lips in Ned's hair. At home there and happy, he breathed in the scent of the man in his arms and let Ned's words pour through him like smoke.

"I'VE WANTED to be with you since the first time I saw you, Joe."

Ned lay tucked up in Joe's arms, the lazy thunder of Joe's heartbeat pulsing in his ear. While his body was exhausted, his mind was a raging turmoil after all the truths he had suddenly discovered. About himself; about Joe. One of Joe's strong hands now lay splayed across his back, while the other lightly stroked the scar at the side of his head. The taste of Joe's seed still danced on Ned's tongue, and that was a wonder beyond anything Ned had ever experienced.

Ned closed his eyes, and before he had even known the words were coming, he had begun to speak. Softly. In a fervent rush. While in his imagination, he spilled the words onto Joe's chest and let them seep in through Joe's pores, in reality the words—words he never thought he would say to another human being—came easily. In fact, they all but gushed out in an unstoppable torrent. Even in the midst of all the other wonders of this remarkable night, it was an inexpressible relief to at long last let them go, and Ned hurried to finish his thought before fear chased it away. "But…. But I kept those feelings about wanting you hidden. At least I tried to."

Joe lightened his touch on Ned's scar but didn't cease caressing it completely. "It's because of this, isn't it?" he whispered. "Because of your scar?"

Ned simply nodded, nestling his cheek more solidly into the pillow of hair on Joe's chest, smiling to himself when Joe's arm tightened around him even more, holding him inescapably in place, right where Ned wanted to be.

"I was sixteen," Ned sighed. "The kids at school found out about me. Found out I was… queer. I was a sophomore. They taunted me with it for weeks. Then one day Bobby Johnson, the quarterback of the football team, cornered me in the shower after gym. I always waited around as long as I could so the others would be gone by the time I had to strip down and shower. Otherwise, the comments they made were just too… painful."

"Couldn't the teachers help?" Joe asked, his finger now resting motionless atop the scar as if absorbing its heat. As if hoping to draw the pain it had caused Ned into himself instead. At least that's how it felt to Ned.

Ned's breath caught. A lump formed in his throat. He tried to connect himself back to the story he was telling. He wanted Joe to understand. For some reason, Joe *had* to understand.

"I was too ashamed to tell the teachers," he said. "Bullying wasn't such a big thing back then. They didn't write slogans about it. You didn't see it on bumper stickers. Nobody passed laws about it in the senate. It was just something that every kid who was different had to suffer through. Like a rite of passage."

"Go on," Joe quietly urged. "What happened?"

A tear slid across Ned's nose. He turned his face briefly into Joe's chest to blot it away. For his efforts, he received a kiss to his hair, and Joe's arms tightened around him even more.

"Tell me," Joe gently pleaded. "I want to know."

Ned let a sigh flutter through him. Then, almost without conscious volition, the words poured out. Somehow, he knew Joe would not judge him for what had happened. Not the way Ned judged himself. Not the way Ned *still* judged himself.

"I was just finishing up with my shower and reaching for my towel when Bobby Johnson came at me out of nowhere. The other kids were gone. We were all alone." Ned paused. He tensed in Joe's arms. "I've never talked about this before. It's not… easy."

Again, Joe pressed a kiss into Ned's hair. "Finish it, Ned. Let it out. Get rid of it once and for all. Tell me what happened."

It seemed the floodgates had opened. Freely now, the tears were slipping across the bridge of Ned's nose and pooling on Joe's chest. Joe didn't seem to mind. He didn't try to brush them away. He merely stroked a comforting circle on Ned's back.

Ned forced himself to continue.

"He… he stood in front of me. Bobby Johnson. He was naked. He started touching himself with a smirk on his face like he knew he was turning me on. He had me cornered against the wall of the shower, still dripping wet, while he stroked himself into an erection. He stepped closer to me and rubbed it across my stomach. I tried to get away. I was crying by now. He laughed at me for crying. Releasing himself, he put his hands on my shoulders and pushed me down to my knees."

Ned's breath hitched.

"The horrible thing was, Joe, I *wanted* him to do it. I'd done things like that before to some of the other boys. That's how the word got around."

Softly, Joe asked, "Did you blow him?"

Ned slipped around in Joe's arms until his face was thoroughly buried in Joe's chest. He breathed in the scent of Joe's skin and wallowed in the comforting darkness there. His answer was muffled, but still it came.

"I acted like I didn't want to, but I think he knew better. He grabbed my hair and pushed himself into my mouth. I cowered there on my knees looking up at him, his cock buried deep in my throat. I could see he enjoyed what I was doing, but there was a mean glint in his eyes too. I didn't understand it until he called out."

Ned stammered to a stop.

"Called out what?" Joe asked.

Ned rose onto his elbows and settled his gaze on Joe's face. "He called out to a bunch of other kids. They were hiding just outside the shower. Out where the lockers were. They filed into the shower, giggling and laughing at me kneeling there with Bobby Johnson's dick down my throat. The minute they were all there, surrounding us, Bobby Johnson pulled back just far enough to shoot his come all over my face."

"Ned…."

But Ned didn't stop because the story wasn't over yet.

"Then the others took their turns with me. I was still crying because I was so ashamed. But they swarmed around me. One of them, I could never remember which one, pushed me facedown onto the cold tile floor and spread my legs apart. He was the first to rape me. I'd never had that done to me, Joe. God, the pain! There were four, I think, who finally did it. One right after the other. By the time they stopped, I had passed out. When I opened my eyes, I was all alone in the shower stall, shivering with cold, splattered with come and filth. There was a puddle of blood at my waist where they had torn me inside. I could barely move. My head was bleeding too. Someone must have kicked me while I was unconscious."

"Ned…," Joe said again, reaching up to squeegee the tears from Ned's cheeks with his thumb. "Please tell me you reported what happened. Please tell me they were charged with rape and assault."

Ned dropped his head back to Joe's chest. It was the only way he could escape Joe's gaze. "Until tonight, I've never told anybody. And I never went back to school. I was sixteen, so I quit. I couldn't go back, Joe. I was too ashamed."

"You were the victim, Ned. You had nothing to be ashamed of."

Ned sighed and shook his head. It was the only answer he offered.

"What about your injuries?" Joe asked.

"My mom took me to the emergency room. They stitched up my head, but I never told them about the other thing. It eventually healed on its own. I was pretty sure my mom suspected what had happened, but she wouldn't talk about it. I knew she was as ashamed of me as I was. She probably went to church and pleaded for my soul. That was mom's answer to everything. She blamed me for what happened. I know she did. And all this time, I've pretty much agreed with her. It *was* my fault. It was my fault for being who I was. I *deserved* it."

Joe slammed a fist into the pillow beside Ned's head, causing Ned to flinch. "But… you were assaulted, dammit! You were *raped*! It wasn't your fault. You were just a kid. What happened should have ruined *their* lives, not yours. Those kids should have ended up in jail. None of the punishment, none of the guilt, should have fallen on you, Ned. It should have fallen squarely on *them*."

"Yes," Ned said. "I know that now. You've shown me that much, Joe. This past year of knowing you has made me face up to a lot of things. Even before tonight, before I was sure you were… the same as me—gay, I mean—you somehow showed me that having these feelings isn't a sin. It isn't wrong. It's just the way some people are. But I didn't know that then. And even if I had known, the shame was too much for me to live with. So I let those kids win. I also let them steal my life from me for the next ten years. Until tonight, I've never been with anybody."

"You kept your desires buried all that time?"

"Yes. The one who finally brought them out was you, Joe. Like I said, I've wanted to be with you like this since the first time I saw you. Somehow getting to know you, becoming friends with you, overpowered the guilt I felt inside. For a while I thought if we were friends it would be enough, but in the long run I knew it wasn't. Still, I was afraid to do anything. Make a first move. Afraid you'd hate me. Or worse, afraid you'd laugh at me like they did. I still hear their laughter, you know. Every day. Every single day. This is the first time I don't hear it, Joe. Right now. Lying here in your arms. I haven't heard it since you first told me how you feel. I haven't heard it since you told me you wanted me in the same way I've been wanting you."

"Oh, Ned." Joe laid his hand to Ned's cheek, and Ned blinked back what he knew was the night's final tear. Hell, it had to be. He was all cried out.

Joe's voice was weak with emotion, as if his anger had drained him. "Is that why you never see your folks? Is that why you've cut yourself off from your family?"

Ned gave a shrug. "It was the only way. There was only my mom anyway. And she wouldn't have wanted me after finding out the truth. After finding out what I'd done. What I was."

"But you were a victim, Ned. What happened wasn't your fault."

Ned dredged up a smile. It had been so long since he wore one, it felt odd on his face. "Yes. I was a victim. But thanks to you, I'm not a victim anymore."

"Good," Joe said, dragging up a matching smile. "And never let yourself be a victim again. All right?"

Ned nodded, making the hair on Joe's chest bristle against his cheek. He lifted his head and gazed toward the window. Only then did Ned realize a burgundy-red dawn was leaking just enough light through the pane to see by. Enough light to see Joe's smile, at any rate, and Joe's beautiful body lying beneath him in that eerie, blush-red morning haze.

Once again, Ned burrowed down and rested his cheek on Joe's chest. Loving the feel of Joe's chest hair on his tender skin, he listened breathlessly for Joe's heartbeat underneath.

"Please, Ned. Don't go back to your apartment. Stay with me until this is all over. I can't bear to think of you by yourself."

"I'll stay with you as long as you want me to," Ned said, touched by the gentle way Joe made his request.

And while an unseen sunrise began to nudge the world from the total blackness of a moonless night into another bizarre crimson dawn, the background hum of electricity, which no one ever really pays attention to, suddenly stopped, leaving an awkward pall of quiet in its wake. The LED readout of Joe's alarm clock on the nightstand blinked out with a beep. The rumble of his old refrigerator in the kitchen stilled. The emptiness left on the air caused them both to lift their heads and listen to the silence.

"The power's out," Joe whispered.

At that moment, every dog within earshot began to howl. The sound of their wailing seemed to come from every direction at once as their plaintive cries suddenly blanketed the city in a wall of mournful sound.

"Holy shit, it's *101 Dalmatians*!" Ned nervously laughed.

Naked, they flung themselves out of bed and rushed to fling aside the curtains on Joe's living room window. Ned's laughter died as quickly as it had come.

Staring out, they saw a world drenched in blood. Or so it appeared. True light did not exist. No shadows fell. Very little of the world was illuminated at all. The closest trees, perhaps. The walls of the building next door. Everything else was lost from sight. Without so much as a hint of the sun rising somewhere in the east, the world was a darkened stage with one red spotlight casting a dim blush past the proscenium, barely enough to light the empty scene.

And around it all, the yips and howls of countless dogs, like a grieving, relentless thunder, rumbled across the city. Their eerie, desperate cries made the little hairs on the back of Ned's neck stand up. Goose bumps peppered his arms.

Ned rested his hand on the velvet softness of Joe's naked hip.

Pressing his lips to Ned's ear, Joe said, "I'm glad you're here."

"So am I," Ned whispered back, savoring the acceptance he'd found in Joe's arms. The acceptance of who he was and all he had done. And the acceptance too of all the hunger he had been feeling for Joe for so long. Along with the blessed, blessed *relief* that Joe hungered just as much for him.

Ned's thoughts fell away as Joe leaned closer to the window, staring out at a day like neither he nor anyone else had ever seen before.

"When you go to work, you're not going alone," Joe said with a worried frown.

"Will the deli even be open? There's no power."

"We'll go and see."

"You mean you'll walk me to work?"

Joe turned away from the window and gazed gently down at Ned's upturned face. "Yes. I won't leave your side until I know you're safe."

Their eyes found each other's. Ned licked his lips and grinned. "Before we go," he said, "there's something I have to do."

And just as Joe was about to ask what he meant, Ned lowered himself to his knees and took Joe's sleeping cock into his mouth. Needless to say, it didn't stay asleep very long.

Ned knelt there, stroking the back of Joe's strong legs while Joe hardened between his lips. Once again, Ned relished pleasing the man he cared about more than any other. Joe's taste was familiar to him now, and Ned knew he would never grow tired of it. Ever.

Moments later, when Joe arched into him and craned his head back, mouth stretched wide in a grimace of release, Ned all but wept with joy as Joe's warm, sweet juices spilled across his tongue. As if the floodgates of one opened the floodgates of the other, Ned scraped his aching cock through the hair on Joe's shin and, with a cry, spilled his seed over the heated flesh.

In the recesses of his mind, Ned heard the same words over and over, echoing inside his head like a benediction. Words he had long wanted to hear. Words he had long needed to believe. And now, suddenly, he did. For the first time ever, the words rang absolutely true.

This is not a sin. This is not a sin. This is not a sin.

Still on his knees, Ned clutched Joe to him while Joe softened between his come-moistened lips.

"Baby," Joe muttered, gently caressing Ned's cheek.

Under Joe's touch, Ned closed his eyes, as peaceful and accepting of himself as he had ever been. Stroking Joe's long legs as if only now discovering how beautiful they were, Ned pressed a smile into Joe's belly and let the scent of Joe's seed, Joe's heated flesh, burrow through him.

He tilted his head back and peered up into Joe's face.

"Baby," Joe said again, and Ned smiled.

CHAPTER THREE

As THE crimson haze deepened, daylight faded, and darkness grew. *Vision was limited to a matter of yards. The third red dawn had barely broken when religious leaders began to speak of the apocalypse, frightening the devout and making a bad situation worse. Politicians railed from their own bully pulpits. Unlike the "men of God," who merely wailed impotently at the heavens, pleading for mercy and laying blame on everyone but themselves, the politicos proposed laws and threatened action, although not even they knew who those laws and threats should be directed toward.*

The night before, two days after the events began and due to fears of a catastrophic collapse, the overstrained power grid that serviced the eastern coast of South America, including Rio de Janeiro, was purposely shut down. This disastrous decision plummeted the city of seven million citizens into impenetrable darkness and launched a crime spree the likes of which no civilized country on the planet had ever witnessed. To prevent further mayhem, Rio's power grid was hastily brought back online. Thirty minutes later, it crashed completely.

In that second avalanche of darkness, the crime wave exploded.

As Rio devoured itself from within, all flights on US soil were grounded due to increasing radiation in the upper tiers of the atmosphere. Soon, the entire world followed suit, grounding aircraft and halting all departures. Thousands were stranded in airports worldwide. Cell phones went silent. GPS signals were lost. No amount of satellite tweaking or recalibration could bring them back.

Due to continued CME activity, radio and television signals in North America were blocked by a massive influx of magnetic emissions. Consequently, few Americans heard about Rio at all. This in turn provided a few extra hours of false security, since they did not yet understand that the continued operation of their power grids was all that prevented their own cities from collapsing under a wave of panic. Nor did they understand that without access to radio waves, neither the media nor the police nor the military could properly function.

The citizens were, in effect, left helplessly uninformed and unprotected. Simultaneously, as all forms of communication failed, the tainted atmosphere around the planet deepened to a ghastly, bloodlike red.

With that third vermilion dawn came, at long last, fear.

And gleefully snapping at the heels of fear… lurked chaos.

AT NINE o'clock in the morning, visibility was less than thirty feet.

It was Joe's night off, and he and Ned clutched hands as they strode down the sidewalk, headed for the deli. Trees, parking meters, and mailboxes kept looming up in front of them through the haze like phantoms springing out to attack. By the time they had traveled two blocks, they were both on edge.

Joe counted back inside his head. This was the third day since the red haze fell. As he and Ned walked along, continuously fighting the urge to start running, a chorus of countless barking dogs bombarded them from every side. The cries of thousands of birds still circling frantically overhead set their teeth on edge. The concrete beneath their feet and everything they passed was coated with bird droppings. The air reeked of it—a bitter, cloying, acidic smell that made them pull their T-shirts over their noses to filter out the stench.

At one street corner, they stepped around a pool of blood on the sidewalk. The blood had to be human. What else could it be? Plus, a trail of bloody footprints led from the middle of it, fading away as they went. The coppery scent of fresh blood soured the air, drowning out for the moment even the stench of bird shit.

"Nobody loses that much blood and lives," Ned whispered, his eyes round with fear.

"No," Joe said. "They don't."

He squeezed Ned's hand to comfort him, and also maybe to comfort himself. Ned eased closer, weaving his fingers through Joe's. They walked on. Their pace was slower now as they gazed nervously about, leery of what might lie ahead and uneasy because they couldn't see more than three or four car lengths in any direction.

Just when Joe began to think it couldn't get any worse, suddenly it was not only bird shit that came tumbling from the sky. It was the birds themselves.

After two long days of endless circling, exhaustion must have finally laid claim to them. One after the other, they plummeted from the sky, their bodies striking the earth with dull thuds, some close enough for Joe to see, others lost in the haze. Ned and Joe jumped when a falling bird struck a parked car not five feet away. The screech of the car alarm ripped through the morning air, startling them even more. Sometimes the falling birds lay limp and lifeless where they landed. Other times the poor creatures tried to pull themselves back into the air, back to where they felt safe. But they were too weak.

Joe had never seen anything so heartbreaking in his life. The birds were everywhere, peppering the ground. Countless breeds—sparrows, crows, dainty hummingbirds, beautiful tangerine-breasted house finches, snowy seagulls, their wingspans surprisingly wide. Some lay motionless in death while others barely stirred, their bodies twitching with exhaustion, wings still flapping in a parody of flight as if they had forgotten the art of stillness. Others were wasting their last ounce of strength fighting with each other, and those were the most confusing of all. It seemed that even as death reached out to claim them, anger had taken root. They clawed and pecked at their dying brethren, even as their own lives slipped away. Between the birds and the howling dogs, the world had gone crazy. Something about this third red dawn had robbed the creatures of their sanity.

And then another thought struck Joe. *Where are all the people?*

He stumbled to a stop, dragging Ned to a halt beside him. "Where has everyone gone?" he whispered, spinning this way and that, looking up and down the sidewalk. And the street. There was no traffic! What the hell was going on?

"Maybe they're hiding under their beds," Ned whispered back. "If I didn't have you with me, that's what I'd be doing."

Joe didn't think Ned was joking, so he didn't attempt a smile. He simply continued to gaze around, wondering where everyone was. Maybe Ned was right. Maybe they *were* hiding, secluded away in closets and basements, waiting for it all to end, waiting for the world to return to normal. He clutched Ned's hand all the tighter, as if afraid he too might suddenly run off and disappear. And that would break Joe's heart.

Frightened but determined, they continued walking hand in hand toward the deli. While the blocks slid by beneath them, Joe's thoughts spun a maelstrom inside his head.

As if the fact that everyone had disappeared wasn't enough to freak him out, Joe suddenly turned his eyes back to Ned. He considered the thought he'd just had. About Ned running away and disappearing into the haze. And what that would do to him.

It was true, he knew. If Ned were no longer here, walking at his side and clutching his hand, it would break Joe's heart. The feelings Joe had for Ned had been stewing for months. And now, after last night, he knew his feelings had turned a corner. They might not be as simple as they had once been, but they were certainly far stronger. It wasn't as if he had fallen in love with Ned after one night in bed together. Or that's what he kept telling himself. But still, looking back at the hours they spent in each other's arms, making love, exploring each other's bodies, made Joe's heart swell inside his chest. Even now, just the feel of Ned's hand in his on this weirdass morning, made his poor swollen heart beat a little faster, a little harder, a little more *contentedly*. It was as if at some point between yesterday and today, he had found his purpose. He had found his reason to go on.

Ignoring the fucked-up world they had woken to—the deepening red haze, the dying birds, the howling fucking dogs, everything coated in bird shit—Joe stopped again in the middle of the empty sidewalk without warning and pulled Ned into his arms. He held him close and laid his cheek to Ned's, relishing the unhesitating way Ned accepted and returned his hug.

"I'm glad you're with me," Joe murmured, his eyes crinkling into a smile as he breathed in the scent of Ned's hair, Ned's skin. "I don't care what sort of shitstorm we've been tossed into here. I don't care what happens to this stupid planet. I'm just glad you're with me, Ned. I'm glad we're facing it together."

Ned rose on tiptoe and laid his lips to Joe's ear. "I'm glad we're together too."

"Are you?" Joe quietly asked, placing his hands at the side of Ned's neck and cradling his head as they pulled apart far enough to stare into each other's eyes.

Ned gazed up at him with such adoration, Joe's eyes burned, and tears began to form. Ned's voice was a whisper, drifting through the haze.

"I'll be with you as long as you want me to be, Joe."

Ned was so beautiful standing there, gazing at him trustingly with those gentle blue eyes, that Joe's heart clenched up like a fist. The spasm was so unexpected it almost hurt. He struggled to find his voice. "Thank you for last night. It was… incredible."

Ned blinked. His eyes were riveted to Joe's lips, and Joe enjoyed having them there. Joe watched as Ned fought to swallow. When he finally found his voice, it sounded all crumpled up, like a piece of paper wadded into a ball, wrinkly and crushed and twisted out of shape.

"Since the day I met you, I've never wanted to be with anyone else." Ned's cheeks burned red, but he didn't look embarrassed. He looked proud and determined. It was as if his time with Joe had made him stronger. Braver and more self-assured. Joe liked that too. "But you probably already know all that," Ned added with a hint of a smile, his eyes as bright as diamonds.

Joe edged closer and laid a tentative kiss to Ned's mouth. He relaxed into the kiss when Ned's arms came up and pulled him close. The kiss went on and on as the birds continued to fall from the sky and the damned demented dogs continued to howl and bark and snarl in the distance. There was a big dog fight going on somewhere. It sounded like they were trying to kill each other. But in Ned's arms, at home in Ned's kiss, Joe wasn't afraid.

He remembered the night before out on the trail. The dogs attacking Ned until Joe rushed in to chase them away. How they could have killed Ned if they had dragged him to the ground. How they could have overpowered him and ripped him to shreds. How it all could have ended far differently than it actually had.

Those thoughts he quickly pushed away. No harm had come to Ned last night, and he wouldn't allow any harm to come to him today. Ned was safe, and Joe would keep him that way. He would take care of Ned, just as Ned would take care of him. He didn't doubt it for a minute.

In each other's arms, they stood in the bloodred haze of a morning that should never have been, in the midst of a city that had gone from an Eden to a bloody nightmare, and lost themselves in the simplicity of a single kiss. There was an innocence and an impossibility about it that did not escape Joe. There was an underlying promise in the kiss too. And the promise flowed silently in both directions, from Joe to Ned and back again. That didn't escape Joe either. While he might not know what Ned was thinking, he most certainly knew what Ned was feeling. Joe knew because his feelings were the same. His feelings were *exactly* the same.

Thank God you're here with me, Ned. And thank God you're safe. While the world crumbled to ruin, a flock of dying birds flopped at their feet, and thoughts and fears tumbled through Joe's head like a load of laundry spinning in a dryer, that one thought came to anchor Joe. His feelings for Ned were crystal clear. There was nothing mysterious about them, nothing strange. They simply were what they were. To a man like Joe who had never given himself heart and soul to anyone before in his life, had never even *wanted* to, it was an astonishing realization. More astonishing even than a world gone head-spinning, batshit crazy.

A scream wrenched him back to the real world.

It was a woman's scream. As quickly as the scream faded, Joe heard a furious yelling. Two men. Cursing. Bellowing horrible words at each other. The woman's scream came again as the unmistakable sound of fists pummeling flesh began to echo through the air. The sounds were made more frightening by the fact that neither Joe nor Ned could see very far ahead. Joe spun first one way, then another, trying to decide which direction the sounds were coming from. In truth, they could have come from anywhere. Just around the corner or a half a mile away, from behind them, in front of them, or directly above their fucking heads. The crimson haze was simply too blinding, too distorting. It made it impossible to pinpoint where sounds originated.

Joe tensed. "What should we do?" He could still taste Ned's kiss on his lips, but the woman's scream echoed in his ears as well. The perfection of the one had been shattered by the terror in the other. And with the red haze still wafting about their heads like a shroud, limiting vision, confusing sound, Joe had to fight against the urge to cower beneath it.

It was hard to be brave when you couldn't see what was coming at you.

Ned plucked nervously at Joe's shirt. Joe's attention was torn from the screams and back to him.

"We should go!" Ned hissed, quietly tugging at Joe's sleeve. "I'm worried about Mr. Wong. He's probably at the deli by himself. He's too stubborn to ever close up shop. We could be nuked by Russia, and he'd still be standing there slicing pickle loaf. And these animals, these people…." Ned cast nervous glances in every direction, clearly disturbed by the distant screams and the tortured, howling beasts. "They're not acting right, Joe. I'm scared."

Ned was right. It *was* scary. Whatever had affected the dogs and the birds seemed to be affecting people too. They were acting crazy.

"Then let's hurry," Joe said. "If he's *not* there, we'll rush back to the apartment and lock ourselves in." A mischievous grin twisted his mouth. "That way I'll have you all to myself again. Naked and delicious."

A flush rose to Ned's cheeks, but standing there in the bloodred haze, his blush was barely visible. On the other hand, Joe enjoyed the fact that Ned's eyes were as bright as spotlights.

"I like the sound of that," Ned purred.

Sharing a secretive smile, they took off once again for the deli. Still holding hands, they sprinted the last two blocks, hoping to slip through the haze before danger could find them. At the final cross street, they looked up the boulevard and spotted a cluster of men a stone's throw away. They were battling with each other, fists flying. There must have been ten or twelve of them. Curses echoed up and down the street. Already inert bodies lay here and there in the melee, knocked senseless or worse. In the distance, police sirens wailed, but the sirens were fading away, not coming closer. For some reason the cops were going in the wrong direction. Whatever the fistfight was about, it appeared the police had decided to let the guys duke it out on their own. Maybe they had bigger fish to fry somewhere else. Or maybe they didn't know about it at all.

A thought occurred to Joe. He fished his cell phone out of his pocket and tapped it on. Nothing happened. There was no signal. Maybe communications were down. Maybe that's why the cops weren't responding to this riot. That must be it!

"They don't know, Ned! I'll bet the cops don't know."

Confused, Ned asked, "What? What are you saying?"

But before Joe could explain, from a stand of trees to their left, they heard a cruel, blustering cry. "Hey, you faggots. Stop!" A second later came the unmistakable sound of a gunshot. Joe ducked as a bullet whizzed over their heads.

"Fucker!" Joe screamed in fury.

Clutching at Ned's jacket to keep him close, Joe tore off down the street, running even faster than he had been before, desperate to get away from the idiot with the gun. Seconds later, the deli appeared through the haze. The windows were dark, of course, since the power was out. The business looked closed, as empty as the street around it. Even the sirens in the distance couldn't be heard anymore. Joe frowned. If they needed police protection, they were piss out of luck.

They approached the deli carefully, not sure what to do. Seconds later, Mr. Wong burst through the front door. He grabbed them both in a steely grip and yanked them inside, almost dragging them off their feet. "Hurry!" he cried. "Get off street!"

The minute they stumbled through the door, Mr. Wong locked it behind them and pulled the blinds. With trembling hands, he latched the dead bolts at the floor and at the top of the double doors. Then he grunted with the effort of sliding a waist-high cooler used for fruit juices in front of the door to secure it further. Sweating and cussing softly to himself, he turned back to Ned and Joe and pulled them deeper into the deli, farther away from the storefront windows and away from the door. Only then did Joe see a smear of blood on Mr. Wong's cheek. With his free hand, Mr. Wong held a bloody wad of napkins to his ear.

"What happened?" Ned cried, rushing forward to lead Mr. Wong to one of the tables in the back, snatching another stack of napkins off the counter as he passed. "What's going on? Why are you bleeding?"

Mr. Wong stared at them, his narrow eyes filled with emotion. Joe wasn't sure if the emotion was anger or fear. His eyes were as dark as onyx, and they skipped like shiny black stones from Ned to Joe, then back again to Ned. "The world go crazy, Neddie," he whispered, as if it was all a big secret and he was the only one who knew it. "The world go fucking crazy!"

"Where's your family?" Ned pleaded, busying himself at the sink behind the counter, dampening the ball of napkins under the faucet. "Are they safe? Are the boys at home?"

Mr. Wong sat obediently still while Ned wrung out the fistful of wet napkins and started dabbing at the blood on his face. Joe watched too. When Mr. Wong's chin was clean, Joe saw there was no cut there at all. The blood must have all come from Mr. Wong's ear. Ned carefully nudged Mr. Wong's hand aside to examine the injury while Joe continued to watch, periodically letting his eyes flit to the door and through the slats of the blinds to make sure no one was sneaking up on them outside. With Mr. Wong's hand out of the way, they saw why there was so much blood. His ear lobe had been completely torn away.

"What the hell happened?" Ned hissed in horror, cringing at the sight of Mr. Wong's mutilated ear. With a grimace, he quickly pressed the ball of wet napkins to it, as much to clean the wound as to block it from sight.

Mr. Wong winced but didn't complain about Ned dabbing at his ear. "Crazy man bite me. He hiding in the back when I come to work."

Joe and Ned turned their attention to the back of the deli. They didn't see anyone.

"So where is he?" Joe asked. "Did you run him off?"

Mr. Wong looked sad, as if he still couldn't believe it happened. "No," he said, his eyes more hurt now than angry. "He still there."

Warily, Joe and Ned moved toward the back, past the fryers and the island where Mr. Wong stood for hours, building sandwiches, mixing salads. They tiptoed past the glass-fronted coolers with the great chunks of meat and cheese inside, all waiting for their turn at the slicer.

They found the man in front of the walk-in freezer. He was lying motionless at the foot of the freezer door. He wore rags and looked homeless. He lay on his back, eyes closed as if peacefully asleep. But sleep was well beyond him at this point in the game, since there was a bigass carving knife protruding from his chest and a large pool of blood congealing on the tiles beneath him.

"My God!" Ned gasped.

Joe rushed closer and knelt by the body. He pressed a finger to the man's neck, seeking a pulse. While he worked, he studied Ned's frightened face. There was an uneasy tremor of recognition in Ned's eyes, and Joe understood the truth immediately. "You know him, don't you?"

Ned nodded. Mr. Wong was suddenly standing there as well. He held more wet napkins to his ear, still trying to staunch the bleeding. While Mr. Wong stared blandly down at the lifeless body, it was Ned who finally spoke.

He sounded confused, like he had just awakened from a dream that made no sense. "It's old Fred. He's homeless. Mr. Wong feeds him sometimes. Takes him a sandwich out back to the alley." Ned offered a desperate frown, clearly trying to make sense out of what might have happened. "He was always *nice*, Joe." His eyes slid to Mr. Wong. "Why would he attack you now?"

Mr. Wong gave an exaggerated shrug. He looked anything but apologetic. "He go crazy, like everybody else. He jump on me and bite me. I think he try to kill me, so I kill him first. What else I supposed to do?"

"We have to call the police," Joe said. "We have to tell them what happened."

Mr. Wong dabbed at a rivulet of blood dripping down his neck. He sounded slightly bored by all the drama unfolding. "I already call. Two hours ago. They no come."

"What do you mean, they no come?"

"What I said. They no come. Why you talk funny?"

Joe didn't have an answer for that. "Then we'll call again," he said.

"You can't. Phone dead now. I just try. Cell phone too. World gone to shit." As if weary of the whole conversation, he suddenly grinned. "You boys hungry? I fix you breakfast. Egg salad fresh."

While Joe grabbed for the phone by the cash register to make sure it was really dead, as he damn well knew it was, Ned still knelt beside the body on the floor. He couldn't seem to tear his eyes off the pool of blood congealing under old Fred.

"He's right," Joe said, staring at the receiver in his hand. "There's no dial tone. The phone's dead."

He slammed the worthless phone back in the cradle, then fished his cell phone out of his pants pocket and tried it again too. He gawked at its blank screen for a minute before he lifted his eyes to Ned.

"Told you," Mr. Wong mumbled, as if nobody ever listened to him.

Joe leaned over Ned and spoke softly in his ear. "Help me," he said. "I can't look at this dead guy anymore. He's giving me the creeps."

He tugged at the freezer door and propped it open with his foot. Reaching forward, he clutched old Fred's shoulders and started dragging him inside. Joe grunted with the exertion. Old Fred wasn't light.

"What about police?" Mr. Wong asked, watching with interest but refusing to lend a hand. "What about forensic science? I watch *CSI*. I know what police do. You're disturbing evidence. Everybody has job to do. They can't do it if you screw up evidence." He still did not offer to help. Apparently he figured *his* share of the undertaking was completed when he plunged a butcher knife into the old guy's chest.

Ned was helping Joe now, each tugging at one of Fred's lifeless arms, dragging him over the threshold of the freezer door while old Fred's head flopped around, his empty eyes gaping at everything and nothing like a couple of marbles rolling around in a saucer.

While he worked, Joe tried to piece it all together. "I have a feeling the police have more important catastrophes to deal with. One dead homeless guy isn't going to beep high on their sonar screens when they've got an entire city going nuts around them."

Mr. Wong clucked his tongue, staring down at the trail of blood smeared across his spotless deli floor and over the threshold of the freezer door. "Look at that. What a mess," he grumbled. He didn't look happy, to say the least.

"Don't worry," Ned said, misinterpreting Mr. Wong's words. "It was self-defense. We're just keeping him on ice until the police show up."

"I not worried about Fred," Mr. Wong snapped. "I worry about my floor!" He snatched a stack of towels from a cupboard and scattered them over the mess old Fred left behind, scooting them around with his foot to blot up the blood.

Joe tried not to laugh. Apparently Mr. Wong no longer cared about maintaining a pristine crime scene. Now he was more worried about keeping his A card with the health department.

Joe and Ned tucked old Fred under a shelf of ice cream containers. Before they stepped out of the freezer, locking him inside, Mr. Wong stepped forward and plucked the knife from his chest.

"German steel," he explained. He huffed out a puff of freezer air while looking wounded, clearly appalled by the way they were staring at him. He shook the knife in their faces. "I build two hundred sandwiches to pay for this knife. Not going to leave it in old Fred."

"Umm, okay," Joe said, still biting back a grin. "So much for forensics, then."

Mr. Wong eyed the old man's corpse a final time while wiping the knife blade clean with one of the towels he had used to sop up blood. "If he keeps, maybe next week we run him through grinder and serve Fred Salad Sandwiches for lunch, hey, Neddie?"

Ned rolled his eyes and groaned so sincerely that Joe and Mr. Wong both burst out laughing.

The three of them exited through the freezer door, leaving old Fred inside to chill—literally. They secured the door behind them, although Fred probably wouldn't be trying to escape anytime soon. The moment they were outside and the freezer was locked, all three sets of eyes settled once again on the deli's front door, which was the only thing between them and a civilization suddenly gone to shit. Somewhere in the distance they heard another gunshot.

"I not open today. World too goofy." Mr. Wong made the announcement matter-of-factly. Like it was something he had decided on the spur of the moment, just for the hell of it. He turned worried eyes on Joe and Ned. It was Ned especially that he seemed to be concerned about. He reached out and patted Ned's cheek, like he might one of his own children. "You boys go home and stay there."

Ned edged closer to Joe, and Joe's face softened when he did. A gentle light lit Mr. Wong's eyes as he watched the two. For the first time he seemed to understand everything. Not about the world falling apart, but about Joe and Ned. About the changes that had taken place since the last time he had seen them together.

He settled his eyes on Joe. Reaching out, he laid a gentle hand on Joe's arm. "Take care of my Neddie," he said, his gaze delving deep into Joe's. "Keep him safe. Old Fred not the only thing dangerous out there."

Joe nodded, even as he slipped his hand through Ned's to anchor him close. "I will, sir. It's my highest priority."

Mr. Wong smiled, first at Joe, then at Ned. "I thought it might be," he said, plucking a key from his pants pocket. He scooted the juice cooler out of the way and knelt to unlock the front door. When it was unsecured, he rose, peeked outside, then stepped aside to let them pass.

"Run," Mr. Wong said, his eyes suddenly serious again. "Run like the wind. I do same. Make sure Mrs. Wong and the babies okay. You boys lay low and protect yourselves. Don't come out till this craziness over. Promise me."

Suffering no arguments and not waiting for an answer, Mr. Wong pushed them through the door and banged it shut behind them before they could protest. A second later Joe and Ned stood outside in the misty red morning, listening to the key turn on the other side of the deli door.

Once again Joe found the two of them facing a world where everything was wrong and nothing made sense. Nothing… but Ned's hand in his.

JOE WAS a little out of breath because he was dragging Ned down the street at a pretty good clip. They ran close together, jostling each other, while trying desperately not to trip each other up.

Ned sounded frightened, but not of their surroundings. "Mr. Wong killed a man, Joe. What's going to happen to him?"

Joe was concentrating on trying to see through the haze. He didn't want any surprises coming at them while he tried to get Ned and himself home. He spoke softly so they wouldn't be overheard by anyone lurking in the shadows. "Don't worry. It was self-defense. They won't blame him for trying to protect himself. And he tried to call the cops, so they can't blame him for not reporting it either. Even we tried to call, so he's got witnesses. The police probably have bigger things to worry about now than one dead homeless guy anyway."

"You think?"

Joe reached over and tousled Ned's hair while dragging up a reassuring smile that was pure show. "Absolutely. As long as Mr. Wong doesn't follow through on his threat to serve up Fred Salad Sandwiches. If he does, then it's a whole new ball game."

He offered up a theatrical shudder, but it didn't seem to amuse Ned much. Not that Joe expected it to.

They stumbled to a stop at the first street corner they came to, looking both ways for oncoming traffic. There was none. The street was an empty ribbon of concrete. Dead silent, it rolled off and disappeared into the haze in either direction. They did a slow turn, cocking their heads to the side, listening. The city was as silent as the street. It was like a ghost town. Before, there had been distant screams and scattered sirens.

Gunshots. Wailing dogs. Now there was nothing. Not even the chirp of a cricket broke the stillness.

"It's so quiet!" Ned hissed. "Where'd everybody go?"

Joe shook his head. "I don't know, but I don't like it. There's a tension in the air. Can you feel it?"

Ned nodded, eyes wide. "Yeah. It's like in a horror movie just before the closet door flies open and a maniac with a chainsaw jumps out."

Joe rolled his eyes and bit back a groan. "Well, that makes me feel a whole lot better." Then, lowering his voice, he said, "Still, I think you're right. Something *is* about to happen. Something bad. Let's get off the street. Now."

Once again, they took off running. They didn't bother holding hands now; they were too busy concentrating on moving as fast as they could while making as little noise as possible. They tried to stay on the grass so the slap of their footfalls fell dead on the hazy air, like the gentle patter of faraway heartbeats.

They ran three blocks flat out as fast as they could. Finally, Ned plucked at Joe's jacket. Sucking in air, he cried, "Wait! Stop! Let me catch my breath."

Joe pulled up short, and Ned ran right into his arms. Joe held him upright while Ned gasped and wheezed. As Ned sucked in oxygen, Joe rested his chin on the top of Ned's head and kept an eye out for anything coming at them.

The city seemed deserted, but Joe knew it wasn't. It couldn't be.

When Ned lifted his head and said, "We can go now," Joe didn't wait around for him to say it again. He once more tugged Ned forward. Walking quickly now, not running, Joe bounced off the balls of his feet to move as silently as he could. After a while, Ned got the picture and did the same.

They reached the place where they had seen the pool of blood earlier and immediately jerked to a stop, crashing into each other. Two bedraggled coyotes were standing on the sidewalk, lapping at the blood. They cowered there, the hair bristling across their skinny backs like they thought the two humans might try to steal their food.

Joe pulled Ned slowly backward until the coyotes were lost once again in the red mist. Only then did he lead Ned back out into the street and around to the right so they could get past the coyotes without being seen by the creatures. He thought he felt Ned trembling against him but, in a stunning rush of awareness, realized *he* was the one trembling, not Ned. And apparently Ned knew it.

"It'll be all right," Ned whispered. "We're almost home."

Joe had to smile. *Who was the brave one now?*

Far away, a cacophony of sirens bleated feebly at the very edge of earshot. The sound was so thin and reedy, Joe knew it had to come from blocks and blocks away. It sounded like every cop in the city was converging on one spot. Quelling a riot, maybe. Or attending some massive disaster. Like the whole fucking world wasn't enough of a disaster already.

A figure loomed suddenly out of the haze directly in front of them. It was a man with what at first glance Joe thought was a rifle. On closer inspection he realized it was a double-barreled shotgun, which was even scarier. The man was young and trim. Handsome. But even at a distance Joe could see there was something wrong about him. He stood sideways to them, leaning slightly forward, peering into the gloom. There was a look of pure hatred on his face like he was itching to use his gun on *somebody*.

Joe's breath froze in his chest. The man hadn't spotted them yet. Thank God.

Holding a finger to his lips to command silence, Joe tugged Ned under the hanging branches of a pepper tree that stood at the side of the walk. The tree's long leaves hung in streamers almost to the ground, covering them like a curtain. It was a perfect place to duck out of sight.

They stood in the shadows, peeking out onto the street at the man with the gun. He hadn't moved yet, but they could hear the incessant *click, click, click* as he nervously flipped the shotgun's safety on and off, on and off.

Joe's eyes flitted to Ned's face and he saw not only fear there, but also cold. Ned's ears were red, his cheeks were flushed, and his teeth were quietly chattering. For the first time, Joe saw his own breath bursting out of him in little white puffs.

With everything that was happening, Joe hadn't noticed how cold it had become. He didn't think San Diego had ever suffered a cold snap like this one. Even the burst of frigid air that rolled over them yesterday when they were in the alley behind the deli talking to Mr. Wong's son wasn't as bone-cracking cold as this one.

He quickly scooped up Ned's hands and rubbed them between his own, chafing them to life, hoping to take the chill away and get the blood moving again. While he did that, he continued to peek between the branches to see what the asshole with the gun was doing. He breathed a little easier when he saw the man was not only still facing away from them but had also moved a few feet farther off. Now he could barely be seen standing there in the mist at the very edge of sight. If he moved away another foot or two he would disappear completely, swallowed up by the fog. Joe wasn't sure if that would be a good thing or a bad. While it would also mean the guy couldn't see *them*, Joe didn't like the idea of an armed maniac hiding in the shadows, waiting to flip his lid and start shooting at anything that moved. The haze might keep them hidden, but it wouldn't do much to stop a barrage of shotgun pellets.

He studied Ned's expression. With a gentle tug, he coaxed Ned down to the ground where they squatted at the base of the tree. If nothing else, it made them a smaller target.

Ned returned his look with a jittery smile. He puckered his mouth like he was blowing smoke rings. "I can see my breath," he said.

Joe spoke in the faintest of whispers behind an equally nervous smile. "Me too."

Ned took a fistful of Joe's jacket, either to balance himself as he squatted, or just because he wanted the connection.

"Mr. Wong was right, Joe. In the blink of an eye the world has suddenly gone crazy."

"Only he said it without articles or prepositions."

Ned snorted, then slapped a hand to his mouth to stifle a laugh. He had no more done that than his eyes grew sad. His hand fell away from his mouth and he clutched a little tighter at Joe's jacket.

"He really killed that man."

Joe sighed. "He didn't have a choice."

Ned fidgeted, drawing a shaky breath, still clearly trying to come to terms with what Mr. Wong had done. "I know. He—he did what he had to, didn't he, Joe?"

"Yes. And that's the same thing we have to do," Joe answered softly, all the while stroking Ned's arm, hoping to keep him calm. Turning away, he peeked through the branches of the pepper tree again. The man was completely out of sight now, and Joe liked that far less than having the man visible.

"Right now what we have to do," Joe whispered, "is work our way around this armed asshole and make it home without getting shot."

Ned nodded. "I'm glad you're with me, Joe. I feel sorry for anybody who's alone right now. Wondering what's going to happen. Trying to stay safe. Not having somebody to…." His voice faded away.

Joe studied his face. "Not having somebody to what?"

The blush in Ned's cheeks blossomed. His ears practically caught on fire. "To care for them," he said quietly, his eyes downcast.

Joe blinked in surprise. His throat constricted as he reached over and touched the back of his hand to Ned's cheek. "I do care for you, Ned."

Again, a tiny smile played at Ned's mouth. He finally looked up. "I was hoping you did."

"Do you care for me too?" Joe quietly asked.

Ned didn't hesitate. The words were freed before he took his next breath. "You know I do."

Joe saw the courage it took for Ned to utter those simple words. Especially to utter them in the middle of everything that was happening. It was as if Ned had arranged in his mind all the things that were most important to him and telling Joe he cared for him ranked even higher than knowing there was a crazy fucker out there with a shotgun itching to blow their heads off.

Joe leaned in and brushed his lips over Ned's mouth. Ned immediately closed his eyes, as if losing himself in Joe's kiss was the most natural thing in the world, regardless of the circumstances. Joe pulled back far enough to watch Ned's eyes as they slipped open again. He didn't see fear now in their blue depths. He saw only… peace. And Joe was pleased by that.

He pulled back and licked the taste of Ned's kiss from his lips. Suddenly he realized how helpless they were, cowering there under a tree. "We have to get home."

There was a calm bravery in Ned's frown that made Joe's heart give a flutter inside his chest.

Ned's eyes narrowed, fearless, even while his mouth turned down in a determined frown. "I know. I'm ready to go when you are."

Joe tapped Ned's chin with a fingertip, causing the frown to disappear. His heartbeat pounded in his ears as he spoke the words for the first time in his life. "I don't just care for you, Ned. I think I'm in love with you."

Ned blinked. His lips parted to become a silent, astonished smile. When his voice came, it was little more than a squeak. "Honest?"

Joe nodded. Once. His gaze was so focused on Ned squatting there in front of him with that sweet smile on his face, that he barely heard himself mutter, "Honest."

Joe leaned in once again to press another kiss to that perfect mouth. Before he got there, Ned's eyes flew open and he screamed in outrage, "No!"

Before Joe knew what was happening, Ned violently pushed him away. Joe struck the ground so hard the air exploded from his lungs. When Ned lunged to his feet and leaped across him, Joe actually flung his arms up in front of his face, thinking he was being attacked.

And he was. Only not by Ned.

Spinning around, Joe saw the reason for Ned's fury. The fucker with the gun had snuck up behind the trunk of the tree. He must have heard them whispering. He was standing there with a nasty, victorious smirk smeared across his face.

As he raised the shotgun to firing height, Ned plowed into him with a roar of fury, fists flying, one knee pistoning up to catch the guy squarely in the nuts. With a feeble whimper and an expulsion of air that must have emptied every ounce of oxygen from his body, the man collapsed under Ned's barrage of anger like a stray dog being mowed down by a speeding car. He didn't stand a chance.

The second he was on the ground, Ned wrenched the shotgun from his hands, and swinging it by the barrel, used it like a club to strike the man in the chest. One, two, three times. When the guy was rolling around in agony, clutching his chest, Ned flung the shotgun as far as he could. It pinwheeled out of sight, swallowed up in the haze. They heard it clatter when it hit the street.

Joe stood there speechless, astounded by Ned's fury, equally appalled and impressed by how quickly Ned had taken the man to the ground and beaten the stuffing out of him. When Ned administered a final kick to the guy's nuts, which really doubled the poor bastard up in agony, Joe finally decided to step in. Not to help neutralize the threat— that job was pretty well accomplished already—but to pull Ned away before he killed the guy.

He yanked Ned away and held on tight while Ned fought to continue his attack on the poor bastard curled up in a ball of misery on the street. Cursing and spitting, Ned was like a rabid dog. Twice, Joe had to grab him tighter to keep him from jumping on the guy. Joe didn't relax his grip until Ned stopped fighting and shaking and twisting in his arms. At long last, Ned finally calmed down.

"He's beaten," Joe whispered in Ned's ear. "There's no need to kill him."

With a last bout of fury, Ned railed, "He would have killed *us*."

And again, Joe stroked and cooed Ned into silence. "But he won't now, so stop, Ned. Just stop."

He stared down at their attacker. He was still clutching his balls and weeping and whimpering like a brat who hadn't gotten his way. Joe nudged him with his foot.

"Get out of here," he commanded softly.

With a cry of pain, the man angled himself off the ground and stumbled away. Joe was pleased to see that in his misery, apparently their attacker's internal GPS was now on the fritz just like the birds. Tipping and blubbering, he took off in the opposite direction from where Ned had flung his gun.

Joe eyed Ned as he stood there watching the man go. He didn't look particularly pleased with himself, but he didn't look ashamed either.

Joe gnawed on his lip to keep from smiling. "Remind me never to rile you up."

Ned sucked in a deep, shuddering gulp of air, obviously still trying to calm himself. There were tears standing in his eyes, and Joe knew instinctively they were tears of anger, not fear. Through the entire attack, Ned had not displayed an ounce of fear. He had shown only fury.

Beneath the hanging branches of the pepper tree, with the cold air once again biting at their ears and fogging their breath, Ned let himself be pulled into Joe's arms.

Joe held him there until Ned's trembling went from weariness to want. When Ned tilted his head back to gaze on Joe's face, Joe planted a tender kiss on each fluttering eyelid.

"Take me home and make love to me," Ned whispered.

"Yes," Joe murmured, taking Ned by the hand. Without another word, he pulled him from beneath the drooping branches of the pepper tree and led him into the haze.

NED LAY on his back, his legs folded upward, knees clamped to Joe's waist. As Joe perched over him with his hot breath bathing Ned's ear, Ned clutched Joe's waist and groaned with every inward stroke.

Joe's voice was a breathless flutter. "Am I hurting you?"

Ned clawed upward, pulling Joe deeper, burying his face in Joe's throat. "No. Oh God, Joe, no. It feels wonderful."

Joe froze, hovering over Ned, his long cock buried deep. Ned lay impaled, his breath stilled by his own pleasure and the knowledge he was pleasing Joe. At the pure joy of feeling Joe's erection buried motionless inside him, he arched his head back, neck straining, lips parted. He fought every urge to whimper, to beg Joe to start moving again. A moan finally slipped out when Joe's mouth fell over his, capturing him in a breathless kiss. Ned writhed in Joe's arms, a worm on a hook, while the beautiful burn of Joe's cock forged a trail of delicious fire into his very core. Lost in the wonder of a hundred sensations tearing through him, Ned was suddenly aware of his tears spilling out, cutting a warm path along his cheek.

"You're like satin," Joe gasped, beginning to move again, slowly, lingeringly. Then in a shuddered whisper, "Please tell me I'm not hurting you."

"Oh God, Joe, don't stop. I'm begging you, don't stop."

As Ned held on, slipping his hands over Joe's sweaty back while still fighting the urge to cry out, Joe's rhythm increased. His long strokes delved deeper. The girth of his cock swelled, stretching Ned's sheath, dragging Ned along with him with every new insertion, every new long slow piercing.

Gnawing at Joe's shoulder, tasting his skin, his sweat, his scent, Ned locked his ankles over Joe's waist. He gasped and thrashed as Joe's cock tore through him. It was moving faster now, relentless, as hard as steel, plumbing his depths, tearing through him like a loving sword. Painless and bulging and razor sharp.

When Joe tensed over him, every muscle in his body quivering with need, Ned knew he could hold back no more.

Sliding his hardness over Joe's belly in a delicious friction, Ned passed the point of no return before he even knew it was coming. With a joyous agony, his seed tore out of him, spilling across his chest. At the same moment, Joe's cock swelled deep inside him, straining at the limit of its penetration, snatching Ned's breath away.

A guttural cry tore from Joe's throat as his juices exploded from him. Both Ned and Joe writhed at the edge of Joe's release for a long excruciating moment amid a tortured, joyous stillness unlike anything Ned had ever experienced before. Just as their simultaneous climaxes began to wane, as their knotted muscles began to relax, Joe found Ned's mouth once again with his. His tongue slid inward, piercing Ned yet again as their two bodies convulsed and his cock gave one last lunge deep into Ned, uncontrollable, mindless, seeking.

Ned dug his fingers into Joe's back, trying to pull him closer, deeper. Joe's lips relaxed over his. The sound of Joe's clamoring heart swelled around him, and Ned pulled away from the kiss to once again bury his tear-stained face against Joe's throat.

He felt Joe's lips on his hair, his warm fingers stroking Ned's cheek. He planted delicate kisses over Ned's scar, and Ned squeezed his eyes shut, loving the gentleness of it. Unashamed of his scar now. Unashamed of anything. A bead of sweat slid from Joe's chin, landing on Ned's lips. Ned eagerly, hungrily, licked it away.

As Joe's cock began to soften inside him, Ned desperately held on, his arms wrapped tight across Joe's back, still not wanting him to slip away. Not yet. Not ever. His own juices, sticky and hot, were smeared between their two bellies. Even that did not shame him. It felt wonderful.

Joe seemed to agree. At the moment when Joe's softening cock at last slid free from Ned's sheath, Joe captured Ned's mouth yet again in a slow, exploring kiss. There was a smile in the kiss this time. With mouths still touching, Joe giggled.

"I can't get enough of you."

Ned could not find the strength to answer. He was too happy, too contented, lying there with the weight of Joe's body blanketed over his, the heat of Joe's skin still burning through him. Inside his head, buried forever in some memory bank or other, he relived the ecstasy of Joe's perfect cock tearing through him. It was a memory he knew would never leave him. Ever.

He struggled to find his voice. When he did, his words were a surprise even to him. "I didn't know it could be like that."

Joe slid off him. Ignoring the mess between them, he rested his head on the pillow and pulled Ned close. "Neither did I, Ned. I—I've never done that before."

A tremor captured them both.

"Me either," Ned said. "At least… not like this." And then finally, surprisingly, his cheeks warmed in a blush.

Joe's bedroom was dimmed to a rose hue by the red haze outside, but they could still see each other in the crimson light. Ned tilted his head up to study Joe's eyes. His blush deepened when he saw that Joe's gaze was welded to his. He watched as Joe licked his lips.

"I can still taste your kiss," Joe said.

Ned broke the connection by scooting down into the bed and laying his forehead to Joe's chest.

"I can still feel you inside me," he whispered, his lips moving through the brush of dark hair on Joe's broad chest. With a shudder, he added, "I hope the feeling never goes away. It wasn't like before. When those boys… hurt me. You were gentle, Joe. Thank you."

"I'll never hurt you, Ned. Please don't thank me for that."

"All right."

Ned emitted a sigh as Joe's cheek pressed into his hair, as his bare body lay snug in Joe's heat. Warmed. Protected. Safe.

"You were so beautiful and brave lying beneath me," Joe whispered. "So accepting of everything I did."

Ned closed his eyes and pressed his mouth to Joe's skin. There was wonder in his voice when he said, "I've never been this happy, Joe."

Joe drew him close, again burying his lips in Ned's hair, one gentle hand stroking Ned's back while the other rested at the swell of Ned's butt, one finger resting in the fissure there, proprietary, laying claim to it all. His voice was a happy grumble, seemingly as astonished as Ned at the feelings surging through him.

"Neither have I," he whispered back.

They both froze when they heard a gunshot in the distance. Then another.

Joe pulled Ned closer, trapping him in his arms. His voice was a lazy wafting of air and sound. His warm breath flowed over Ned. Ned peered up and saw Joe staring through the bedroom window.

"It's amazing," Joe said.

Ned had to struggle to find his voice. "What is?" A lazy smile twisted Joe's mouth. At the same moment, Joe's gaze left the window and returned to Ned's face. "It's amazing," he said, "that I should find the brightest light of my life in the middle of all this darkness."

Ned tried to understand what Joe was saying. Maybe he was too well fucked for coherent thought. "What light do you mean?" he asked.

"You," Joe said, and he passed a thumb stroke over Ned's bottom lip, smiling down as he did. "You're the light. The brightest I've ever seen. You blind me, Ned. You burn my eyes right out of my head."

"Joe...." He watched Joe's gaze slide back to the window. His own eyes followed along.

"It's getting darker," he said, and Joe nodded.

"Yes. The red stuff is thicker now. It's not even noon yet, and it might as well be sunset. The day looks like it's over."

Ned pressed a kiss to Joe's chin. "I'm glad you're with me."

Joe smiled down at him. "Me too." Again, his eyes trailed back to the window and the encroaching darkness. His strong arms pulled Ned closer, his one hand returning to lay lightly across the curve of his butt, which again made the blood surge to Ned's cheeks.

"Don't be afraid," Joe said. "I won't let anything happen to you."

Ned breathed in Joe's scent. He pressed his lips to Joe's chest and tasted the come he had spilled there earlier. A surprising rush of desire tore through him. He longed to feel Joe's cock buried inside him again. Right now. Right this minute. But he knew that would be asking a lot. He grinned at his own brazenness for even thinking it. Instead, he answered softly, "I know you won't, Joe. As long as you're with me, I'm not afraid."

Joe smiled. "No?"

"No."

Slowly, inexorably, they both were drawn to the darkness outside the bedroom window. Even as they watched, wrapped in each other's arms, the darkness seemed to grow.

For the first time, Ned wondered what would happen if the light disappeared completely.

STILL NAKED but wrapped in blankets because the apartment was cold, they sat across from each other at Joe's tiny kitchen table and ate peanut butter and jelly sandwiches. Since the power was still out, they were also trying to drink up all the milk. Joe kept refilling their glasses. Their bare knees touched under the table, and Joe had captured one of Ned's feet between his. At the moment he was fully enjoying stroking Ned's ankle with his big toe. Occasionally, Joe reached down and brushed his fingertips through the hair on Ned's thigh. He was already addicted to the feel of Ned's skin. Having lost himself more than once in its satin softness, he could no longer leave it be.

It took all the willpower he possessed to drag himself back to practical matters.

"As far as I know, I still have to work tonight," Joe said, sipping at the last of his milk. "While I'm working, if you want to bring some of your stuff over, you can. Toothbrush, some clothes, whatever."

Ned laughed. "I'm just next door. I could simply run over and get stuff as I need it." Joe frowned. "What if it gets to where we can't go outside?" He hooked a thumb at the kitchen window. "Look how dark it's getting out there. With all the whack jobs running around, I'd rather you stay inside while I'm not here. There are still dogs out there too. They seem to be running in packs now. They almost brought you down last time. I have no intention of letting it happen again. Plus I have a dead bolt on my front door. All you have is that crappy chain thing. A three-year-old could bust through it."

"I can't just move in with you," Ned laughed. "Your apartment isn't any bigger than mine."

Joe frowned. Again, he reached under the table to caress the warmth of Ned's thigh. With his thumb he gently prodded the hardness of Ned's knee while the second half of his sandwich lay forgotten on his plate. "I don't care," he said. "Just until it's over, Ned. Please. I want you here. Do it for me. You'll be safer, and I'll be…." Joe let the sentence go unfinished.

"You'll be what?"

Embarrassed, Joe picked up his sandwich again, more to fiddle with it than to eat it. "I'll just be happier," he said.

Ned's face softened, and he carefully returned his own sandwich to his plate. By the time he looked up again, his eyes had filled with tears.

Joe sat breathless, watching the crystal droplets gather atop Ned's long pale lashes.

"All right," Ned said quietly, smiling in spite of the tears. "If that's what you want, I'll stay here."

Joe reached across the table and dabbed his napkin at a tiny blob of jelly at the corner of Ned's mouth. When a tear finally spilled over Ned's lashes and skittered down his cheek, Joe dabbed that away too. Ned sat obediently still while Joe fussed, and at that moment, a thought occurred to Joe that would solve everything. His pulse quickened.

"Or better yet, you could walk to work with me," he said, watching Ned's eyes, wondering what Ned would think of the idea.

Ned blinked away the final blur of tears. "Really? What about the trails? Do you think they're still safe?"

Joe considered, and quickly came to a decision. "It'll be safer than taking the car. We can sneak through the darkness on foot better than we can sneak around in the car. If we get stuck in a mob of people in the car we won't be able to get away or get out or anything. We'll be trapped."

He turned to stare through the window at the growing darkness outside. Was it his imagination, or did it seem even darker than it had only a few minutes before? He made his mind up before he returned his gaze to Ned's face. "Sorry, kid. I just made an executive decision. You're going with me whether you want to or not. I'm not leaving you here alone. And I have to go to work. Not only do I need the money, but we're feeding the animals now. They need our help." He eyed the gathering darkness through the kitchen window. It was noon and the light was almost fully gone. "I have to go," he said again, looking worried. "I have a terrible feeling half the workforce won't show up tonight."

Ned stared out at the darkness too. He seemed to be calmly considering the matter. "There's a high fence around the zoo. We might even be safer there than we would be here."

Joe blinked. "You're right. I hadn't thought of that. We *will* be safer there."

"Okay," Ned said, his forehead furrowed with determination, his eyes fearless. He turned from the window to study Joe. "I'd rather be with you anyway. We can protect each other. You don't think they'll mind if I tag along?"

"No. They won't mind. They need all the help they can get. They'd probably welcome another pair of hands."

"In that case, sure, I'll go."

Relieved, Joe offered him a lopsided grin. "Then it's settled."

Ned nodded, his own smile slipping in. "Settled."

Joe reached over to the kitchen counter and grabbed his cell phone. He checked to see if it was working yet. It wasn't. Exasperated, he tossed it aside.

"Technology sucks," he muttered to himself. His forehead furrowed. "We should have kept the shotgun we took from that guy. We shouldn't have thrown it away."

"Guns scare me," Ned said, shaking his head. "Too many bad things happen because of guns."

Joe looked uncertain. "I guess."

"It'll be all right," Ned quietly insisted. "Things will get back to normal soon. I know they will."

Joe resumed gnawing halfheartedly at his sandwich, all the while staring at Ned sitting across from him. Despite all the talk of guns and protecting themselves, he was more than aware that the delicious bristle of Ned's leg hair brushing against his own had caused his cock to fill with blood. It was standing upright beneath the table, pulsing in time to his heartbeat.

"You were amazing this morning," he said, his voice already deepening.

Ned looked up. He seemed to understand instinctively what Joe was feeling.

"So were you," Ned said. "I—I've never felt anything like that. To feel you inside me...." His words trailed away. His gaze caromed around the room, as if seeking the right words. Words he couldn't quite grasp.

"What, Ned?" Joe pleaded softly. "Tell me. Tell me how it felt."

He watched as Ned lifted his hand and laid his fingertips to the scar at the side of his head. He did not stroke the scar, he simply rested his fingers over it, as if seeking comfort. Joe wondered if Ned even knew he was doing it.

Ned's lips twisted into the faintest of smiles. His eyes settled on Joe, and Joe sat mesmerized by the sweet intensity in them, their gentle burning light.

"It just felt *right*. It—it felt like I had been hanging around all these years, vamping to the music, waiting for fate to make use of me in some way I hadn't figured out yet. But then today, lying under the weight of you, Joe, being possessed by you like that... it was beautiful. When you slid inside me, it was like I suddenly knew who I was. Like what had been missing was suddenly there. There was pain, but it only lasted a minute. When the pain receded, there was only you. Filling me up. Using me to please yourself. And pleasing me at the same time. It was— unexplainable. You were the missing piece I'd been waiting to find my whole life, Joe. You made me whole. You made me complete. I thought I would be terrified after what happened to me before. But I wasn't. I wasn't scared at all, Joe. Not with you."

Joe reached over and took Ned's hand, pulling it gently away from the scar and laying it on the table, cradled between both of his. He slid his thumb over the hair on Ned's forearm, then circled Ned's slim wrist with his fingers just to feel that he held Ned safely in his grasp. That neither one of them could get away.

Joe's eyes flicked to Ned's scar. "Have you really been with no one since that happened? Was I honestly the first?"

Embarrassed, Ned gazed down at their hands. "Yes. Yesterday and today. They were both firsts."

Joe stared at the simple openness in Ned's gaze, the light of pure truth in his pale blue eyes. "Was it worth the wait?" he asked in a breathless hush. "I know it was for me, but was it for you too? Was it— what you hoped it would be?"

"No," Ned said with the tiniest shake of his head. A fire rose in his eyes. In the fading light, they shone like embers. "It was more. It was everything. Most of all, it was you, Joe. Just you. Wanting me. And that made it perfect."

Joe brought Ned's hand up to his lips and laid a soft kiss to his palm. When he did, Ned stroked his cheek with a fingertip. "I *still* want you," Joe said on a sigh.

Ned smiled. "I know you do. I can feel it."

Joe's eyes slid back to the tousled hair hiding Ned's scar.

"I'm sorry that happened to you," he said, his voice frail. "I'm sorry you missed so many years of being who you really are."

"Don't be," Ned said. Again, his gaze was focused, determined. "It was worth the wait."

"Why, Ned? How can you say that?"

"I can say it because waiting for me at the end of all those years was you. And this morning, feeling you inside me, knowing I was pleasing you, it made me realize I had come full circle. I went from being a sixteen-year-old kid, interrupted just as he was discovering himself, to a full-grown man who finally found himself in the arms of someone who really cared. You, Joe. You care for me. You have no idea what an astonishing thing that is to me."

Ned sucked in a quaking breath. His gaze slid from Joe's face. He looked uncertain suddenly, as if he thought maybe he'd said too much.

Joe pulled Ned's hand to his mouth and rested his lips against it as he spoke. "Don't ever be ashamed to look at me. Please. Don't ever turn your eyes away after you've shared yourself with me."

"I'm sorry."

Joe offered him a sad little smile. "Don't ever be sorry either. You have nothing to be sorry for."

"Don't I?" Ned asked.

"No. Not with me."

Joe dragged his chair closer to the table just to get an inch or two nearer to Ned. He rummaged through his brain for a second, trying to organize his thoughts, trying to find the exact words he wanted to say. While he did that, Ned waited patiently, stroking Joe's cheek again. Ned's eyes never once left Joe's face, and there was not a single moment that Joe was not aware of their gentle blue fire settling over him.

"I've waited too," Joe muttered, letting his voice escape on a desperate rush of air. "I lost faith in people a long time ago. I've spent my life not wanting to be close to anyone. I've never wanted to let them in. I'm not like other people, I guess. I like being alone. I like being by myself."

Here, Joe lost his momentum. His words floundered before he finally discovered the truth of what he was really trying to say. And even he didn't know it was the ultimate truth until he heard it with his own ears.

"I never felt lonely until the day I met you. Outside. On your front step. I'll never forget that day. I'll never forget how you looked that day. I'll never forget how my heart hammered inside my chest when we shook hands for the first time. How your skin felt on mine. How suddenly I wasn't as bulletproof as I always thought I was."

He released Ned's hand and reached up to slide his thumb through Ned's hair until he felt the hard flesh of Ned's scar beneath his touch.

"This scar," Joe said, "is not who you are. You're so much more than this. And now that you're with me, I'm so much more than I ever was too. I think we were both scarred, Ned. I think maybe we were both broken people. I think maybe we would have stayed broken if we hadn't found each other. I also think...."

Ned leaned in, waiting, his eyes bright and alive. There were tears standing in them again. He didn't ask the obvious question; he simply waited for the answer to come, as if he knew Joe would give it to him when he was ready.

Joe's fingers slid from the scar and brushed across Ned's tender cheek and its pale sprinkling of downy hair. "I also think... I love you," Joe said softly. "I think I've loved you since that very first day when I saw you standing by your door."

Joe watched as Ned closed his eyes, squeezing a tear free. It spilled over his bottom lash and slid across Joe's hand, forging a delicate path down through the dark hair on Joe's forearm. The luscious, tickling heat of it sent a chill through Joe.

"You don't have to say these things," Ned whispered. "You don't have to make a commitment to me. I'm happy to be with you either way. With or without promises."

Joe's breath caught. He fought the will to weep, to cry out, to laugh out loud, at himself, at the world, at everything. "I didn't say what I said for you, Ned. I said it for me. I said it because I couldn't go on *not* saying it." He took a deep breath to calm himself. "And I said it because it's true. In fact, I think it's maybe the truest thing I've *ever* said."

Ned's lips trembled as he formed the words. "Then, you love me?"

"Yes," Joe said, so innocently believing of the answer he gave that the clamoring of his heart suddenly quieted, his pulse slowed. An unexpected calmness settled over him.

They sat motionless, staring into each other's eyes.

"I've never been loved before," Ned whispered into the hush.

"No," Joe softly replied. "Neither have I."

IT WAS strange getting ready for work in the tomblike silence of an apartment devoid of electricity. The juice hadn't come back on yet, and that was starting to worry Joe. Through the course of the long day, the light outside had progressively dimmed as well. The red haze was so thick and heavy now, it lay like a film before the eyes. More than once Ned and Joe found themselves standing at Joe's front window trying to see across the lawn outside. Trying to spot the street. Trying to discern the landmarks they knew so well. The palm tree on the corner. The big blue mailbox on the sidewalk out in front of the building. The movement of traffic that always before had thrummed up and down Sixth Avenue in an endless procession. Not only could the cars not be seen, even the sound of them was lost in the haze. Or maybe there was no traffic at all. From where they stood, it was impossible to tell.

Whatever was going on out there, it was goddamn creepy. Joe knew that much.

Visibility was now reduced to ten feet or less. The haze was like a blood-soaked curtain, blocking everything.

"Don't worry," Ned whispered at his side. "We'll get to the zoo and everything will be all right."

It was almost time to go. They were dressed, Joe had his flashlight, and they were wearing the heaviest coats they owned because not only was the day outside a big red mess, it was also freezing cold. The temperature had continued to drop. And since the power was out, the apartment was cold too. He and Ned had spent most of that day burrowed under the covers in Joe's bed, snuggled against the icy air, talking quietly, falling deeper in love.

And now, standing at the front window, looking out with Ned at his side, Joe knew he was a different person. Every time he gazed at Ned's face, or felt Ned's hands on him, or simply heard Ned's laughter shimmering through the unholy twilight, he knew he finally understood what being in love was all about.

It was a wondrous discovery. Wondrous and beautiful.

"Maybe we shouldn't go," he said now. He cast another worried glance through the window, more hesitant by the moment. "God knows what's going on out there. Maybe we should stay here. Barricade ourselves. Lay low."

This time it was Ned who pulled Joe into an embrace. He pressed his lips to Joe's throat and gave his Adam's apple a playful nip. "We have to take care of the animals. You said so yourself."

"I know."

"We both have to keep working. This red shit isn't going to last forever. We don't want to come out of it unemployed. That wouldn't be a very good way to start a life together."

"I know."

"And most of all, I want to see the zoo. I've never been able to afford to go. I've never been there."

At that Joe grabbed Ned's shoulders and pushed him far enough away to look at his face. "Well, we can't have that! Why didn't you tell me? I work there. I have free passes."

Ned grinned but still managed to look embarrassed. "I figured, but I didn't want to ask."

"Dumbass," Joe muttered, causing them both to laugh.

Their laughter slowly died as Joe peered once again through the living room window. "When we go, I want you to stay close to me."

"I will."

"In fact, hold on to me like you did before. If we get separated, we may never find each other again."

"I promise," Ned said. "I'll be a barnacle. I won't let go."

"A barnacle." Joe smiled. "I like the sound of that."

Ned blushed. "So do I."

A moment later they were out the door and standing in a world that was as alien as anything they had ever experienced in their lives.

Somehow, out in the open, their vision seemed even more limited than it was when they were standing at Joe's window. And the air was infinitely colder. They could see their breath. They stood on Joe's front steps and listened for a minute. They couldn't hear much of anything. No traffic, no dogs howling, no birds.

As for the silence of the birds, it was easily explained. The ground was covered with their corpses. A few still flopped around, as if beating broken wings, but most lay either dead or too weary to move.

"Poor things," Ned said, clutching Joe's hand.

Joe hardened his heart, tearing his eyes from the unfortunate creatures. Stepping off his front step, pulling Ned along beside him, he said, "Let's go. Stay close."

"Yes," Ned said, more to himself than to Joe. "I'm here. I'm close."

Seconds later they had disappeared in the crimson mist. Only moments into their trek, Joe heard the sirens. They were far away and numerous. So numerous they seemed to fill the air but buried deep within the red muck. Muted. Like a niggling itch below the skin. Down by the bone. Down where you almost couldn't feel it at all.

Then Joe smelled smoke. Like the distant keen of sirens, it was buried deep, hidden within the haze, and suddenly Joe understood. A great pall of black smoke had blended with the red air. The smoke hadn't been there before. It had fallen over the city sometime while he and Ned were secluded in his apartment. In his bed. Falling in love.

On the southern horizon, Joe saw a faint gleam of light trying to pierce the haze. The gleam was more yellow than the vermilion shadow it lay buried in. The colors of blood and light blended into a palette of heat, almost like a raging sunrise. Bright and hot and devouring. For the first time, Joe thought he could discern the crackling of flames in the distance. The crackling of flames and the cries of a thousand terrified voices. Or were those noises simply inside his head?

And then, like a theater curtain opening wide to reveal the stage behind, Joe suddenly saw the truth. He finally understood.

"It's downtown!" he hissed, clutching at Ned, pulling him close. He pointed at the swatch of glowing yellow light radiating across the horizon. Toward the crackle of flames and the tumult of voices warring in the distance. They were real voices. They weren't imaginary at all.

"It's burning!" Joe cried. "The city, Ned. Downtown. It's on fire!"

JOE TUGGED Ned down the street, down the hill, in the opposite direction from where they were supposed to go. Away from the zoo. Away from where Joe said they'd be safe.

Ned stumbled, trying to keep up. "Where are we going? What about work, Joe? What about the animals?"

A figure loomed out of the mist in front of them. A man—no, *two* men. They didn't appear to be armed or even particularly threatening, but clearly Joe wasn't taking any chances. With a shush to keep him silent,

Joe steered Ned off the street, and they ducked among the bushes next to a chain-link fence that separated the park from an eroded, trash-filled gully where homeless people lived and where God knows what went on at night. Joe tugged Ned along between the bushes and the fence. He didn't slow his pace. He was still heading downtown, not more than a mile away. Toward the weird glowing light and the smoke. And whatever the hell was happening among the screams and the sirens and all the racket.

As they drew nearer, the cries of terrified people grew louder too. Joe tugged Ned harder, trying to increase their speed.

But Ned wasn't having it. He suddenly dug in his heels and stabbed his fingers through the wire fence, grabbing on, pulling Joe up short, refusing to go another step. He tugged at Joe's coat, forcing him to turn around and look at him.

"This isn't safe. Why are we doing this?"

The air was freezing, but a sheen of sweat peppered Joe's forehead. His eyes looked a little crazy. Somehow Ned couldn't find a connection between the man who'd made love to him only hours before and the man he was staring at now.

Joe hissed his reply. "I need to know what's happening."

Ned gave him a shake. "No, you don't. Whatever it is, there's nothing you can do about it. We have to go where we'll be safe. We have to get behind the walls of the zoo. That's what you promised me we'd do. We can hide there, you said. We can help with the animals. We can—"

"Ned…."

"Please! I can't lose you! I can't let anything happen to you. It would kill me, Joe. Don't you understand that? Whatever is happening downtown is bound to be dangerous. Why the hell are you dragging us into the middle of it?"

Finally, the fire in Joe's eyes softened. He glanced back over his shoulder at where the sirens and the flames and the screams could still be heard. But he turned back to Ned just as quickly, and Ned could feel his gaze burning into him. Joe's eyes were no longer hot and furious like the heat seeping through the haze from the fires but once again warm and caring and kind.

"You said you'd protect me," Ned softly said. "Remember?"

Joe nodded. "I remember."

Suddenly, from down the hill, came a loud explosion. The glow of light that couldn't quite pierce the red haze brightened in a furious flash. Frantic voices cried out all the louder. Panicked. Terrified. Ned thought they sounded like firefighters battling a blaze, but he couldn't be sure. Maybe it was just horrified onlookers. Whatever and whoever it was, Ned knew he didn't want to be a part of it, and he didn't want Joe to be a part of it either. Life was dangerous enough right now. What was the point of throwing themselves into the middle of even more danger? The smoke was so thick now, he could barely breathe anyway. What would it be like if they got closer to the inferno?

"Come on," he pleaded, tugging again at Joe's coat. "We have to get out of the open. We have to get farther away from the fire, not closer to it. We have to get behind the zoo walls where you said we'd be safe. If you love me, *please!*"

Joe stepped closer and pulled Ned into his arms. "Yes," he said, his lips in Ned's hair. "You're right. I'm sorry. I just got a little... nuts."

Ned tried to smile. "The world is nuts enough. You don't have to join in."

Even as they cowered by the rusted fence, the encroaching darkness deepened yet again. Ned didn't know if it was the smoke or whatever was happening in the heavens that caused it, but he could see on Joe's face that he was aware of it too. In a matter of minutes, their visual range had deteriorated even more. Ned could hardly see five feet in front of him now. And the only good part of that was that no one could easily see them either.

It was time they moved. Time they left the street and headed into the park. Down the trails. Over the zoo's back fence and into the compound where they'd be safe. Where Joe had promised they would go all along. Evening was coming on. On a normal day, this was the time Joe would be heading to work and Ned would be heading home, his own workday ended. Of course, this was anything but a normal day. Or a normal world.

"We should check on Mr. Wong," Ned said. "Before we strike off down the trail, we should veer past the deli and make sure he's okay. He should still be there. Maybe the police came. Maybe he's in need of his two witnesses about now."

"You're right," Joe said. "With the phones down, he can't reach us if he needs to. It's only a few minutes out of our way. Let's go."

Relieved, Ned mumbled, "Thank you," and moments later they were retracing their steps back up Sixth Avenue. They didn't run, but they kept up a good pace, as much to get Joe to work on time as to hopefully slip past any threats they might find waiting for them along the way. After spotting the two men earlier, Ned supposed Joe had learned his lesson. Ned followed obediently along as Joe steered them once again away from the streets and off the sidewalks, making sure they were well hidden among the bushes and trees along the outer edge of the park.

As they moved farther from downtown, the noise of the fire receded behind them. The knife-sharp wail of the distant sirens buzzed in Ned's ears like the whine of a pestering insect, but he was too worried about Mr. Wong to pay it much mind.

They picked up their speed. After a few minutes, Ned took stock of where they were and panted, "We're almost there."

"YES," JOE said. He blinked the haze from his eyes and pointed to a wisp of movement he had spotted between the trees up ahead. "And look who's coming to meet us."

It was Bobby Wong. He was creeping through the fog like a tiny ninja. Maybe because he was an innocent twelve-year-old and didn't know any better, or maybe it was sheer desperation, but he didn't look frightened. He simply looked determined, sneaking along, hunkered low to make himself as small a target as possible. If the circumstances hadn't been so bizarre, Joe might have thought he was playing cowboys and Indians. But the serious look on Bobby Wong's face soon told him the kid wasn't playing at all. He was deadly serious.

Bobby was moving at an angle toward the path Joe and Ned were taking, so Joe spotted Bobby before Bobby spotted them. When Joe gave a soft whistle to get the kid's attention, Bobby jumped about three feet straight up into the air. He whirled around, squinted into the haze to see who was making that sound, and a moment later, he ran up and threw himself into Ned's arms. Only then did Joe see that Bobby was crying.

Joe gently pulled the two apart. "What is it?" he asked. "What's wrong? And what are you doing out here all by yourself?"

Bobby wasn't wearing his white work apron or one of the silly paper hats Mr. Wong made everybody wear. He looked like he was dressed for school, but the schools were surely closed.

Bobby was shaking from either the cold or an overdose of adrenaline. When he finally calmed down enough to speak, he directed his words to Ned, not Joe, probably because Ned was still clutching his arms. Ned looked as scared as Bobby did, so Joe stepped closer to offer his support to both of them.

"What are you doing out here all by yourself?" Ned demanded again. "This is no time to be playing in the park."

Bobby's back stiffened. "I wasn't playing! I've been looking for you!" He sounded offended, like they should have known better than to treat him like a kid after all he'd been through.

Joe laid a gentle hand to the back of Bobby's neck and gave it a gentle squeeze. "It's okay, Bobby. We're sorry. We're just surprised to see you out here all by yourself. So now you've found us. What's wrong?"

"It's Pop!" Bobby sniffled, appeased. Still, he had enough sense to keep his voice low. Apparently he knew full well what a precarious position they were in, out here in the park in the open, unprotected. He explained everything while his eyes continually ricocheted from Ned to Joe, then back again. "Looters are breaking into all the stores around the deli. Pop was hoping you could come and help us protect it."

"We were on our way there," Ned said. "Are your mom and the rest of the kids okay?"

"They're home, but they're okay," Bobby said, wrapping his arms across his chest to fend off the cold. He was practically dancing around, hopping from one foot to the other, trying to keep warm. His hurried breath puffed out little clouds of steam that disappeared as quickly as they formed. His dark eyes were big and hyperalert, snapping like firecrackers in every direction at once. "Mom's the one who sent me to the deli to make dad come home. But he can't leave the shop. The crowd will tear it apart if he does. Maybe they will anyway, if Pop doesn't get somebody to help him. You guys got a gun?"

"No, sorry," Joe said, regretting yet again that they had thrown the shotgun away.

"Well, come anyway. Please. The street's overrun. We'll have to go around back through the alley. Pop has barricaded the shop windows with everything he could push against them." Suddenly Bobby's eyes got even bigger. "Did you know there's a dead guy in the freezer? Pop killed him! He's frozen solid, like a big Popsicle. If I'd known Pop had it in him to do something like that, I wouldn't have bugged him so much over the years."

At long last, Bobby's face melted into a grin. Ned laughed too while Joe gazed on, wondering if they were both crazy. If there was anything funny in the situation, he was having a hard time figuring out what it was.

"Let's go, then," Joe hissed, staring out into the mist again, trying to gauge its dangers, trying to plan which path would be best to take. After a moment of consideration, he headed straight across the open lawns, counting on the haze to keep them hidden. It was the quickest way to get where they were going. The three of them crouched low and moved fast, as Bobby had done earlier.

Before they had gone a hundred feet, Joe began to hear sounds of mayhem coming from up ahead. It sounded like a mob, all right. He didn't doubt for a second they should try to help Mr. Wong, but he had to wonder what they were getting themselves into. Still, Mr. Wong had always been good to Ned. Anyone good to Ned deserved all the protection Joe could give.

They peered through the last rim of trees out onto the street where Mr. Wong's deli was located. They couldn't see far. Not even to the other side of the avenue. But they could see part of the mob, milling around in the middle of the street, chucking rocks, a few of them fighting each other for stuff they had already stolen. Debris was scattered everywhere, and not a few inert bodies lay sprinkled around too. Again, no cars moved past. So many people acting like maniacs impeded the passage of traffic. Besides, headlights couldn't pierce the haze any better than living eyes. Trying to drive through this red gunk would have been asking for trouble.

Without thinking about it, Joe grabbed both Bobby and Ned and shoved them straight out into the crowd, bringing up the rear to keep an eye on them and protect them. Single file, they tore through the mob as quickly as they could, and the looters seemed not to notice them at all. With almost a sob of relief, Joe shepherded them behind a row of dumpsters at the end of the block and into the alley that opened on the back of the businesses along the street, including Mr. Wong's deli. The last time Joe had been in this alley was when he and Ned had sat out here on trash cans, swinging their legs, scarfing down one of Mr. Wong's sandwiches. The day the first cold snap had barreled through the city. And the first time Joe had almost declared his true feeling for Ned.

Funny. It seemed like ages ago but couldn't have been more than a couple of days.

Bobby snagged Joe's coattail. "Wait!" he hissed. "There's somebody there! Just ahead. Look. In the shadows next to the building. See?" Bobby gasped. "It looks like Pop!"

Joe and Ned both leaned forward, squinting into the haze to try to see what Bobby was pointing at. When Bobby started to run toward the figure, Ned grabbed him and pulled him back. Bobby fought for a moment, then gave up, surrendering himself to Ned's grasp.

Seeing that Ned had Bobby under control, Joe touched Ned's shoulder to show his approval, then took a step forward. Then another. He could see the figure now. It was a man but not, thank God, Mr. Wong. The stranger was sitting upright behind the dumpster, his back to the brick wall, his legs sticking straight out in front of him. His mouth was open like he was sleeping. There was a slash of color across his throat, like a red scarf.

As he took a step nearer, the haze thinned enough for Joe to see everything. The man wasn't sleeping; he was dead. And that wasn't a scarf across around his neck, it was blood. His throat had been cut. Maybe another looter had killed him for what he'd stolen. Or maybe he'd just run afoul of one of the crazies populating the city now. Like the homeless guy who'd attacked Mr. Wong. Or like the fucker with the shotgun who had tried to kill him and Ned only—when was it—yesterday?

The days were beginning to blend together. Like they do in war, Joe thought. Like they do when soldiers stumble from one battle to the next with no real end in sight. Like they do when death is facing them at every turn and normality has receded to a distant memory.

Joe shook these thoughts from his head. He returned to Bobby and Ned and pulled them both into his arms. He leaned his head in and whispered to Bobby, trying to comfort the boy. "It's not your dad, son.

It's just a stranger. But he's dead, and he's not pretty. So don't look at him, okay? Both of you, just keep your eyes on me. The back door of the deli isn't far. When we get inside, we'll be safe."

Joe forced a smile and tousled the boy's hair. Bobby was standing with Ned's arms around him, both to comfort and to control. Clearly Ned didn't want the boy running off and getting into trouble. Joe switched his gaze to Ned and gave him a wink.

"Let's go now," he said. "You guys ready?"

Solemn-faced, both Bobby and Ned nodded.

Joe turned to lead them the rest of the way down the alley to the deli's back door. They moved carefully through the fog. In a normal world, it would have been the brink of sunset. Dusk.

They crept forward as quietly as they could. The deli was in the middle of the block, a few doors down the alley. Towering above their heads were the rear balconies of twelve stories of luxury condos. Mr. Wong's deli was tucked into the ground floor of the high-rise, sandwiched between a bookstore and a travel agency.

"There," Bobby cried. "There it is!"

The three of them rushed forward, quickly covering the last few feet to the deli's back door.

Joe tried the knob, but of course it was locked. He tapped lightly at the metal security door, hopefully loud enough to be heard from inside but not loud enough to draw anyone else's attention.

He heard footsteps, and a familiar voice whispered around the edge of the door, "Bobby? That you?"

Joe started to answer, but at that moment the alley was plunged into utter darkness. It was like in a theater, when the curtain goes up and the house lights dim. In an instant, the ambient light of the red haze was erased from the landscape, leaving nothing behind but endless black. *In a normal world, darkness approaches quietly on catlike feet*, Joe thought. *In this world, it crashes down like an avalanche of blinding rock.* And it had happened in the space of a heartbeat.

It was as if God had at long last pulled the plug. The world was suddenly plunged into total, relentless night. Both Bobby and Ned plucked at the back of Joe's shirt, drawing close, anchoring themselves to him, cowering away from the darkness.

With the loss of light came the immediate absence of sound. The city lay hushed around them. Even the looters in the street were stunned to silence.

Joe reached around and pulled Ned and Bobby closer, cradling them in his arms. The darkness was so intense, he was blinded. Lost. The silence that lay on the air was almost as unnerving. The world and everything in it seemed to have been hurled into a shadowy, soundless pit.

"God help us now," Ned whispered from the lightless depths.

Just then, the door they stood in front of flew open, scaring them to death. Before they could even cry out, a tiny Asian man with a paper hat perched jauntily on his head yanked them inside.

CHAPTER FOUR

A NEW flurry of sunspots erupted. Immense in size and fury, they dwarfed the eruptions that came before. Boiling across the surface of the sun, they spewed more waste matter into the solar system.

As Rio and all of South America floundered in shadow, these planet-sized blisters of exploding energy created more darkness, further draining already weakened electrical grids. Lights across the Midwest blinked out. Limitless night descended on Canada from Manitoba to British Columbia on the Pacific Rim. The power grids in Europe, Asia, and Africa sputtered to a stop. All US cities, both small and large, fell to darkness only hours later.

San Diego was the last to go. Temperatures plummeted. Silence and shadow descended on the California city at what should have been the hour of nightfall on June 27.

As in mankind's ancient past, people were left with only fire for light and heat.

Civilization—and civility—immediately crumbled. The world was brought to its knees. In the aftermath of total defeat, the brightest minds on the planet sought skyward for answers, and to their joy they found a red moon, flushed to life once again by the latest cataclysmic explosion of sunspots, glaring back. A pale, shimmering field of pink stars returned to fill the darkened firmament from one horizon to the other. Hearts soared, seeing them there again.

But it was a short respite. In moments, utter darkness descended once more as both the moon and stars disappeared completely.

On a blinded Earth, the silence they left behind was deafening.

A PALE light flickered inside the deli. The burners on the gas stove, Ned noted, were lit for illumination and what little heat they might offer. It would have been pitch-black and freezing cold without them.

Joe and Ned moved to the window to peer out at the city street and at the wide empty sky arching overhead, now devoid of light entirely. It was as if a gazillion miles away, the sun had finally died, its spark of light at long last flickering out. A chill tore through Ned. He wondered if this new development was permanent. And if it was, what it could mean. For the world. For all of them. Without the sun, would they simply freeze to death? Had the planet suddenly become a frigid, lightless tomb? Was this how it all would end? With a billion voices whimpering in frozen shadow?

"It's gone," Joe muttered beside him. A hand snaked out and rested on Ned's shoulder. Ned detected a tremor in the hand. Joe's voice was taut with worry. "I wonder what will happen now."

"I can't believe it," Ned said. "I *won't* believe it. The light will come back. I know it will."

Softly, sadly, Joe said, "I hope you're right."

Ned turned as Mr. Wong grabbed his son and pulled him into a fierce embrace. Tears stood in Mr. Wong's eyes, sparkling in the flickering orange light cast by the flames on the stove. Stepping back, he pushed Bobby to arm's length and his eyes traveled over him from head to toe, as if reassuring himself that his son was truly safe and in one piece. Then he gave Bobby a teeth-rattling shake before pressing his hands to the boy's cheeks and squeezing them so hard Bobby's eyeballs pooched out.

With those bulging eyes, Bobby cast furtive glances at Ned and Joe, clearly embarrassed by his father's attentions.

"You're gonna pop my head like a pimple," Bobby groused, barely able to move his lips and wiggling like a worm on a hook, trying to free himself from his father's clutches. "Stop it!"

"You're back," Mr. Wong cried, ignoring Bobby's complaints. If anything, he squeezed Bobby's cheeks even harder. "I not see you leave. I turn around, you gone!"

Bobby's lips were so puckered by his father's viselike grip, he could barely talk. "Adverbs, Pop. Conjunctions. And I went to find Ned. We needed help."

Mr. Wong tore his gaze from Bobby's face and let them fall on Ned and Joe. White teeth shone through a radiant smile even while tears dribbled off his chin. "And you bring them both. Number one son did good."

Bobby finally went limp in his father's grip, hanging by his head in humiliation. "Oh God, Pop. Knock off the Charlie Chan shit."

Mr. Wong winked at Ned. "Bobby big man now. Cuss like sailor."

Turning back to Bobby, he grabbed the boy's shoulders and gave him another shake, this one less gentle and considerably less fawning. In fact, it rattled the kid's teeth like castanets. "Number one son end up with sore butt if he say 'shit' again."

Bobby blanched. "Sorry."

Apparently appeased, Mr. Wong gave Bobby a final pat on the head and let him go. Bobby rubbed his cheeks and quickly stepped out of reach, as if afraid his father might snatch him up again.

Suddenly all business, Mr. Wong shivered against the cold and crooked his finger, beckoning all three of them to follow.

"Come in. Come in. There's heat." Mr. Wong glanced back at Joe, his eyes sad. "Something burning downtown. Did you know?"

Ned and Joe answered in unison. "We knew."

They moved as a group. Watching Ned stay close to Joe, Mr. Wong perked up a little. He even gave Ned a secretive smile.

"You boys different now. Not just friends, I think. Lovers, maybe."

Bobby giggled, and Mr. Wong chucked a loaf of bread at him to shut him up. He offered Ned and Joe an apologetic glance. "My son not understand. I do. We leave it at that."

Ned flushed, but Joe said, "Thank you, sir. And you're right. We're not just friends anymore. I don't think we ever really were."

Mr. Wong shot him a wink. "I not think so either. But sometimes person in love the last to know." He turned a fond gaze to Ned. His eyes softened. "You look happy," he said gently.

Ned's face burned all the more. "I am, sir."

To that, Mr. Wong said, "Good," and turning away, he stared across the deli at the front window, his shoulders slumped, his posture suddenly weary. "Sound like looters left. Maybe the dark scare them off."

"I sure hope so," Bobby said. He sounded like he meant it. But even while he obviously still worried about the dangers outside, his gaze kept slipping to the freezer door, causing his father to roll his eyes.

"Yes!" Mr. Wong snapped. "Dead body still there. And no, you can't look at it."

Bobby offered up a slightly guilty smirk. "Did I ask?"

"Number one son not as smart as number one son think he is."

"Jeez, Pop. Give that Charlie Chan *shi*—I mean, *stuff*—a rest! It's genetically and racially humiliating."

Mr. Wong giggled.

Ned watched this latest exchange with bewildered amusement, wondering how these two could be bantering at a time like this. "So what are we going to do?" he asked impatiently. His own gaze kept slipping back to the storefront windows, afraid he'd see a face there, peering in, searching for them. The face of a man maybe, a *crazy* man with a club or a gun in hand. Or a fucking bazooka. He suddenly realized that even with Joe at his side, he didn't feel safe barricaded inside the deli. What he really felt was trapped.

Still, Ned saw nothing to really frighten him as he stared at the empty window. What had been dusk outside only minutes earlier was now a soul-killing, fathomless black. Only far in the distance where fires in the center of the city still burned did a shimmer of light gleam across the horizon. Poor downtown. Ned knew those streets and buildings like he knew the back of his hand. He wondered if when this was all over, there would be anything left of the city he knew at all. That was assuming this mess would ever *be* over. At the moment, it looked doubtful.

Joe moved up behind him, and Ned sensed him gazing over his shoulder. He was staring through the window too. Ned directed his words to Joe's ears alone, already relishing Joe's nearness, Joe's heat. Thankful for his presence. "Night fell early," he said softly.

Joe pressed his chest to Ned's back, closing the gap between them even more. "I'm not sure it's really night. It might actually be…."

"No!" Ned pleaded. "Please. Don't say it. It's not the end. I know it isn't."

Gently, Joe relented. "All right. I won't say it."

Ned shook himself, seeking something a little less soul-crushing to think about. Anything to take his mind off the avalanche of inky darkness that had suddenly crashed down upon them. "Do you think we're safe here?"

"No," Joe said. "The light's completely gone. Until the morning comes, I'm not sure we're safe anywhere. That's assuming the morning comes at all."

A chill shot through Ned to hear such words from Joe, but he wasn't surprised Joe had said them. Like Joe, Ned was pretty sure the danger had intensified too. With this sudden loss of light, even Mr. Wong seemed to think it had. But still, it couldn't be as bad as Joe was implying. He wouldn't believe it. Not yet.

Ned leaned back into Joe, who was holding his hands out to either side of Ned, waving them near the gas flames on the stove, trying to get them warm.

"What do you think?" Ned quietly asked. "What should we do?"

"I'm thinking," Joe said, slipping sideways to stand beside Ned so they could both absorb a little of the heat. "I can't believe the police still haven't come about the dead guy in the freezer."

"Me either," Ned said. "I guess they really do have bigger fish to fry." The heat felt good. Having Joe near felt even better. Not knowing what was going to happen next felt terrible. Ned's throat was dry, and his stomach was a tight ball of misery. He had never known such fear. The total loss of light in the evening sky had rattled him severely.

A sputter of gunfire erupted outside. It sounded close, but not too close. Ned instinctively ducked, waiting for the deli's front window to explode in a spray of glass. When it didn't, he allowed himself a sigh of relief.

"Idiots still being idiots," Mr. Wong carped. He and Bobby were sitting side by side on the floor in the corner, hugging their knees. They too were staring at the front window as if uneasy with the fact that little more than a quarter inch of plate glass separated them from the crazy people on the street. A siren wailed in the distance, but it was moving farther away, not closer. It didn't sound like a police car anyway. It sounded like a fire truck. Again Ned worried about downtown, wondering if the people had escaped the buildings that were burning.

Joe took Ned's hand and pulled him gently toward the opposite corner of the kitchen—in the back, far away from the flickering rings of flame on the stove—where the shadows lay deepest. He tugged him down to the floor so they could sit together with their backs to the wall. Joe wrapped his arm around Ned, and like Mr. Wong and his son, they tucked their knees up under their chins and settled in close to each other. Ned had never felt so loved and protected in his life. It was colder in this dark corner, farther away from the heat and light of the stove, but Ned didn't mind. He was with Joe. That was all that mattered.

While Mr. Wong and Bobby talked softly in their own little well of shadow across the room, Joe leaned in, pulled Ned's hand to his lips, and whispered for Ned alone to hear.

"Are you okay?" he asked. His voice was soft. His warm lips were even softer, moving like folds of satin over Ned's knuckles.

Ned had to smile. "Oddly enough, even scared to death, I've never been better."

Joe's lips twisted into an answering smile. Ned could feel it on his hand.

Another explosion of gunfire echoed down the street. Once again, a scream rang out, then silence.

Ned let his head drop to Joe's shoulder. He spoke as quietly as he could so he wouldn't be overheard by Bobby or Mr. Wong. "Can I talk about us for a minute?" Ned asked. In his imagination he saw his breathless words sliding through the darkness to Joe's ears, like birds, winging home.

Joe hadn't shaved before they left the apartment, and now, as Joe used the back of Ned's hand to stroke his own cheek, Ned shivered with sexual energy at the bristly, masculine feel of it.

"My favorite topic. Us," Joe cooed, snuggling closer, exciting Ned even more.

Ned let the shadows and the cold settle around them while he tried to forget about the rising bulge in his pants. He cast about for the words he wanted to say. Then, unplanned, the words simply spilled out in a fevered rush. "I always thought the world hated me, Joe. I mean, the world the way it used to be. I even understood the hatred, because I hated myself too. Ashamed of who I was, *what* I was. Disgusted being me, being queer. I realize now it was the people who put this scar on my head, and other people like them, who made me feel that way." In the dark, the fingers of his free hand navigated toward the welt of scar tissue under his hair. He stroked it idly, absentmindedly, like a child twiddling the corner of a favorite pillow. "Because of you, Joe, I'm not ashamed anymore. I don't care what people think. Being gay is a blessing now. It's a blessing that brought me to you. And you to me."

Joe pressed a kiss to Ned's brow. "It's a blessing for both of us. I wasn't ashamed of who I was, but I think I used my gayness like a shield. To push people away. To seclude myself. I think maybe if you hadn't come along, I could have spent the rest of my life alone and not even minded much, not even regretting I had no one in my life."

"And now?" Ned quietly asked.

Again, Joe's smile brushed warm across the back of Ned's hand. Joe's breath bristled the little blond hairs there, sending a jolt of happiness through him.

"And now," Joe said, "the very thought of being alone, being without you, scares me to death. I promise you I'll do everything I can not to let anything happen to you. I can't promise I can protect us if the world decides to blow up in our faces. But I do know if the world survives all this, then we'll survive with it. If there's even a semblance of the old planet left to live on, I fully intend to live on it with you. Trust me, Ned. I won't let anything but death or the end of the world tear us apart."

"I believe you," Ned whispered, the burn of tears in his eyes.

He twisted around to tuck his head under Joe's chin and nestled his cheek into the warm softness of Joe's jacket. He slid a hand under the hem of it, then burrowed under Joe's shirt too, so he could feel Joe's warm belly against the palm of his hand. The soft pelt of hair sprinkling Joe's stomach and chest tickled his fingertips. He ached for sex, but at the moment, simply touching was enough. And knowing he was loved was *more* than enough. It was everything.

"We're on the same side now, Joe. We're allies. A team. We're both fighting the same battle. The battle to stay together. I'm sorry about the city, about all the poor people out there. Not for those assholes on the street, maybe, but for everybody else. They're just like us. Fighting to hold on to what they love. I don't know what's happening with the planet, but I think if we all pull through this, we'll be better people for it. We'll have caught a glimpse of what it means to lose everything. That has to change us for the better, Joe. It's changed me already. I know it has."

Joe brushed Ned's forehead with his lips. "It's changed me too. Loving somebody does that, I guess. Even with all this crap going on, I feel blessed having you here in my arms. Feeling blessed is a new feeling for me."

Ned's heart felt like a balloon pumped full of too much air. "Joe...."

He burrowed deeper into Joe's embrace, his fingers sliding over the warm wales of Joe's rib cage now. Again, his body almost bucked with his need for Joe. To feel Joe's iron cock buried inside him, maybe, or taste Joe's juices spilling across his tongue while Joe's back arched beneath him in release. To know he had pleased Joe in some way. To know he had pleased Joe in the same way Joe could please him, with nothing more than a look, a touch, a caress. A really fantastic fuck.

Ned squeezed his eyes shut and curled himself into a fetal position with his head in Joe's lap. When Joe's arms folded around him, Ned felt protected from whatever might come. He breathed his answer into Joe's belly. "Love does change us," he whispered back. "It changes *everything.*"

Ned heard the squeak of a cooler door, then the rustle of cellophane and the rattle of knives. He realized suddenly that Mr. Wong, true to form, was stirring about making sandwiches. *When in doubt, eat.* That was the Wong philosophy. Ned knew this because he'd been working for the man for two years.

As if Mr. Wong could read Ned's thoughts, he started mumbling while he worked. "Have to keep up strength. And this pastrami too good to waste. Bobby, fetch pickles. The fat ones."

Joe snorted softly. "After all, what's Armageddon without a pastrami sandwich and a pickle?" To Mr. Wong, he said, "Ned and I have to go soon. We have to get to the zoo. We'll be safer there, and the animals need our help."

"No," Mr. Wong said. "You not taking my Neddie anywhere. Not yet. First you eat. Maybe when street calms down. Then you go."

Reluctantly, Ned said, "I guess we can wait for a while."

"Good!" Mr. Wong barked happily. "You like horseradish, yes?"

JOE PATTED his stomach. Mr. Wong had given him and Ned two sandwiches each. And chips, a pickle, a little tub of yogurt, and a Coke. He was stuffed. He glanced at his wristwatch. It was getting late. Almost eleven. It would be midnight soon. He was already hours late for work, and he knew he couldn't cower here much longer. He thought Ned seemed antsy to get moving too. It wasn't for fear of being fired that Joe worried about being late for work. He suspected there wouldn't be many zoo employees showing up tonight anyway. They had more important things to worry about than keeping their jobs. Survival for one. Protecting their loved ones for another.

Like he was protecting Ned.

He glanced at Ned now, sitting next to him in the shadows. He was concentrating hard, using a plastic spoon to dig out the last of his yogurt. Farther away, Bobby had finished eating and was now curled up in the corner, snoring softly. He had fallen asleep. Mr. Wong had thrown his coat over the boy to keep him warm. Joe watched now as Mr. Wong stared at his son for the longest time before finally turning to Ned and Joe. Moving closer, Mr. Wong slid his back down the wall next to Joe until he was sitting on the floor beside them.

"My heart hurt," Mr. Wong said quietly, his voice barely stirring the darkness. "Bobby right to worry about body in freezer. I worry too. I never murder anybody before."

"You had no choice," Joe said. "It was kill or be killed. That's not murder. It's self-defense." Ned leaned in, listening to what they said. He had sat up and was resting his head on Joe's shoulder again, peering across Joe's chest at Mr. Wong on the other side. Joe laid his hand over Ned's knee, still glad to have him close.

Mr. Wong heaved a leaden sigh. He was staring at his hands, flexing his fingers as if mesmerized by the way they moved. "I always good to that man. I feed him. I let him sleep in the alley. Not run him off. Gave him big box in the winter for a house. Life not easy for someone like that. I try to help. But still…."

"Still he tried to hurt you," Joe said.

"Yes. He try to hurt me. I don't understand."

While Bobby softly snored in the corner, the eyes of the other three drifted toward the door of the walk-in freezer, where the homeless man lay, getting colder and stiffer and deader by the minute.

To Joe's surprise, Mr. Wong turned back to him and said, "I have to go. Take Bobby. My family need protection too. You and Ned welcome to come with us. Or stay here if you want. There's food and a little heat. You might be okay."

"No," Joe said. "We have to go too. But how will you get to your family? Where are they? Where do you live?"

"Not far. Maybe fifteen, twenty blocks. We might take car. What you think?"

"It would be safer to walk," Joe suggested. "You might get trapped in a car. The street could be blocked. There are a lot of people out there with guns. Anything could happen."

Mr. Wong nodded. "I think you right. We walk. Slip through dark like Chinese cats. Little and sneaky."

Joe and Ned laughed. Mr. Wong didn't. He merely sat there in the shadows, staring across the kitchen at his sleeping son. "I wish you come too," Mr. Wong fervently added.

Ned responded before Joe could. "I'm sorry. Like Joe said, we have another route to take. You'll be safer without us anyway. Less noticeable." Joe watched as Ned offered Mr. Wong a lovely, gentle smile. A twinkle of mischief lit his eyes. "You'll be littler and sneakier on your own."

Mr. Wong only nodded, as if expecting the refusal. He reached over Joe and took Ned's hand. "You be careful."

"Don't worry," Joe said. "I won't let anything happen to him."

"No," Mr. Wong smiled. "I don't suppose you will."

Mr. Wong heaved a sigh, as if prodding himself to get started. "Best wake up number one son."

Before Joe could respond, a horrendous crash jarred the darkness. The blinds were ripped from the window on the street. Shards of glass tore across the deli, strafing the place like bullets. Struck with debris, the display case by the cash register exploded as well, shattered by the flying glass. The brick that caused all the damage tumbled to a stop at Joe's feet.

Wrenched from sleep, Bobby cried out and scuttled across the kitchen on his hands and knees, flinging himself into his father's arms. What was once a front window was now a black hole opening into the night. Icy air poured through the wound. Joe realized they were suddenly unprotected and unhidden, laid bare to all the chaos outside. He rushed across the room to quickly turn off the flames on the stove so they wouldn't be seen by anyone on the street.

"We have to go *now*!" Joe hissed. "All of us. It's not safe here anymore. Out the back. Hurry!"

Ned dove toward the workstation and grabbed a fistful of kitchen knives. He handed one to each of them—Joe, Bobby, Mr. Wong—and kept the last one for himself. "Weapons," he said, as if an explanation was necessary.

"I'd rather have a bazooka," Bobby groused.

To which Joe replied, "Wouldn't we all?"

Mr. Wong took a final look around his shop. He scooped the paper hat off his head and dropped it on the floor. "Don't suppose deli be here when we come back."

Ned laid a consoling hand on the little man's shoulder. "It might, Mr. Wong. It might."

Bobby stepped close and slid his arms around his father's waist. "If it's not, then we'll open a Chinese restaurant."

Mr. Wong gave a disgusted grunt. "Chinese restaurant more work."

Bobby reached up and gently bopped his dad on the chin with his little fist. "You live for work."

"No," Mr. Wong whispered in the darkness. "I live for my children. From number one son on down."

"And what about mom?" Bobby quietly asked.

"I live for her most of all." He tousled his son's hair. "If you're ready, we go to her now."

Bobby nodded bravely. "I'm ready."

They stepped away from each other, and Mr. Wong moved to unbolt the back door. They stepped into the pitch-black alley with Mr. Wong leading the way. When all four of them were outside, Mr. Wong firmly latched the door behind them and locked it with a key. "If anyone chasing us," he said, "that slow them down."

Clutching Ned by the collar of his jacket, afraid he would lose him in the darkness, Joe groped around in the shadows until he felt Mr. Wong's arm. He grabbed it and tugged him close.

He spilled a tense whisper into the darkness. "You're going west, I think. We're headed east. Be careful. Stay in the park as long as you can. Avoid the streets."

"Yes. You too."

"We will."

Mr. Wong bumped into Joe in the dark and, reaching around him, pulled Ned into a bone-crushing embrace. "You listen to Joe. He take care of you."

"Yes," Ned said. "And I'll take care of him. You and Bobby stay safe."

Mr. Wong gave a self-mocking snort. "I kill one man already. What's a few more?"

Bobby gave a dry laugh from somewhere in the shadows. "Sheesh, Pop. You sound like Jackie Chan doing his Rambo impersonation."

Totally unamused, Mr. Wong said, "Tonight, I think, being Rambo not a bad thing at all."

Joe fumbled in the shadows until he found Mr. Wong's hand. He squeezed it and pulled him into a hug. "Stay safe," he hissed in Mr. Wong's ear. "And thank you."

Before Mr. Wong could answer, Joe tugged Ned away, leading him down the alley. Hand in hand, they slipped into the darkness.

"THEY'LL BE all right," Joe whispered.

Ned swallowed his fear for Mr. Wong and the boy and said, "I hope."

Moving as silently as they could, they reached the end of the alley. The air was colder than Ned had ever known it to be in San Diego. And the night was darker. From where they stood, he couldn't see the glow of fires burning downtown. And without it, the darkness here wasn't really darkness at all but a solid black bubble that loomed over them, blinding them to everything that lay ahead or behind or above. Ned waved his hand in front of his face and saw nothing. If Joe hadn't been standing next to him, holding on to his sleeve, Ned would have felt adrift in a sea of ink, alone and lost and drowning.

"I'm glad you're here," he muttered. "I'm glad you're with me."

"Me too," Joe said. "Come on." With a little prodding, he coaxed Ned out of the alley and onto the sidewalk that led past the deli.

On this stretch of boulevard, the night was silent, but Ned knew they were anything but safe. That brick hadn't chucked itself through the deli window. There was somebody out here. Probably a lot of somebodies. Hiding. Lurking. Plotting. And Ned seriously doubted any of them had civic improvement on their minds.

Joe stopped abruptly and sucked in a breath. "Oh, no!"

"What?" Ned hissed, alarmed.

"I forgot the flashlight. I left it back at the deli." Joe chewed on his lip and then shrugged. "Well, we can't do anything about it now. Stay close to the buildings!"

Trying to move silently, Ned didn't answer, but he edged closer to Joe and took a fistful of his coattail to assure they wouldn't become separated. Joe still had hold of him too, but Ned wasn't taking any chances. He didn't release his grip on Joe's jacket for a second.

Up ahead, they heard the crash of glass. Another plate glass window had been shattered. It sounded like it too was coming from the deli. Muted curses followed the shattering glass along the darkened street. The crackle of countless footsteps scraped through shards of windowpanes. Hushed voices rose up, then just as quickly fell away. Ned knew that, even if he couldn't see them, the looters were climbing through the deli window, moving in to see what they could plunder, who they could harm. He and the others had gotten out in the nick of time.

"Mr. Wong was right, Joe. He won't have a business when he comes back."

"No," Joe whispered sadly. "He won't. Quickly now. There's nothing we can do. Let's get across the street."

It was almost impossible navigating through the Stygian darkness. Good thing they knew the area so well, or they wouldn't have been able to move at all. It didn't matter so much, now, that they had lost the flashlight. Using it would have been like luring moths to a flame, snagging the attention of every bad guy in a three-block radius.

There were no cars moving on the street, and now Ned understood why. All four lanes of the boulevard were effectively blocked, littered with refuse. Overturned trash cans. Mailboxes torn from the curbs. Uprooted bushes. Even bicycles and stuff pulled from looted parked cars had been flung everywhere. Ned tripped over something soft and bulky in the darkness, and it was only because Joe had hold of him that he kept his feet. It took him a few seconds to realize that the soft thing he had tripped over was a body. A human body. It was imminently still, that body. Imminently… dead.

"There are c-corpses out here," Ned stammered. "These people must be killing each other."

Joe didn't sound like he much cared. "All the more reason for us to get off the street." With another tug, he dragged Ned through the obstacle course of discarded junk and pulled him into the park on the other side of the street.

Here in the open, farther from the buildings, they were once again in a position to see the light in the sky where the fires downtown left a glow on the horizon. It didn't light the ground around them, but it was sufficient to set their course. They could at least see in which direction they needed to go.

They ducked under a stand of trees where the air was colder and the darkness inkier. By the smell of the trees and his own familiarity with the area, Ned knew they were pines. They took a moment to catch their breath and gaze back to where Mr. Wong's shop would be. They couldn't see it, but thanks to the glow of the distant inferno, they could see the outline of the twelve-story building that towered above the deli.

They had no more lifted their eyes to stare at the roofline far above their heads than a small flame surged to life near the summit of the building. A scream pierced the night as the flame quickly grew. Inside the blossoming ball of fire on one of the building's uppermost balconies, they saw the outline of a person, upright and writhing. Be it man or woman, they couldn't tell. But circling the burning man or woman was a handful of spectators. The spectators were laughing. One held a red gas can, another a torch. The twisted human outline inside the ball of fire screamed again. This scream was quickly stifled, as if by the inhalation of flames crisping the victim's lungs. The body, wreathed in fire and still writhing in agony, flung itself forward, trying to outrun its own agony. Teetering for a moment at the edge of the balcony, it slowly, oh so slowly, went silent and tilted out into the night. In a mute pinwheel of fire and light and thrashing limbs, the body somersaulted through the air for what seemed countless minutes before it struck the street with a bone-crushing thud directly in front of the deli. Still shrouded in flames, there at last the victim lay still, its torment over.

Far above, Ned heard cruel laughter. In the weakening illumination from the flames devouring the burning body lying sprawled against the curb, he could see the gaping black hole where the deli's window had once been. A sea of faces peered through the frame of shattered glass. They were staring at the dying ball of fire still sputtering on the street with the broken and twisted stick figure of a person, blessedly dead, inside. Some of the faces were smiling. Some of the faces were laughing. They looked inhuman there in the orange light of the feeble flames. Like demons or something. And for all Ned knew, maybe they were.

Suddenly overcome by the horror of what he had seen, Ned spun away and pressed his face into Joe's chest. He bit back bile, his mind racing with either fury or terror, or both. "They did that on purpose, Joe. Did you see? They set that person on fire—and *laughed*."

Joe turned away too, using his body to further block Ned's view of what had happened, of those pitiful remnants of flame still flickering on the sidewalk, of the ugly leering faces in the window. In a voice weak with emotion, he pleaded, "Don't think about it. Let's keep going. Please. Our only ally now is the darkness. We'll hide ourselves inside it while we take the trail through the park. Hopefully, we'll be alone there. No one will see us. We have to get to the zoo, Ned. We'll be safe there. I know we will."

Ned had to force himself to leave Joe's arms. Using his knuckles to wipe the tears from his face, he said calmly, stubbornly. "You lead. I'll be right behind you."

"Brave man," Joe said. "Let's go."

Once again, Ned clung to the tail of Joe's jacket as they slipped away into the night. Moving as quickly as he could to keep up with Joe, Ned desperately closed his ears to the sound of cruel laughter still ringing out from the building behind them. He ached to gaze back one last time at what lay crumpled on the street—the burning pile of refuse that was once a human being. But he didn't. He knew that one more glance would change nothing. The memory of that tumbling figure, wreathed in flames and falling through the air, would never leave. There could be no unseeing what he had just witnessed. No matter what he did, there could be no disremembering.

"Hurry," he pleaded to Joe's back, aching to get as far away as he could from the site of such horror. "Please hurry."

Obeying, Joe reached behind him and clutched Ned's hand, pulling him quickly into the forest and onto the familiar path that threaded a trail down through the trees.

Up ahead, for the first time in hours, they heard the yelp and cry of dogs. And farther away, the whooping bleat of a howler monkey, its razor-thin wail slicing through the night like a serrated knife.

Ned almost smiled. In spite of the dogs, the raucous cry of that monkey was like a flashback to happier times. Back when the most troublesome thing Ned had to worry about was how desperate he was to tell Joe he loved him. The good old days indeed.

The zoo, he thought, focusing his attention on the trail ahead and the feel of Joe's coattail clamped in his fist. *We have to get to the zoo.* The words kept repeating themselves inside his head like a mantra. Over and over again.

Joe whispered from the shadows. "Don't worry. I'll keep us safe."

Ned's heart gave a quiet thump inside his chest. "I'm not worried, Joe. I'm not."

Staying close, staying vigilant, they burrowed deeper and deeper through the tunnel of darkness beneath the trees. The shadows were deep and unrelenting, the air so cold it gnawed at Ned's cheeks and brittled his ears.

Despite his brave words to Joe, Ned was terrified. He could barely remember the crystal clearness of light and the sensation of sunlight on his skin. The only warmth he felt at all was his love for Joe. That fire was alive and hot inside him.

It was the flame that kept him going.

THE FERAL dogs kept barking in the distance, but none of them approached. Joe and Ned were moving more slowly now, planting their feet carefully, the darkness so deep it was like walking through soup. Ned had taken Joe's hand a while back, and Joe couldn't begin to express to himself how much comfort that gave him.

The trail was leading downhill now. Joe knew where they were by the tilt of the land and the feel of the colder air in the more shadowy places. The clean scent of pine lay heavy around them, the familiarity of it comforting. Especially after the stench of smoke and burning flesh back on the street.

"Joe?" Ned ventured beside him, his voice hushed. He was clearly trying to be quiet.

"Hmm?"

"Those people back there," Ned whispered. "Why were they acting like that? Why were they hurting each other?"

Joe had been wondering about that too. He had come to a few conclusions while he and Ned worked their way down the infernal trail. "I think it's only the ones who were evil to begin with. It's almost as if the darkness makes them brave enough to let themselves go, be who they really are."

"You mean cowards and bullies," Ned said.

"Yes. Cowards and bullies. Like you see on the internet. They figure they can't be seen, they can't be identified, so they act out their most vicious fantasies. Hurting people. Trying to prove to themselves they are really brave, when in reality they're just the opposite."

A gentle silence settled around them, and in the midst of it, the bleating cry of the howler monkey sounded off in the distance once again.

"I wonder who it was," Ned asked, his words almost sleepy, as if he wasn't really asking but just pondering aloud. Or maybe he was just worn out by the horror of it all.

"You wonder who *who* was?" Joe asked, edging closer to Ned to wrap an arm around his waist while they plodded down the trail, walking more carefully now because there were roots in the path to trip over, loose stones to twist an ankle on.

"The person they burned," Ned said, his voice fragile. Joe felt him shudder as if the memories he dredged up were frightening him all over again. "The person they… murdered."

"Probably even they didn't know. Maybe it was random. Senseless. Maybe they just killed for the sake of killing. I don't understand it either, Ned. Maybe no normal person could *ever* understand it."

Joe stopped and turned to face Ned. He pulled him into his arms and coaxed Ned's head down onto his chest. He spoke softly in Ned's ear even while listening for anything approaching from either direction on the trail. This was no time to let their guard down.

"Try not to dwell on it," he whispered, his lips brushing Ned's flaxen hair, the beautiful color of it lost in the darkness but yet alive in Joe's memory. "The person is no longer suffering. That's enough for us to know."

Ned's lips rustled on the front of Joe's jacket when Ned answered. "Do you think they'll ever be punished for what they did?"

Joe sighed. He had been thinking about that too. "Yes. I think they'll be punished. Either in this life or the next, they'll pay dearly for what they did."

"That's what I think too," Ned said. "Evil like that can't go *un*punished. Not if there's still good in the world."

Joe smiled at that, at the simple innocence in Ned's response. "There will always be good in the world, Ned. Hell, as long as you're in it, how could there not be?"

"You're making fun of me."

Joe's smile broadened. "No, actually, I'm not. I mean every word I say."

He gently pushed Ned to arm's length as if to study his face, but it was pointless. It was so dark he couldn't see anything, least of all Ned. "It's time to keep moving," he said, picturing the white puffs of their breaths mingling on the frigid air, though the sight itself was swallowed in the enveloping darkness. "Besides, I'm freezing. We need to get inside."

"Yes, please," Ned said amid a shiver signaled by the clatter of teeth.

Joe laid a hand across Ned's icy cheek as if to say, "Good, then, we understand each other," and a moment later they were once again headed down the trail. A shimmer of light appeared somewhere up ahead. Joe squeezed Ned's hand, and by some sort of sensory uplink, he was sure Ned had seen it too.

More quietly now, they moved farther along the trail. They walked carefully because the path was steep here. And that steepness was like a guidepost to Joe. He knew exactly where they were.

Up ahead, somewhere in the shadows, the tiny footbridge stretched over the freeway. Joe knew they would be safer on the bridge, away from the trees. So he tried to hurry.

Staying as close as possible, Ned matched him step for step. Something was about to happen. Joe could sense it.

More slowly now, leery of the steepness of the trail and wary of those blinking lights he could see up ahead, Joe led Ned carefully down the trail.

NED SAW it first. A caravan of automobiles. Cars, pickup trucks, vans, all packed with people like troop carriers, headlights beaming. They were moving in a convoy along the Cabrillo Freeway, slipping under the little bridge, heading toward downtown. Here and there along the caravan, people waved black banners, as if rallying the world to a cause.

Joe and Ned stood side by side, their noses pressed to the wire mesh encircling the footbridge, watching the lighted caravan pass below. The pickup trucks especially filled Ned with fear. In the truck beds, packed to bristling, stood dozens of men, women, and children, every one of them packing a weapon. Guns, machetes, knives. Ned saw one young man with a fistful of rocks in his hand. Another with an ax over his shoulder. Like a bloodthirsty army, fueled by anger and misplaced patriotism, they screamed obscenities into the night. Like madmen they shook their fists at nothing but the lights of the other vehicles around them. Their insane cries filled the air.

Who were they setting out to fight? Ned wondered. Where was their fury directed? Who, for fuck's sake, was the enemy here, and who did they think they were protecting? Or were they setting out to protect anyone at all?

"It's like they're declaring war," Joe said, clearly not understanding what was happening either. He edged closer to Ned so he could be heard over the roar of the engines and the screams of mounting fury below.

"Yes," Ned said. "But who are they declaring war *on*?" He could hear his own confusion. And he could sense his own fear in the way the goose bumps slithered up and down his arms. He had never seen this much anger, this much *crazy*, in his life. He was stunned.

"Look at all the guns," Joe muttered. "It's like this mob is aiming to take over the streets. As if there isn't enough looting and killing going on already. And where are the cops? Do you think they know what's going on?"

"God, I hope so," Ned breathed. He pictured the throng of looters swarming through the deli's front window after smashing it open with rocks. Saw again the body, doused in flames, tumbling through the air, voiceless in its own agony, sailing to its death. He remembered the sound the body made when it hit the street. The whoosh of flames, the crack of bones, the sudden stillness. And he remembered, most of all, how relieved he had been knowing that person's suffering was over. "There's enough looting and killing already."

"More than enough," Joe said, his trembling hand clutching Ned's.

The long caravan passing below seemed endless. Stuck in here and there among the cars and trucks, Ned spotted bright yellow school buses. They too were packed with armed civilians. Gun barrels protruded through open windows like thickets of weeds. Faces, both old and young, both eager and murderous, peered out as well. Here too some of them looked little more than kids. And those, Ned thought, were the most frightening faces of all.

Ned's gaze kept falling on the black banners scattered around. Was that the emblem they had chosen to proclaim who they were? A strip of black fabric, as dark as the air around them? As featureless and empty as the shadows that had fallen over the planet?

"The flags…," he sputtered. "What do they mean?"

Joe shrugged. "Doesn't matter. We have to get to the zoo and lay low. If there's going to be a battle, I don't want us stuck in the middle of it."

Ned scanned the sky, seeking the comfort of a single star. A mere glimpse of moon. But there was nothing. The only illumination anywhere came from the train of headlights below. And the sparks of light glinting off thickets of polished gun barrels.

Ned focused his attention back on the caravan passing beneath their feet. "There are so many of them!"

"Too many," Joe answered. "I have a terrible feeling things just got worse."

"So do I." Joe turned to gaze at Ned in the flicker of lights below. His eyes appeared worried as they slipped away from the lights below and once again surveyed the darkness surrounding them. That darkness hadn't eased up one little bit. And with an army of crazies moving into the city, all the horrible things the world had seen already were now compounded.

"Joe?" Ned asked again. "Do you think it will be okay? I mean, before it's all over. The darkness. Everything. Do you think we'll survive it? I mean, people. The population. The world."

Joe tensed at his side. His only answer was brief, whispered softly. "I don't know, Ned. Come on. Let's go."

A moment later, they were huffing and puffing up the steep path on the opposite side of the canyon, and darkness reclaimed them. The trees had thinned out, but with the lights from the caravan left behind in their wake, the night was just as dark as it had been before. It didn't worry them, though. The shadows were a blessing now, not nearly as frightening as that mob of armed idiots back on the freeway. Happily, the zoo was just ahead, and the trail was straight. They were almost there.

As if to prove it, Ned heard the chuff and bellow of a big cat. A panther, maybe, or a lion. It sounded so close that a chill shot up his spine.

Joe seemed to understand. "Don't worry. Their voices carry. He's not as close as he sounds. And he's locked up."

"Thank God," Ned said on a shivering breath.

A moment later, Ned heard another sound. This time it was a throaty, stuttering growl, coming from the darkness to their left.

Joe stopped in his tracks, and Ned plowed into him. He instinctively wrapped his arm around Joe's waist as the two of them stood on the path listening. Both men were ramrod straight and rigid with surprise.

"That didn't come from far away at all," Joe whispered.

Another snarl came from their right.

Ned's words snagged the air like fishhooks. "Neither did that."

"More dogs!" Joe spat. "Stay close."

"If I was any closer," Ned hissed back, "I'd be climbing up your ass." Suddenly he missed the heavy cudgel he had used the last time he ran into feral dogs.

A scuttling sound arose in the underbrush at either side. Loose stones clattered down the hillside behind them. The dogs were blocking the trail at their backs, cutting off any retreat. By the sounds they were making, they were drawing closer too. Stalking. Preparing an attack.

"Where's the fence?" Ned pleaded through chattering teeth. He wasn't sure if they were rattling because of the cold or because of his fear. Probably a little of both.

Joe tensed at his side. "It's a ways. It's too dark to run for it, so we'll have to make a stand here. Still got your knife?"

Ned all but slapped himself in the forehead. The knife he'd taken from the deli! He'd forgotten all about it. He fumbled around at his back and pulled it out of his belt. It felt flimsy and light in his hand. While the darkness was so dense he couldn't see the blade, he knew it was no more than eight or nine inches long. For it to be any use, he would have to be nuts and eyeballs to the creature he was using it against, and that prospect didn't please him at all.

When a growl suddenly erupted directly at his feet, Ned instinctively kicked out and caught the beast smack in the head. A lucky shot. A very satisfying yelp of pain accompanied the kick, and Joe chuckled at his side.

The chuckle died quickly enough when Joe cried out, "Fuck!" Joe was no longer at Ned's side. He had been wrenched away amid a flurry of snarls that erupted around them from every direction. Ned groped in the darkness and discovered Joe a couple of feet away. Ned reached out for him and found him jerking and swaying, clearly in battle with *something*.

"It's got my leg!" Joe cried. "Get it off me!"

Ned didn't think twice. He dropped to his knees at Joe's side, flailing blindly at the darkness with the knife. Joe was hopping around, trying to keep his balance, while whatever had hold of him kept yanking at his leg, trying to tug him off his feet.

Ned's hand came in contact with a furry flank, and without thinking about it, he stabbed the blade into the creature's flesh. A horrific wail split the night as the beast retreated, almost jerking the knife from Ned's hand. Around them another chorus of growls erupted. Ned didn't know how many animals there were, but he did know he and Joe were outnumbered.

He pulled himself to his feet and clutched Joe to him. "Dark or not, we have to run for it. There's too many of them, and it's too dark to fight. Lead the way, Joe. I'll follow."

No sooner were the words uttered than sharp teeth clamped on to Ned's ankle in a viselike grip. One of his socks ripped loudly as a piercing pain tore through him. He kicked out, but the beast wouldn't let go. This time it was Joe who dropped to his knees at Ned's feet, and when the dog let out a mournful yip of terror, Ned knew Joe's knife had found its mark.

Ned had no time for thanks or congratulations. A second later, Joe was pulling him up the trail. The hillside rose steeply here, so they couldn't really run. All they could do was try to stay ahead of the pack of dogs snapping at their heels.

Ned snagged his toe on a great tree root that lay across the path. As he fell forward, as if in slow motion, he unwittingly dragged Joe to the ground with him. They hit the trail hard, but ignoring the pain, Ned quickly flipped onto his back and held the knife out in front of him. He could sense Joe doing the same beside him. The beasts moved carefully closer, signaling their movement only by the scrape of stones around them. They were wary of the knives now, but they were still hungry, or crazy, or whatever else had made them decide to attack in the first place.

"This ain't good," Joe gasped, scuttling closer to Ned, obviously still hoping to protect him even as the battle had turned in the dogs' favor.

"Get up!" Ned seethed, suddenly as furious as he had ever been in his life. "We've been through too much to be killed by a pack of stupid dogs. Goddammit, I won't have it!"

In spite of the situation they were in, Joe barked out a laugh. "Well, somebody's got his dander up!"

He allowed Ned to pull him to his feet. Instinctively, they turned to face the trail they had just climbed, blinded by the lack of light, relying on their ears and reflexes to protect themselves. Again, Ned heard the dogs closing in. They were panting now, their footpads scattering pebbles. Even now an occasional growl tore through the night, clearly aimed at them. Apparently the dogs were as pissed off as Ned. But they were leery too. They didn't like those knives at all.

Ned was about to give in to his fury and run screaming directly at them, waving his knife like a maniac, when the night sky screamed to life above them. Ned cowered in shock as a roar of sound enveloped them both, all but pushing them to the ground. The bushes at either side whipped and thrashed about in a sudden gale. The wind was so strong, so furious, that a cloud of dirt and grit as sharp as bee stings exploded up around Ned, tearing at his eyes and skin. Squinting through the dust, Ned was astonished to see long streaks of light stabbing down from the sky, crisscrossing the trail and piercing the trees. In their scattered beams, Ned spotted the attacking dogs hightailing it back down the path, a cowardly pack of six or seven of them, terrified by the racket and the light, their bravado gone, their will to kill supplanted by an uncontrollable urge to run from this mysterious new threat.

Ned was sort of feeling the same way. He didn't understand the noise and lights either.

He looked up as Joe edged in beside him. Together they scanned the sky above their heads, trying to figure out what this noisy, airborne monster was that was making such a racket and had saved their skins by scaring off the dogs.

"A helicopter!" Joe cried, his voice muffled because he had pulled the collar of his coat up over his nose and mouth to filter out the dirt whipping through the air.

Ned did the same, and shielding his eyes with his hand, he squinted skyward. Joe was right. It was a helicopter. It had SDPD painted on its side. The cops had finally shown up!

Before he could stop himself, Ned raised his fists in the air and jumped up and down.

"Give 'em hell!" he screamed. "Blow their asses to kingdom come!"

Joe laughed. "I presume you're talking about the bad guys."

"Hell yeah! And the dogs too! Fuck 'em all! Blow 'em to smithereens!"

Ned continued yelling, spinning toward Joe and raking him into his arms. Together, they hugged and laughed and watched the helicopter tilt to the side, then sail off across the sky. At last, when Ned had calmed down and they were both about finished choking to death from the swirling dust thrown up in the downdraft from the spinning rotors, they ducked away from the onslaught of noise and dirt and resumed their trek up the climbing trail.

Ned was still deliriously happy. "I *know* it will be all right now! I *know* it will!"

Joe held him close as they once more navigated their way through the darkness.

"I hope you're right, but until that happens, I still want to get inside the zoo," Joe said. "I won't be happy until you're out of harm's way. Where nothing can happen to you."

"Not me, us. Where nothing can happen to *us*."

Arm in arm, they climbed on. The trail was really steep here, and it was hard work. Blinded again by the darkness, they crashed into the zoo's back fence before they ever saw it coming.

Cursing softly, Joe fumbled around in the dark for the secret opening, a loose flap of chain-link fencing that only he and maybe a few homeless people knew about. The moment he found it, he and Ned ducked inside. Joe took a moment to secure the flap behind them. Ned supposed that was so the dogs couldn't follow them through.

They were on the zoo grounds now, and Ned figured they were safe. He breathed a sigh of relief. They stood still for a moment, listening to the single helicopter thumping away to silence in the distance. As soon as it was gone, the night moved in to take its place. Suddenly noise erupted everywhere. The chitter of crickets in the bushes. The gentle exhalation of Joe's breath stirring his hair.

And above it all, a cacophony of countless animals shrieking, roaring, snarling in their cages.

A chill shot up Ned's back. "What's going to happen now?" he asked in a worried hush.

Joe's arms tightened around him. "I don't know."

Ned stepped closer. "Whatever it is, I'm glad you're here with me."

Joe pressed a kiss to Ned's forehead. "I'll always be here with you."

Ned smiled and closed his eyes. "I know," he softly answered. "That's because you love me more than life itself."

Joe chuckled in the dark. "Now you're catching on."

JOE WOVE a careful path, leading Ned between rows of long tables filled with potted plants and huge tubs containing seedling trees, all lined up like sentinels on either side. The night air seemed colder here than it had in the park.

"This is the nursery," Joe explained. "Not the nursery for baby animals, but the nursery for the plants we use on the grounds. This is where I work."

Ned could smell the flowers and the heavy musk of rich loam, but he couldn't see a thing. The sweet scent of oleander clung to the frigid air. The moon was still hidden, and clearly the power was still out. Here, away from the fires in the city, the darkness was absolute, as dense and unrelenting as a brick wall. Not for the first time that night, Ned flapped a hand in front of his face and saw absolutely nothing. He sighed, hating the endless darkness more and more as time went by.

Nearby—*too* nearby—he could hear the shrieking wails and furious bellows of a dozen beasts, each cry different than the other. If he hadn't known he was within the walls of a zoo, and if he hadn't known those creatures were penned up behind impregnable moats and walls and bars and screens, the cries would have scared him to death.

"So we're going to feed the animals?"

Joe reached back, groping for Ned's hand. "We can't feed them all, but we'll do what we can. I'm worried, though. I don't hear anyone. We may be the only humans here."

"How can that be?"

"I don't know. Maybe everyone thought it best to stay home and protect their families."

"But we're still safer being here than in the city?"

Joe's squeezed his hand. "Yes, we're still safer being here."

Their fingers entwined, Ned followed Joe through the groundskeepers' compound. Apparently Joe had worked here long enough to have the layout memorized, which was a good thing. Ned would have been plowing into trees and tripping over pots and tables every time he turned around. As it was, he only knew what they were walking through, or around, or between, because he reached out continually to feel what was sliding past. The brittle frond of a baby palm. The velvet blossom of some flower or other. More than once he hissed in pain and drew back from a thorn.

Suddenly a macadam path unrolled beneath his feet. The sidewalk was still rising with the slope of the hillside, as it had in the park. Their footsteps echoed over a small wooden footbridge. The path continued to wind around here and there until it finally leveled off. Somewhere close at hand, Ned detected a gentle splashing. The scent of wet fur and chlorinated water wafted through the air. He heard a grunt in the darkness, and this time it didn't come from Joe. The air was colder than it had been before, and Ned tried to figure out what they were approaching.

"Polar bear tank," Joe whispered, as if he could sense the question in Ned's mind. "We'll go past this way," he added, steering Ned around the enclosure.

As the hill crested, the path widened into what, in the darkness, might be a one-lane road, maybe for tour buses to carry zoo visitors through the compound. There were no tourists present tonight, however. By the utter lack of a single human voice, Ned suspected there weren't any people around at all. Aside from the animals, he and Joe were on their own.

Gentle chomping sounds rose up on either side of them, and Ned edged closer to Joe.

There was amusement in Joe's voice. "We're next to the antelope compound. They're being friendly, hoping we're going to feed them."

"Are we?" Ned asked. "Going to feed them, I mean?"

"I hope so. As long as the hay barn isn't locked."

Ned reached out his hand in the dark, and sure enough, he touched a rubbery muzzle. A long, hot tongue slipped around his fingers, but no teeth came into play. The animal was saying hello, as friendly as a cow.

"What about the big cats?" Ned asked. "Will we feed them too?"

As if wondering the same thing, a lion in a far-off enclosure roared its dominance over its neighbors. In respect, all other animal sounds fell silent until the echo of the lion's cry receded. Clearly here, as on the plains of Africa, the lion was offered a begrudging respect. *Once a boss, always a boss*, Ned thought.

Joe sounded less than impressed. "That's Namba. He's always bitching about something."

"Will we feed him?" Ned asked again. "Him and the others?"

"No. We can only do so much. You have to know what you're doing to feed the big cats. Some of them have to be hustled into a side cage so the meat can be inserted. That involves keys we don't have. Others, like the lions, reside in a big pit. We could toss food down to them if we had the food, but we don't. The meat lockers are locked. We can't access them on our own. But don't worry. Big cats don't eat every day in the wild. They can go a long time without making a kill. They'll be all right for a while."

Ned heard the bang and rattle of a metal door squeaking open. He was engulfed in the heady aroma of fresh hay. A beam of light pierced the darkness, shooting this way and that. Joe had snagged a flashlight off a shelf inside the door.

"This is the hay barn. We'll make it our base of operations," Joe said, gazing around the large tin shed. "I know it's not the Ritz, but we can lock ourselves in. There's also running water in a service sink along the back wall and a porta potty in the corner."

Ned studied the electric-blue monstrosity Joe was illuminating in his flashlight beam. "Gross, but cool," he said.

With a kindly smirk, Joe said, "Thought you'd like that. We'll feed the camels first. They're at the back of this building." He pointed to a wall of baled hay stacked in front of them. Then he aimed the light at a hand-pulled wagon parked against the wall. "We'll load the bales on the wagon and cart them around. There's a little tractor, but I want to make as little noise as we can. No sense broadcasting our whereabouts." He cast an apologetic glance Ned's way. "I'm afraid I really did mean it when I said we'd be working."

"Well, good." Ned grinned. "I like work."

Spotting a pile of gloves, Ned grabbed two pairs. One for him and one for Joe. He tugged the empty wagon closer and immediately began loading it with wired bales.

"Gee," Ned said. "They're light."

"It's straw," Joe explained with a smile, resting the flashlight in a convenient place so they could see what they were doing. Working together, they packed the wagon in no time.

"Come on," Joe said. He snatched up a pair of cutters to clip the baling wire and tugged the filled wagon toward the open door. "I'll introduce you to the camels. Don't get too close. They spit."

"Lovely," Ned muttered under his breath.

The next thing he heard was Joe saying, "Hello, you ugly fuckers," and like pets, the camels came galumphing up to meet them, grumbling happily. They were hungry, yanking the straw out of Ned's hands before he could toss it over the fence.

And so they worked, proceeding from one enclosure to the next. The frigid night deepened. With only a flashlight to find their path, Ned followed Joe's directions to the letter. Interrupted by endless reloadings, they pulled the wagon along the roadway, first on one side, then on the other. By the time they were finished a couple of hours later, the camels, antelope, bison, and most of the other hoofed beasts had been fed. They returned the wagon to the barn, and Joe closed the door, sealing them inside.

In a nest of hay, they plopped themselves down to take a break, their backs propped up against the wall of bales with a scattering of loose straw beneath their butts. After a while, the straw helped keep them warm.

Before he knew it, Ned fell asleep. He opened his eyes hours later. He squirmed closer to Joe and rested his head on Joe's shoulder as he listened to the bay and howl of wolves somewhere close by—*caged* wolves, thank God. Their eerie cries were probably what woke him up. Beyond the wolves, out past the walls of the zoo, far off in the distance, Ned thought he heard the clatter of gunfire. His heartbeat quickened.

"It's started," Joe said. "The cops. They must be taking back the city from all those goons with guns."

"But what good will it do?" Ned asked. "If the darkness stays, what good will any of it do?"

To that Joe didn't seem to have an answer. He hesitated, then said, "I don't know."

"Do you think it's over now?" Ned asked. His voice was barely audible, but he couldn't help it. The thought of this unforgiving darkness lasting forever horrified him. "I mean, if the light doesn't return, if the sun doesn't shine anymore, how can the planet survive?"

Joe flicked on the flashlight and stabbed the beam around the barn as if checking to make sure they were still alone, which they were. He just as quickly switched it off to preserve the batteries.

"Ned, I don't know what's going to happen. If it is the end, we won't be facing it alone. Somehow, for me, that kind of takes the sting away."

Ned snorted back a wry laugh. "In other words, fuck the human race. We've got each other."

"And the camels," Joe smirked. "We've also got the uglyass camels." Snuggling close, they sat in their little nest of scattered straw and laughed at themselves, at the world, at the darkness. And yes, even at the camels. In the distance, the staccato clap of gunshots filled the night.

After a while, Joe checked his watch. "It's too dark to tell from in here, but the sun should be up by now."

"Do you think it is?" Ned asked. "Up, I mean? I hated it before, but now I'd give anything to see that red, hazy light again. At least you could navigate through it. You could see things."

Joe pulled himself to his feet. Ned followed him, wading through the scattered hay. He stood waiting while Joe slid the barn door open. Ned's heart sank. There was nothing to see past the sill of the door but a wall of implacable black, merciless and unyielding. It was as deep as the darkness that had fallen when they were standing in the alley behind Mr. Wong's deli. Staring into it was like being submerged in ink.

Ned heaved a leaden sigh.

"We should have known," Joe muttered sadly.

Ned moved up to press himself to Joe's back.

Quietly Joe asked, "Do you think we've seen the last sunrise we'll ever see?"

"No," Ned said, all but commanding the heavens to obey. "Don't even think that."

With a sigh, Joe said, "All right. If that's what you want." His tone brightened. "Are you ready to get back to work? The animals still need our help."

A great sadness rolled over Ned at the weariness in Joe's voice. He stood on tiptoe and slid his lips over the back of Joe's neck, mumbling gentle words onto his warm skin as they stared out at the lightless morning. "It'll be all right, Joe. I know it will."

"Will it?" Joe asked. He squirmed around in Ned's arms until they faced each other. Softly, he said, "You never give up hope, do you?"

"Well…." Ned hesitated. "Not yet."

"So what do you suggest we do, oh optimistic one?"

"I suggest we get back to work. We came here to help the animals. You said so yourself. Let's do some more of that, and then we'll see what we can do for ourselves."

"All right," Joe said, ducking his head to rest his cheek against Ned's.

With Joe so close, Ned closed his eyes, awash in his love for the man before him. They both needed a shave. Touching was like two porcupines having a smooch. But it was a turn-on too. Ned shuddered at the sensation of his cock lengthening in his pants. But they had no time for that now.

Straightening his shoulders, Ned pulled back a bit, tapped Joe's chin with a kiss, and said, "Let's do it, then. The animals are waiting."

"Greedy bastards," Joe growled, but with a smile in his voice. Hearing it, Ned smiled too.

Then Ned's smile widened as a sudden thought struck him. Here he was facing what might very well be the end of the world, and he was doing it with a boner.

Now what could possibly be wrong with that picture?

THROUGH ALL the long, dark day that followed, it took every bit of Joe's willpower to fight the despondency that bore down on him. The only thing giving him the strength to carry on was Ned's relentless determination that everything would somehow turn out okay. And here Joe had thought *he* was the strong one in the relationship.

He glanced skyward for the hundredth time, praying for just a single spot of sunlight to pierce the blackness, like the blade of a merry knife worming its way into the inky canopy to allow the entry of a single spear of light. But no merry knife appeared. No light shone down. And quite possibly it never would.

Joe quickly pushed that thought away. He would at least *try* to bask in Ned's optimism a little longer.

They had done a lot the night before, but today Joe knew they probably couldn't accomplish as much as he'd hoped they would. There were simply too many limitations, too many locked larders. Too many beasts to feed.

He supposed he understood why the other workers had failed to show up to care for the animals. They had their own lives to worry about. Still it broke his heart. The animals they couldn't tend to tonight would be okay for another day or so, but what would happen then? Would they lie in their cages, slowly starving to death? He couldn't call his bosses because the phones didn't work. He couldn't access the larders where they kept the food each individual species required because he didn't have the keys. Many of the larger and more dangerous beasts—and consequently some of the rarest and most beautiful—he didn't have the skill to feed anyway.

Joe was exhausted. He and Ned had not rested nearly long enough. But still, there was work to be done. They might as well do as much as they could.

He led Ned down the macadam path toward the patio area where dozens of umbrellaed tables were scattered about. At the edge of the area, Joe used the beam of his flashlight to find the popcorn cart that was always parked there. Without thinking too much about it, he picked up a large stone from the ground and crashed it through the window at the front of the cart. Carefully reaching in, he grabbed a fistful of candy bars and handed them to Ned.

Ned accepted them gladly. "Ooh. Breakfast!"

Joe snatched up a few more bars for himself, unwrapped and bit into a Snickers bar with relish, and then stuffed the rest of them into his pockets for later.

Ned spoke around a mouthful of chocolate. "That's vandalism. You'll get in trouble for that." He didn't sound any more concerned about it than Joe did when he answered.

"Hey, we're saving their very expensive animals from starving to death. Surely they'll cut us some slack for that."

"Well, we can hope."

Chomping happily, Joe led Ned on through the compound.

At the back of a gift shop, inside a small fenced area that wasn't locked because there was really nothing valuable inside, they scooped up armloads of eucalyptus branches, previously cut by the animal handlers.

"What are these for?" Ned asked, his arms full.

"You'll see."

When they had gathered up all they could carry, Joe led Ned up a winding wooden walkway with the flashlight tucked under his chin so they could see where they were going. They caught the glimmer of golden eyes in the darkness at either side. Sweet fuzzy faces turned toward the approaching light.

"Oh!" Ned cried. "Koalas!"

"Yes," Joe said. "This is all they eat. Eucalyptus leaves." Without any further explanation, he dumped his load of eucalyptus branches over the side of the walkway into the enclosure. Ned did the same. They stood side by side for a minute, watching by the light of the flashlight as the koalas slowly meandered their way toward dinner, as unconcerned as if the world ended every day of the week, thank you very much.

A moment later, Joe tugged at Ned's sleeve. "Come on. Let's see what else we can do."

They scattered pellets through the feeding pond in the flamingo pen by the zoo's front gates. Stumbling around in the dark until they found the door to another shed, they finally hefted a few bales of hay—not straw this time, so they were considerably heavier—and manhandled them over the iron fence into the elephant pen after cutting the baling wire away. The elephants accepted their dinner with far more enthusiasm than the koalas, trumpeting and swaying their great bodies back and forth in pleasure. The bales had barely hit the ground when they were reaching down with their agile trunks and stuffing their faces with hay. While they fed, Joe switched a spigot at the side of the barn and filled their drinking trough. When that was done, they moved on.

Astonished to find how many things they *could* do to help the animals, Joe and Ned passed the long day joking, laughing, and barely minding the darkness at all.

Almost sick with all the candy he had eaten, Joe at long last checked his wristwatch to see that the day was almost over. They needed rest again. They needed sleep.

They wended their way back to the barn where they had slept the night before, and collapsing on the straw, they wormed their way into each other's arms. Joe smiled to himself when Ned immediately fell sound asleep. His flaxen head rested on Joe's chest while Joe cradled Ned's hand in his, slowly, gently stroking the blond hairs on the back of it, relishing the feel of his new lover's skin.

Lover. He still couldn't believe it had happened. He still couldn't believe he had committed himself to Ned, and how lucky and proud it made him feel.

And with his usual impeccable timing, he did it just as the world decided to breathe its last gasp before flickering out like a fucking candle!

Even so, there were bigger things to worry about now, incredibly enough.

Society was at war with itself. Somehow the darkness had robbed people of their common sense. Or worse, had dragged them back to the Stone Age. Slowly, over the last twenty-four hours, Joe had come to the inescapable conclusion that if he and Ned were to survive the battles raging out there, they would have to leave the city. But where should they go? And how would they get there?

He had sworn he would keep Ned safe, and he meant to keep that promise. But was it even possible?

Still trying to decide what they should do about their own survival, Joe slipped into an uneasy sleep. When he opened his eyes again, he immediately glanced at his watch and saw it was after two in the morning. They had slept for hours.

Gently, he nudged Ned awake. Leaning close, he touched his lips to Ned's ear and whispered, "Are you ready to go back to work? I want to finish before dawn."

"If it's like yesterday, there won't be any dawn."

"You never know." When he spoke the words, even Joe knew he was being overly optimistic. Still, it pleased him to think a dawn *might* break apart this suffocating darkness. And how the hell could a little optimism hurt?

Ned seemed to agree. His head slipped around as he squirmed closer and pressed his lips to Joe's. Joe's heart thundered happily for a moment inside his chest.

Ned's voice was husky with sleep, his breath warm and sweet. "What did you have in mind? More camels?"

"No. The birds. We can feed some of them and whatever else we can find that will eat seeds. The meerkats, maybe. Some of the marsupials. I know where the birdseed is kept. It isn't locked."

"There's still nobody else here?"

"I don't think so. I haven't heard anyone."

"What will we do after we feed the birds, Joe? Are we going to stay here? Do you still think it's safe?"

In the far distance they could hear what sounded like a battle raging. Gunfire, the scream of machinery, and beneath it all, a constant roar. Angry wailing. Fury and fear. But it wasn't the wail of animals this time. These were human cries. Human voices. Joe hoped he was wrong, but he feared the voices were drawing closer.

"I've been thinking," he said quietly, leery about telling Ned what he'd decided, not sure how he would react. "I have a plan. But first, let's see what more we can do here. Are you rested enough?"

Ned laid his cheek to Joe's. His eyelashes fluttered over Joe's skin. A hunger rose in Joe that left him almost breathless.

"If you are," Ned said, "then so am I. But afterward, what's the plan? What is it you want to do?"

Ned listened once again to the war being waged in the distance. The war that would probably determine their future. Hell, maybe it would determine everyone's future in this one little corner of a beleaguered world.

"I want to see the fighting, Ned. Then I'll know what we have to do."

Ned tensed beside him. "See the… fighting?"

"If you'll come with me. I won't leave you anywhere on your own."

Joe waited only a scattering of heartbeats before Ned answered. And when he did, it was the answer Joe knew it would be.

"I'll follow you, Joe. Wherever you lead me, I'll go. You know that."

"Yes," Joe whispered, laying his hand over the crisp coldness of Ned's ear and stroking it gently with his thumb to stir some warmth into it. "Yes, I do know that."

"I love it when you touch me," Ned murmured.

"Oh, really?" Joe teased.

He slid his hand down Ned's chest, then burrowed it under the hem of Ned's coat, only to discover a very intriguing bulge pooching up the fly of Ned's pants. "You're hard." He chuckled. "And what do you know, you're getting harder."

"Yeah, I've had that little problem off and on for a while now."

"Have you really? And who says it's little?"

After sliding Ned's zipper down, Joe squirmed his fingers through and grasped the warm stiff flesh inside, gently easing it out into the cold night air.

"Oh God…," Ned muttered, lifting his hips off the straw to meet Joe's touch.

Joe bent and took Ned between his lips. At the same time he used his free hand to press Ned back into the hay. When he had him where he wanted him, flat on his back and trembling, legs spread wide, Joe used his mouth to carry Ned to climax. Afterward, since turnabout is fair play, Ned did the same for him. When Joe came, filling Ned's mouth with hot cream, both men cried out, clutching at each other. Joe could feel Ned smiling around his cock, even as his heated lips coaxed the last drop of semen from him.

Afterward they rewarded themselves with a few minutes of cuddling.

"If it wasn't so damned cold, I'd rather have you naked," Joe breathed, still basking in the memory of how hungrily Ned had fed from him. And how hungrily he had fed from Ned.

"Me too," Ned replied, still unable to do much more than groan. His come-moistened lips slid across Joe's eyelid, and his hand still caressed Joe's softening cock, his fingers slick with spit and semen. "But having you like this will do in a pinch."

A dingo howled and yipped nearby. Joe lay quietly in Ned's arms and listened to the plaintive cry. Languidly, as if they barely had the strength for it, they pulled themselves from the hay, readjusted their clothes, and went back to work.

A short time later, they were strewing seeds in the aviary and the individual bird cages while Joe lamented the fact that the big birds, the raptors, would be left unfed because they had no meat for them. When Ned suddenly clutched his arm, Joe stood stock-still, his fist still filled with birdseed.

"What is it?" he hissed.

Ned's voice was drenched in wonder. His fingers tightened on Joe's arm. "Listen! The animals, Joe. They've gone quiet. And feel the air. It's not as cold as it was before."

Joe might have been a statue, standing there in the dark. Holding his breath, he tilted his head to gather the sounds around him. Ned was right. The lions, the tiger, the dingos, *all* of them had fallen silent. And the air too. It really *was* warmer. Not much, but a little.

They stood in the massive aviary, with stairways angling off in different directions, while flocks of birds fluttered about their feet, snatching up the scattered seed. Joe set his bucket of seed aside and stared upward through the arching mesh ceiling high above their heads. In the midst of a blank, black sky, dimmed slightly by the mesh he had to look through, Joe saw a single star, glittering in the velvet dark.

His flashlight clattered to the sidewalk.

"Good God," he said, dragging Ned closer and pointing a trembling finger skyward. "Look at that!"

Together, arm in arm, they stared upward at the single, shimmering star piercing the heavens.

"Light," Joe whispered in awe, his fingers tightening over Ned's. "Look how beautiful it is."

At that moment, as if it had never been there at all, the single blinking star winked out, leaving the world once again hooded in an endless canopy of black.

"No," Ned whispered. "Don't go." But the darkness did not yield. The brief glimpse of beauty it had allowed them did not return.

Turning away, Ned buried his face in Joe's chest. He didn't weep; he didn't sob. He merely stood there, pressing himself to Joe, seeking comfort, perhaps, holding on. Ned's sadness leaked into Joe. He clutched Ned close, cooing nonsensical words, stroking Ned's back. Desperate, he continued to scan the sky, trying to remember exactly where he'd seen the star. Where it had appeared. How beautifully it had shimmered. Oh, how he wanted to present it to Ned one more time. To make Ned smile. To make Ned's fears fall away.

Unmoved by the wants of one puny human drowning in a sea of black, the darkness remained aloof. It showed him nothing. Long minutes later, Joe finally accepted the truth.

The star was gone. And with it, any hope of another dawn was gone as well.

The world had once again slipped into unbroken darkness around them.

CHAPTER FIVE

WITH THE first dawn after all electrical power was stripped from the planet, people learned they had yet to see the worst of what the solar storm could bring. For in truth, that dawn did not come at all. The sun did not appear on the eastern horizon. Not so much as a semblance of daylight spilled down onto the planet to chase away the shadows and bring illumination to an anxious, terrified world.

The planet's day and night were both swallowed now in darkness, total and absolute. The lightless shadow had devoured all. The blood-red haze had disappeared. Even the memory of its pale light seemed to have died in the night.

Above the forty-ninth parallel, for a brief moment during the predawn hours, the northern lights had been seen shimmering like neon in the darkened sky. In the midst of it a single burning star appeared. It was a spectacular show, drawing every eye, stalling every breath. But the aurora quickly faded, the star blinked out, and the sky—and all the hopes centered upon it—were left blacker than before.

In San Diego, too far south for the northern lights to be visible, only one brief glimpse of that single burning star would show itself. Before, only the moon and stars had been buried behind a vast black sky. Now the light of day lay hidden as well. While the air blew slightly warmer across the southern edge of California, as opposed to the more northern stretches of the hemisphere, it was still more frigid than a temperate summer climate should allow. Clearly, the world had been turned upside down and inside out.

And its turning had not ended yet.

NED AWOKE in Joe's arms again. They were still lying on their mattress of straw, but this time they were tucked beneath a dusty padded blanket—the sort of blanket a mover might use to protect furniture—that Joe had found in the barn. Ned lay still, listening to the faint grumble of Joe snoring beside him. It was a sound he knew he would never grow tired of hearing, not if they lived to be a hundred. Of course, a contented old age was a prospect growing more and more remote. Even Ned was smart enough to know that.

Peeking out from beneath the blanket, his first thought was that the air was still warmer, and that gave him hope. His second thought was that the darkness had not gone. It still cloaked everything in sight—or more correctly, everything *not* in sight. Beneath its weight, he fought desperately to battle hopelessness. If Joe had not given in yet, neither would he. Even beyond that, one inescapable conclusion remained. They still had each other. That had to count for something.

His body ached from all the work they had done. He was more used to cooking bacon and chopping veggies than hoisting bales of hay over neck-high fences.

He automatically reached for the flashlight, groping around until he located it atop a bale of straw behind them where Joe must have left it before they fell asleep.

They had worked long hours the night before. When they finally collapsed in exhaustion it was approaching dawn—or what *would* have been dawn if the world were not standing on its head. The birds and the ruminants—from kookaburras to toucans and bison to giraffes—had all been fed. A lot of the other beasts as well. The work had consumed much of the night, and Ned had never in his life felt such a sense of accomplishment, knowing all the good they had done. They had saved a lot of lives, and they had done it all by themselves. For still, even this morning, there seemed to be no other humans on the zoo grounds. No one else had come to help feed the animals. Ned supposed the other workers were too busy worrying about themselves and their families to take the time to tend the beasts in their care. Or maybe they thought the world was coming to an end, so what was the point?

Ned squeezed his eyes shut to empty that thought from his head. Still feeling uneasy in the darkness, he switched on the flashlight and sent its beam dancing across the hay barn, making sure they were alone. He stopped surveying the barn long enough to study the dust particles floating in the flashlight beam, thinking how alive they looked. He finally settled the light on Joe's sleeping face. The moment the beam touched him, Joe fluttered one sleepy eye. A moment later, he blinked the other eye open. Squinting into the flashlight's glare, his first action upon awakening was to reach out and caress Ned's cheek. Ned lowered the light. His breath hitched when Joe's fingers touched his skin.

Joe seemed to like Ned's reaction, for he offered a gentle smile. "My God, Ned. How long did we sleep?"

"All day and part of the night, I think. I'm stiff as a board. And it feels late. Or early. I'm not sure which. But it feels like a lot of time has passed. Could we really have slept that long?"

"I think we did," Joe said, clearing his throat, waking his voice, forcing a yawn to get the blood moving. He coughed up a rueful laugh. "Stress and lugging those bales of hay around must have worn us out. I'd kill for a toothbrush."

"Ditto," Ned said around a grin. "A toothbrush and a Big Mac."

"With fries and an apple pie. And onion rings."

"And a chocolate shake. No, scratch that. No chocolate." He had consumed a dozen candy bars the night before. "I've had all the chocolate I can handle. How about a big, juicy steak?"

"Oh God. Don't toy with me." Joe squinted against the glare of the flashlight beam and glanced at his wristwatch to check the time. "Please, turn that thing off."

Ned switched the flashlight off, and the darkness instantly closed in around them.

"It's almost three in the morning," Joe said, tapping his watch with a fingernail. "Not that it matters, I guess. Day is the same as night now. I wonder if it will be like that from now on."

Ned groaned. "God, I hope not." Once again, Ned tried to squeeze those thoughts from his head. *How can the world survive without light? How can plants grow? How can man feed himself?* Ned dug his fingernails into the palm of his hand, and the pain finally pushed the thoughts away. "Honestly, Joe. The sun can't stay hidden forever. The light has to peek through sometime." Ned grabbed at the only smidgeon of hope he could find. "Did I really see that one little star last night, or did I dream it?"

"You saw it. So did I. I had hoped…."

Ned finished the sentence for him. "You had hoped it would signal this was all about to end. All this endless fucking night."

"Yes," Joe sighed, nestling closer to lay his head on Ned's chest. "That's exactly what I hoped. But now it looks like the dark is just as deep as before. We'll have to wait and see what daybreak brings."

Daybreak. The word drifted around in Ned's brain, lost, as if the definition of it had faded from his memory banks. When was the last time he had seen a real dawn, with golden light spilling across the toes of his shoes, with the hot California breeze blowing through his hair and pleasantly warming the back of his neck? Good Lord, he honestly couldn't remember. Daybreak? Dawn? Morning? What the hell was that?

The darkness pressed down on him now with an almost physical weight. Ned feared if Joe hadn't been at his side, if he had been alone, he would have gone mad staring into it. He would have run screaming into this endless night until he ran himself to death. Like the birds that had tumbled out of the sky from sheer exhaustion.

"I don't think anyone has come," Ned said, tearing his thoughts away to concentrate on more practical matters. "It's been so quiet."

Joe gently untangled himself from Ned's embrace and sat up with a groan. "It *is* quiet!" He held his breath.

"What?" Ned asked. "What is it?"

"The animals," Joe answered. "Even the animals are quiet again."

Ned jerked upright. My God, Joe was right. The beasts were silent. They weren't howling at each other or bellowing their frustrations into the lightless world. How had he not noticed it the moment he opened his eyes?

He gripped Joe's arm. "What does it mean?" he asked, his voice as tense as a drawn bowstring.

"I don't know," Joe whispered back. "But I have to see the sky. We have to try to figure out what's happening. Maybe the world is beginning to right itself. Why else would the animals grow calm again? Why else would the air be warmer than it was? Why else did that one little star appear last night, even if it was just for a minute?"

Joe struggled to his feet and groaned his way to the barn's sliding door. Ned followed close behind, listening to Joe rake the sliding door open with a horrendous rusty screech. Just as Ned feared, no light spilled in. From their vantage point, the darkness was still absolute.

They stepped outside. Ned prayed for at least a *glimpse* of light, a *trace* of morning sun shimmering in the heavens. But there was nothing.

The daytime darkness that had fallen two days ago had not lifted at all. If anything, it was denser than the darkness of the night before. Ned had to grope to find Joe standing less than two feet away.

"Damn!" Joe muttered under his breath.

"I'm sorry," Ned whispered, clutching Joe's sleeve, burrowing his fingers under the cuff to stroke the hair on Joe's wrist. To comfort either himself or Joe, he wasn't sure which.

Joe turned to drag him near. He tucked Ned's head under his chin and spread his hands over Ned's back, trapping him in his arms. He ducked his head and kissed the top of Ned's head.

"We have to find some breakfast," he said. "I can't do anything else until I've eaten. You must be starving too."

"I am. And I need real food. Not candy."

"Me too. Come on. I have an idea."

"Where are we going?"

"Down to Big Cat Canyon. There's a restaurant there I think we can pillage."

"Ooh. Lead the way."

Taking Ned's hand, Joe led him away from the hay barn along the roadway. In every direction, the world was soundless and dark. No wind stirred the branches of the towering eucalyptus trees peppering the grounds.

Without the animals throwing a fit, the morning was deathly still. Even the hoofed creatures penned along the road—okapi, impala, zebra—were silently sleeping off their recent feast, or so Ned imagined, since he couldn't see them in the dark.

Ned followed Joe's flashlight beam to a steep bank of winding stone steps leading downward. The steps had once followed a gurgling man-made waterfall through what was meant to be a tiny rain forest. Without electricity, the pumps had stilled and the waterfall stopped gushing. When Joe aimed the flashlight to where the water once tumbled downhill, Ned saw algaed stones and an empty artificial creek bed. They carefully navigated their way down the rustic stairs through eerie stillness. Around them, a chaos of lush ferns stood tall and green, shimmering with dew.

Their path leveled out when they hit a second broad macadam pathway at the bottom of the stone stairs. Suddenly a chuffing sound tore at the darkness. It came from near at hand, and it clearly came from a lion. Only then did Ned realize they were standing next to the deep pit that served as the lion enclosure. Somewhere down below, inside a deep stone cage open to the sky, prowled three lions, a male and two females. Joe had told him about them often enough that Ned felt he had seen them with his own eyes, although he really hadn't. Still, he knew the tourists peered over a railing down past fake stone walls to where the lions lived, spying on them as they slept and ate and fought the boredom of a captive life. The chuff came again, trailed by a low rumbling growl. It was as if the lions had heard their footsteps and assumed they were handlers. Now they were waiting, tense, ready to pounce on any food that might be coming their way. Or hell, maybe they were as unhinged and as rattled as Ned himself, not hoping for anything, really, but simply suspicious of what the world would do to them next.

Ned shuddered at the hungry growls below. Somehow, not knowing exactly what the lions were up to made their noises more frightening.

"The flashlight must be making them nervous," Joe said, pointing it down at the ground.

Ned scrambled around for something to say that would take away his fear, or at least hide it from Joe's ears. Something normal. Something that might have been said back when the world was a familiar place, back before it blew up in their faces.

He smiled to himself when he settled on the words. He uttered them almost happily, surprised by how comforting they sounded to his own ears. "My lover is taking me out to breakfast. Mimosas and strawberry crepes. Scrambled eggs and hash. Sausage gravy and biscuits, maybe with a huge pile of hash browns steaming on the plate."

Joe huffed a laugh in the darkness, competing with the lions. "Yes, that *would* be nice. But let's not be *too* optimistic. The power has been off for a while, you know. You might have to settle for a couple of cold hot dogs and a tub of potato salad if it hasn't spoiled yet."

"Even better."

Joe dragged him to a stop. Again he hissed, "Listen!"

Ned froze. It was another burst of gunfire somewhere off in the distance. With all the canyons around them, it was hard to pinpoint the direction, but he suspected it was coming from downtown again, three or four miles away across the park toward the bay.

"They're still at it," Joe said. "They're still fighting."

"You mean the cops and those goons with the guns on the freeway?"

"Yes. And I still want to see it."

Ned couldn't believe what he was hearing. "You still want to *see* it? Why?"

"I want to know what's happening. We have to talk to somebody. We have to decide what to do."

"You mean whether we should leave the city or stay?" Ned asked.

"That's exactly what I mean."

Ned edged closer, as if afraid Joe might slip away in the dark. "It scares me to think about it. Where would we go? What would we do?"

"I'm not sure." Joe clutched Ned's hand. Ned could sense him standing tense in the darkness beside him. Maybe he was worried about how Ned would react to what he said. They were both standing as still as they could, listening to the far-off gunshots.

Ned scanned the horizon for a glimpse of light from the fires, but he saw none.

"I think the fires are out," he whispered. "Downtown isn't burning anymore. Maybe it was just one building. Maybe the firefighters put it out."

He could sense Joe scanning the same horizon. "Maybe," Joe said. "We'd have to get closer to know for sure." Joe turned and gripped Ned's arms. "As soon as we find something to eat, I think we should leave. Head for downtown. Now. Tonight. There's nothing more we can do here for the animals. We've fed all the ones we can."

"But you said we'd be safe here. Are you sure we should leave?"

Joe gently traced his thumb along Ned's jawline. His cool fingers stroked Ned's ear. "It's the only way we can know what's happening. It's the only way we can decide what we have to do next."

Ned hesitated but not enough for Joe to notice, he hoped. He trusted Joe, after all, and he had no intention of leaving him no matter what happened. If Joe thought they needed to do this, then Joe must be right. Even if Ned knew Joe was *wrong*, he would follow him. Because that's what people in love do. They stay together. No matter what.

"I love you, Joe. Wherever you go, I'm going with you."

"I love you too. So it's settled. Come on. Let's dig up something to eat, then we'll be on our way."

"Now what do we have here?" a lazy voice inquired from the shadows behind them. Ned heard the ratchet of a shotgun being cocked, and a chill shot up his spine. Joe's hand tightened on his arm.

Joe's flashlight beam stabbed a path through the shadows, falling on a man standing less than ten feet away at the edge of the road. "Get behind me, babe," Joe hissed, the words clearly meant for Ned.

The brittle rumble of mocking laughter scarred the night. "Queers," the man said. "Just what I thought. Now don't move, and get that light out of my face or I'll blow your faggoty heads off. I don't like queers, you know. They're ungodly."

"The only ungodly thing I see around here is you!" Joe spat, and before Ned knew what was happening, Joe sprang at the man. In the careening beam of the flashlight Joe carried, Ned saw Joe reach the man with the gun before the man even knew he was flying at him out of the darkness.

A fist struck flesh and a groan of surprised pain erupted. The shotgun rattled to the pavement, and the man cried out. Ned watched the man's face strobe past as the flashlight banged him in the head. Joe was using it as a club!

With another cry of pain, haloed in the flashlight's beam, the man tried to wheel away and flee, clearly deciding he had bitten off more than he could chew. Before he could run two steps, Joe dragged the man backward by the collar of his coat. Flinging him around, Joe raised his foot and pressed it to the man's back. With a kick, he propelled the man forward, arms flailing, toward the rail overlooking the lion enclosure.

"No!" the man screamed in terror, as if suddenly understanding his fate.

Before Ned could scream too, and before Joe could arrest the man's momentum, for Ned knew instinctively that this had not been Joe's intention, their attacker's body sailed over the waist-high railing and a second later landed with a scrambling thud on the rocks below!

A lion growled, quickly followed by another, and then a third. A second of stunned silence ensued before the man in the lion pit screamed again. This time his scream lasted only a moment, instantly deteriorating into a terrified gurgle before it was cut off completely. Ned imagined the lion's teeth clamping on to the man's throat, piercing his neck, spilling his warm blood, which the hungry lion eagerly lapped away. The horror of what Ned imagined—and what was really happening down below— stabbed at Ned's heart like a knife. He clapped his hands over his ears to block out the horrible sounds. But it was too late. Even Ned knew that. Those sounds would be with him forever.

Joe rushed to the rail and peered over, aiming the flashlight beam down into the enclosure below. Ned ran to his side, and together, they watched the man being dragged away. Already, the two lionesses were fighting over their prize, while a third lion, the male, lurked alongside, waiting to snag a piece for himself.

The man was lifeless now, his head lolling, mouth agape, face bloodied perhaps by the fall, while the lionesses hauled him away by his outstretched arms, back toward the cave in the rear of their pen. Back where the shadows were deeper, where they could dine in peace.

Joe quickly flicked off the light.

"I didn't mean to kill him," he gasped, his voice stricken. "But when he called us queers, I saw red. He had no right to do that, Ned. He had no right to mock us or look down on us because we are who we are. Hell, we're all in the same boat here. People, I mean. We're all… fighting for our lives."

Ned laid an arm across Joe's shoulder. Turning away from the sounds below, he forced Joe to turn away too. "You did what you had to do. And you're right. He shouldn't have done what he did. He shouldn't have threatened us. Did you know him? Did he work here?"

"No," Joe said. "He was a stranger. And—and if he had left us alone, he would still be alive. What a stupid thing to die for. It's not like we had anything to give him. Why the hell did he do it? Why did he attack us?"

He had switched the flashlight off. Ned was glad. For the first time in days, he *longed* for the darkness to come flooding back in. To block out what they'd seen, what they'd heard, what they'd done. To block out the guilt he heard in Joe's shattered voice.

Ned found Joe's hand and brought it to his lips. "Who knows why he did it, Joe? Maybe there is no explanation. The whole world is nuts. He just did what everybody else is doing. Something about this constant darkness drives them crazy, I think. Like those people who threw the burning body off the roof back by the deli. Then they *laughed* about it! Maybe it's fear that's driving them to it, I don't know. But it doesn't make any sense. None of it. All you have to know is that you did what you said you'd do. You kept us safe. You kept *me* safe. This guy's death was his own fault, not yours. Don't waste any time feeling guilty about it."

"You're right," Joe murmured, as if more to himself than to Ned. His voice was still broken, weak. Ned had never heard him sound so defeated. "I did what I said I'd do. I kept us safe. But still. The poor guy. What a terrible way to die. And he was young too. Did you see him? He couldn't have been more than twenty."

The lions were still fighting over their prize below. Listening to them, and listening to Joe, Ned found an odd anger welling up inside. Not at the man this time, but at Joe for feeling guilty about what had happened. He gave him a shake. "I don't care how young he was! I'd rather it be him down there than you. Or me. Let it go. Please. He got what he deserved. He would have hurt us, Joe. Maybe he would even have killed us. I'm not going to waste a tear on him. Neither should you. If we're going to survive, we have to live like the animals do. Survival of the fittest, Joe. That's how we have to think of it now."

Joe took a long shuddering breath. He switched on the flashlight and aimed it at the ground between them to throw out a little ambient light for them to see by. His hand reached into the light and stroked Ned's arm. "My lover, the hardass," he muttered feebly. "You're always on my side, aren't you?"

"Yes," Ned said. "Always. And I'm not finished being a hardass yet. Give me the flashlight."

Joe handed it over. "What are you going to do?"

"I think it's time we armed ourselves." He cast the flashlight beam back and forth along the path. After a quick search, it came to rest on the gun lying alongside the opposite curb where Joe had flung it earlier. Ned hurried over and snatched it up. He handed it to Joe.

"Maybe you'd better carry it," he said. "I might be a hardass, but I'm not hardass enough to know how to handle a rifle. I'd probably shoot myself in the foot. If it's even loaded, that is."

Joe gave a sympathetic cluck, but he took the gun and examined it. "It's not a rifle. It's a shotgun. A 10-gauge pump. A hunting gun. Holds three rounds at the ready." He ejected the fat shells into his hand, said, "Yep. Three," then just as quickly he reloaded them into the chamber. He showed Ned where the safety was, how to click it on and off, how to fire the weapon.

Ned listened politely, looking more nervous by the minute. Guns scared him to death. "But you'll carry it, right? It'll be safer for both of us in your hands. Trust me."

Joe laughed. "Sorry. You'll have to carry it for a while because I'll be needing the flashlight. Just try not to shoot me, okay?"

Reluctantly, Ned took back the gun and relinquished the flashlight. "I'll try not to," he said doubtfully.

Ned glanced across the road at where, by the sound of all the guttural grunts and growls, a hearty meal was being merrily consumed by three happy lions down below. He gave a shudder.

Motioning Joe away, he lured him down the path, away from the sounds of feasting coming from the lion enclosure. "At least we can say we fed the lions," Ned muttered, a wry smile twisting his mouth.

Joe gave an incredulous snort in the dark. "Yes. I guess we can. And now we're armed as well, God help us."

Ned shuddered at the sound of tearing flesh. "Let's get out of here," he snapped, his voice taut.

Without another word, they hurried down the path in search of a decent meal.

Leaving the lions alone to enjoy theirs.

JOE AIMED the flashlight straight ahead. The beam ricocheted back in their faces when it hit the glass door in front of them. Joe quickly turned it off.

"Where are we?" Ned asked.

"The Sabertooth Grill," Joe answered with a smile in his voice.

"You mean a restaurant?"

"Yes, a restaurant."

"How do we get in?"

Joe allowed himself a sardonic laugh. He'd already killed a man and trashed a popcorn cart. How could a little breaking and entering hurt? "How do we get in? With a brick," he said, and before he gave Ned time to argue, if that was his intention, Joe picked up a brick from the edge of the sidewalk and heaved it through the plate glass door.

The crash and tinkle of shattered glass sounded really loud in the dark. Joe switched the flashlight back on, surveyed the damage, and carefully kicked out the bottom part of the window that hadn't yet fallen. That job finished, he simply stepped inside like he owned the place while Ned humbly followed.

"You'll get fired for this for sure," Ned whispered.

Joe gave a mocking grunt. "We fed the animals, didn't we? Even the lions have dined, as you so blithely pointed out. So fuck 'em. I figure the zoological society owes us a meal. You can leave some money on the counter when we're finished if it'll make you feel less guilty."

He didn't have to wait long for Ned to think about it. "Nope. You're right. Fuck 'em."

They both laughed.

They weaved around tables, past an empty salad bar and drink machines, and entered a kitchen in the back through swinging doors. Joe played the flashlight around, checking into every dark corner to make sure they were alone. When he was convinced of that, he sent the light skittering over the equipment to see what they might be able to use.

"Ooh," he said. "A gas grill."

"Meaning?" Ned asked.

"Meaning we can cook something."

"Like what?"

The light fell on a tall stainless-steel door that looked remarkably like the entrance to a massive walk-in cooler, not unlike the one in Mr. Wong's deli where poor old Fred was laid out like a side of beef. "I guess it depends on what we find through that door."

The two advanced on the door, and Joe yanked it open. Sure enough, icy air wafted out to greet them.

"Maybe no one has opened this door lately. The food should be okay. The power's been off for a while, but it's still cold inside."

"Heck, why wouldn't it be?" Ned asked. "The whole world is cold."

"Oh hush." Joe stepped into the cooler and played the flashlight beam around, pinpointing different items scattered about. Before them on a stack of shelves reaching ten feet in either direction lay a selection of chicken cuts, fish, and vegetables. On a far wall, on another stack of shelves, rested pies and boxes filled with cheesecakes and cookies.

Ned gripped Joe's waist and stared from behind while his chin dug a hole in Joe's shoulder. "You hit the mother lode," he said, breathless with awe.

Joe found himself grinning. "I know," he said. "I'm clever that way."

He slipped out of Ned's grip and rushed back through the door. Holding his breath, praying it would work, he found what he thought was the knob that would switch on the gas grill. Sure enough, flames erupted through a bed of fake charcoal. Joe let out a whoop. The grill itself was about three feet square. Back in the days when the zoo was still welcoming guests, which seemed like ages ago, Joe had seen it covered with chicken breasts, burgers, and kabobs, all sizzling away to perfection at the hands of a troop of white-clad chefs with jaunty toques perched on their heads. The chefs were no longer here, but the flames and the meat hadn't gone anywhere, and that's all Joe cared about.

He rushed back to the cooler with Ned outlined in the flickering light behind him, watching his every move like a hawk. Shuffling around through the inventory for a minute, Joe suddenly announced, "Look what I found!" Proudly, he held up a rib eye steak as big as a hot water bottle.

"Holy mother of God," Ned gasped. "I don't suppose you see another one of those lying around."

Seconds later, Joe held up another slab of meat, bigger than the first. "Will this do?"

A moment later, the steaks were on the grill, and while they started to sizzle, Joe and Ned rummaged through the cooler again, digging out salad fixings, a gallon jug of macaroni salad, and two separate cheesecakes—cherry and one strawberry because they couldn't settle on a flavor that pleased them both.

They carted the food to a table as far in the back as they could find. Once the steaks were cooked, Joe intended to turn off the broiler to draw less attention to themselves if anyone should walk past outside.

Joe spotted utensils hanging on a pegboard. Grabbing long tongs, he flipped the steaks. The smell rising from the grill made the spit puddle in his mouth. Waiting no more than two minutes longer, because that was about all he could stand, he scooped the great slabs of meat onto big plates and turned off the flames.

Ned hadn't been idle, he saw. He had set the shotgun aside, and now their table was set with eating utensils and neat glasses of wine with a carafe of merlot standing ready at the side for refills. Their desserts were neatly displayed on an adjoining table so that all they had to do was reach over and grab what they wanted.

For the next twenty minutes, while they consumed their meal, they didn't utter a word to each other. To his horror, Joe realized halfway through his steak—which was delicious and just as rare as he had hoped it would be—that he hadn't thought once about the man he had killed less than an hour before.

Joe stood the flashlight on its nose, which allowed them just enough light to eat by, but not enough to draw attention from outside. Their knees were pressed together under the table, and the clatter of knife and fork was the only sound that accompanied their meal. Periodically, Ned would reach over and touch his hand with a fingertip, as if to reassure himself Joe was still there. Every time he did, Joe felt a rush of pride soar through him.

When the steaks were down to smears of grease and a couple of nubbins of bone, they stuffed themselves with cheesecake, each man sampling both flavors before unfastening their belts and collapsing back in their chairs.

Joe smiled at how handsome Ned looked sitting across from him, his face barely lit by the flashlight pointed down on the table between them. Ned's plate, he noticed, was just as empty as his own. They had been starving.

Ned politely burped. "Great meal."

Joe nodded in agreement. "Cheap too," he added with a smirk. "Free actually."

"That's because it's stolen."

Joe's grin broadened. "Precisely." And for no reason at all, his gaze burrowed through the dark to where Ned had propped the shotgun against the wall by the cooler door. It was still there. His face softened as he turned his attention back to Ned.

"I have a question," he said softly.

Ned stopped fiddling with another wedge of cheesecake and looked up. "Shoot."

Joe sucked in a deep breath, which gave him enough time to get the words in the proper order inside his head. "Why do you think we admitted our love for each other now, Ned? I mean, just as the world fell apart."

Ned sat stone-still for a moment, then answered quietly. "Maybe because that was when we needed each other the most."

Joe gave a little nod, as if Ned's answer agreed with him. "You know, it wasn't when I actually said the words that I first started loving you. I loved you for months before that."

Ned's eyes glittered in the darkness. "I felt the same way about you."

"Why didn't you tell me?"

Ned looked down at his hands, then back to Joe's face. "I was afraid. I thought you liked me, but I was afraid you didn't like me the same way I liked—*loved*—you. I mean like a gay man loves another gay man." Color rose in his cheeks. His eyes skittered away again. "Sexually, I mean."

Joe reached across the table and captured Ned's hand. "Would you have ever told me if I hadn't spoken the words first? Would you have trusted me enough to do that?"

A fog fell over Ned's eyes. He chewed his lower lip with teeth that gleamed white in the subtle light. "I don't know. I'd been hiding my gayness for years. Ever since I had it beat into me that it was the wrong way to be."

Just as Joe knew he would, Ned lifted his free hand to find the scar at the side of his head. He wondered if Ned even knew he was doing it.

Joe smiled at Ned and gripped his hand a little tighter. He was glad when Ned's gaze bravely centered on him, no shame, no doubt, no sorrow. Ned had found his strength again. Joe could see it in his eyes.

"You're not damaged, you know. Sometimes you seem ashamed by what happened to you, as if that day, that *scar*, has left you physically handicapped in some way."

A tiny furrow formed in Ned's forehead as he considered what Joe had just said. "Didn't it?"

"No. You're no more damaged than anybody else. To tell you the truth, Ned, I always thought I was sort of damaged too. I mean, I hated being around people. I hated sharing my life with anybody. It never bothered me that I was alone, because I never felt loneliness like other people did. Well, not until I met you. Then suddenly I didn't want to be cut off from the world anymore. I wanted to be a part of something. I wanted to be a part of you. Nobody else. Just you. It was like a switch had been flipped. One minute I was the same old me, and the next minute, I was somebody else."

A smile teased at Ned's mouth. "Still, we must both be a little brain damaged. It took us a year before we admitted the truth to each other about how we felt."

Joe grinned back. "Maybe a slow flame burns longer."

At that, Ned dropped his hand from his scar and barked out a laugh. "Sure, Confucius. That makes a lot of sense. We're not goofy, we just burn slower."

Joe snorted a laugh, then leaned over the table and dragged Ned's hand to his lips. He pressed a kiss into Ned's palm.

"I would have hated to face the end of the world alone, you know. As selfish as it sounds, I'm glad you're here with me."

"Me too." Ned's thumb stretched up to stroke the bristle on Joe's cheek. "If it really is the end of the world, I can face it now. I've spent time with you. We've made love. I can let it go, I guess. Life, I mean. Although God knows I don't want to. It's like you and I had our dessert first. Now we're ready for our main course and the kitchen is being closed in our faces. Growing old together, Joe. That's what love is really about. I don't want to see this world end before we can do that. I want it to end on our own time. When *we're* ready. And that time hasn't come yet, because God knows I'm not ready to let you go yet."

Touched by Ned's words, by the look of love in Ned's crystal-blue eyes, Joe took a long, shuddering breath. His mind was suddenly filled with the image of Ned lying beneath him, naked, warm, and oh so beautiful. "I'm not ready either," he whispered. "As long as you're around, I don't think I ever will be. That's why we have to get away. Out of the city. Somewhere off on our own where we won't have to worry about someone sneaking up on us with a gun."

"So you think the darkness is here to stay."

"I don't know. But if it is, I don't want to be living in fear every minute. I want to keep you safe. I want to keep us both safe. Maybe we'll have a shot at growing old together yet."

Ned's mouth twisted into a lazy smile. "You're not still wondering if I'll come with you, are you?"

"No," Joe said. "I'm not wondering."

"Should we go now, then?" Ned quietly asked. "Is that what you want to do?"

Joe glanced through the restaurant window at the darkness outside. It hadn't let up one iota. Nor had he expected it to. "Yes," he said. "I know it doesn't look it, but it must be getting well toward morning now. If we're going to leave, I think we should do it now."

Without hesitating, Ned gently pulled his hand from Joe's and pushed himself up from the table. "I'll pack some food," he said, suddenly all business. "You take your trusty brick and visit that souvenir shop I saw a couple of doors down with the backpacks in the window. Get us each one. God knows when we'll have another chance to eat. We'll take as much food with us as we can."

"Good idea."

Joe headed for the gun. Grabbing it up, he laid it across his shoulder, then turned back to Ned. "You're not just sexy, you know. You're also brave and smart and cuter than hell." He waited to hear Ned mumble a mocking "Thank you" in the shadows, then added, "Now what did I do with that fucking brick?"

AN HOUR later, Joe sported a backpack with a big fluffy smiling koala on the front, while Ned's displayed a grinning polar bear. The backpacks were clearly meant for kids, but Ned liked them anyway. They were roomy. They cheered him up. And it seemed a long time since he had done anything silly. Having a full belly for a change was pretty enjoyable too. Ned's pack was heavy, laden with extra food. Joe's pack was stuffed with food as well. Plus extra sweaters, socks, gloves, and spare flashlights lifted from the same gift shop. The sweaters and socks were bedecked with images of animals too. They both wore long woolen scarves wrapped around their necks, with the San Diego Zoo logo knitted up and down their length. The scarves were necessary because it might be less frigid than it was a day or two earlier, but it was still far from warm. Away from shelter as they were about to be, hypothermia was a real threat, so they dressed as warmly as they could. Plus with the world gone dogshit crazy, one never knew when the temperature might drop again. Or for all they knew, spiral all the way down to a brand-new Ice Age.

Ned adjusted the straps across his shoulders. They stood in the gift shop surrounded by all the touristy crap the San Diego Zoo had to offer, which was a lot. Ned laughed out loud when Joe pulled a credit card from his wallet and slapped it down on the counter by the cash register.

In the flashlight beam, Joe looked impish. A second later, he shot Ned a wink, then reclaimed the credit card and stuffed it back in his wallet. "Guess they don't want my money," he mumbled. "Can't imagine why."

Getting back to business, Ned watched Joe tie the shotgun to his pack to free up his hands. That was necessary because he had found hiking sticks, which he said might come in handy while traversing the canyon trails in the dark. Ned, of course, had another opinion. He thought the sturdy sticks might be useful for smashing in a few dog brains if the feral bastards should decide to attack them again.

Ned gazed down at himself, then eyed Joe with his koala pack and tall wooden stick. "We look like a couple of overgrown Von Trapp kids setting out to tackle the Alps."

"Yes, and we're going to do it as quietly as we can," Joe said, "so don't yodel."

Ned bit back a laugh. "Gotcha." His mood just as quickly sobered. "Is it dawn yet, Joe? Has the day begun?"

Joe dutifully checked his watch and smiled up at Ned in the flashlight's beam. "Yes, babe. Somewhere behind all this darkness, the sun is up. In a normal world, we would be bitching about the heat and wishing we'd remembered our sunblock and parasols."

Ned's answering grin was feeble, and he knew it. "I miss that world," he said softly, then added with a snicker, "not that I've ever used a parasol in my life, like you apparently have."

Joe offered up a good-natured snarl. "I miss that world too. Snide gay insults and all."

Still grinning, Joe adjusted the weight of the pack on his back and reseated the straps digging into his shoulders. He reached behind to make sure the shotgun was secure. Apparently satisfied, he said, "You ready?"

Ned nodded, his smile fading. "I'm ready."

"Then stay close. And try to be quiet. We have no idea what—or who—is out there."

"I know."

"And don't be afraid."

"I won't," Ned said. "I'm not. I trust you, Joe. I'll trust everything you decide."

"You mean until I do something stupid, right?"

"Exactly."

Joe turned off the flashlight, and no sooner had he done so than Ned felt Joe's strong hands pulling him close. Joe's warm lips sought his in the dark. They kissed and clung to each other for a long minute, and finally Joe eased himself from Ned's arms.

"All righty, then," Ned muttered, still tasting Joe's kiss. "Now I really am ready. Lead the way."

Joe's hand slid through Ned's hair in a gentle caress, lightly brushing the scar beneath. As if the feel of it gave him strength, Joe turned his back and set off. Ned stayed two steps behind, adjusting the weight of his pack and wielding the unfamiliar walking stick like a cane. He quickly decided the walking stick helped a lot, not only in maintaining his balance in the blinding darkness, but it also felt sturdy enough to be used as a weapon if the need arose, just as he'd thought it might.

Single file, navigating by Joe's memory, they wound their way along the zoo's walkways without any light to show their way. After long minutes, when Joe slowed his pace and began to zigzag around an array of unseen obstacles, Ned was confused. Then the scent of flowers and loam hit him, and he knew they were back in the nursery. The chain-link fence to the outside would be just ahead.

Joe flicked on the flashlight long enough to find his secret hole in the fence, then just as quickly switched it off. The fence rattled when Joe peeled back the flap of snipped wire that constituted a trapdoor. A moment later, Joe tugged at Ned's coat, steering him toward the opening. With a whispered "Watch your head," he ushered Ned through the fence first, then quickly followed.

Joe replaced the flap of wire, crunching it into place, and the next thing Ned knew they were on the trail leading down the canyon into Balboa Park. The familiar piney scent of fir trees lay thick on the air. And something else lay on the air as well. It was a smell Ned couldn't quite place.

"Cordite," Joe whispered as if reading Ned's mind. "It's used these days in place of gunpowder. Creates less smoke and doesn't wreck the gun barrels as fast. The fighting must have come closer than we thought."

"What *don't* you know?" Ned asked, dutifully impressed.

Joe laughed. "A lot. The trail is rough here. Give me your hand."

Ned complied. "I don't hear any gunfire now. Do you think the fighting is over?"

"I don't know."

"I don't hear any crazyass dogs either."

Joe grunted in agreement. "Neither do I, thank God."

They hurried along the trail as quickly and quietly as they could. Ned understood Joe didn't want to use the flashlight any more than they had to, so he did his best to tread carefully and not fall on his face. When the trail grew rocky, or a root tripped him up, he reached out and Joe was always there to offer support.

"The air is still warmer," Ned whispered. "I think it's even warmer than it was before."

"I know," Joe said, sounding cautiously hopeful. "I thought I felt a breeze a minute ago too. The air hasn't moved for days. It must mean something."

Ned peered through the surrounding pines to pan the sky from one horizon to the other, or as much of it as he could see. The heavens were still as black as pitch. That one single star they had glimpsed in the night had not returned. Ned wondered if it ever would.

Joe grabbed his arm and yanked him to a stop. "Listen!"

Ned froze. Sure enough, he heard a faint rumbling noise. It seemed to be coming from far away, like a gentle continuous thunder.

He began to detect human voices buried inside the sound. Furious yelling and screaming. Then his straining ear captured other components of the noise. The metallic clang of machinery. Breaking glass. The roar of engines. Trucks maybe. And once again the sputter of gunfire ricocheted through the air—the staccato chatter of small arms, the heavy concussive thuds of what sounded like heavy artillery.

"It's a riot!" Joe hissed. "Somewhere in the city. The cops must be using everything they've got to break it up. Those loud booms you hear are from stun grenades, I think. Like SWAT guys use."

Fear clutched at Ned's heart. "And we're walking *toward* the fighting?"

Again, Joe said what he'd said back in the hay barn. "We need to know what's going on. It's the only way we can decide what we have to do. Come on."

"Joe...."

Joe turned from the path before him and, fingers splayed, pressed his hand to Ned's chest, as if seeking his heartbeat. "Don't be afraid," he whispered again. "I'll take care of you. I'll keep you safe. But we have to get closer!"

"I—I know. It isn't that."

"Then what is it?"

Ned pointed a trembling finger down the trail. "There's a light up ahead. On the footbridge. And I can see something… hanging there."

JOE HAD been so concentrated on the sounds of distant fighting, he hadn't noticed what lay straight ahead. Ned was right. Down the trail where the path met the footbridge that crossed the freeway below, a pale light hovered, encasing the bridge. It didn't come from passing traffic because the light wasn't moving. But the light didn't originate on the bridge either. It glowed from beneath it.

And in that light, Joe could see that Ned was right again. There *was* something hanging on the bridge.

He slipped his fingers through Ned's, as much for his own comfort as Ned's. "Come on. Stay close. Don't wander off."

"Trust me. I'm not going anywhere."

Joe smiled. Then looking closer at what lay ahead, or more correctly what *hung* ahead, he felt the smile slip from his face like a cold slice of pizza sliding off a plate.

Moving slowly closer, he discerned what was hanging there in front of them in the same instant Ned did. He knew by the way his fingers popped when Ned convulsively squeezed them tight.

Both men jerked to a stop.

"It's a body!" Ned gasped.

"Y-yes," Joe stammered. "It is."

They warily stepped closer.

Hanging from the crossbeam that arched across the footbridge—the crossbeam that the surrounding mesh was anchored to—hung the body of a woman. Her hands were tied behind her back and a heavy rope was wound about her throat, clumsily knotted into a hangman's noose. The rope idly creaked as the body lazily spun in the faint breeze that Joe suddenly felt wafting up from the canyon floor. The woman was dressed in rags. One battered shoe was missing, nowhere to be seen. The toenails on her bare foot were black with filth. A few feet away, overturned on the footbridge, lay a rusty shopping cart, its contents spilling out. Rags. A dirty water bottle. A book, mushy with age, its pages ripped out and scattered about. Perhaps this woman was one of the many homeless who made Balboa Park their home. Perhaps she had once enjoyed the balmy summer days here before the sun took a swan dive and left them all in the dark. But what had happened to her now? How could she have ended up like this?

Ned must have been asking himself the same questions. "Was it suicide, Joe? Did she kill herself?"

"No," Joe said, since that was the first thing he had figured out. "There's nothing for her to have stood on or stepped off of after she adjusted the rope. The shopping cart is too far away to have been any use. Plus her hands are tied."

Edging closer, Joe, with Ned on his heels, took his first step onto the footbridge and peered down through the mesh surrounding it to the freeway below. And the source of light.

It was a car. An old station wagon with a bunged-up front fender and bigass fins on the rear end, straight out of the sixties. The passenger door was wide open. It had been abandoned. Joe knew it must have happened a while back since the battery was growing weak, the headlights beginning to dim. It seemed even the crazies had ceased using the freeway to get around, since there was no traffic moving in either direction. While its battery might be draining, the flickering headlights of the abandoned vehicle still had just enough power to shine upward and illuminate the gruesome scene in front of them.

That thought brought Joe's eyes back to the woman twisting idly in the breeze.

He averted his gaze from her face, turning to Ned instead.

"You all right?"

"It was murder, wasn't it? Somebody did this to her. She was… lynched."

Sadly, Joe answered, "Yes. I think she was."

In the distance, the sound of stun grenades increased. A flurry of them. *Thump. Thump. Thump.* The concussive pulses pounded through the air like frightened heartbeats. Ned moved closer. He slipped a hand into Joe's coat pocket and leaned in to whisper hoarsely, "Let's go back to the zoo, Joe. There's food there. And walls. We can lock ourselves in the hay barn. We'll be safer than we are out here."

Joe pulled Ned against him. At the same time, he twisted Ned around so he wouldn't have to look at the poor woman hanging by her neck from the bridge. "But the zoo *isn't* safe. We were attacked there once already. More people will find their way in. We need to leave the city, Ned. I think it's the only way for us to protect ourselves."

He captured Ned in his arms and pressed his lips to his ear. "It took me a lifetime to find you. I don't want to lose you now. Please trust me. You said you did. Now show me you meant it. Please. Let me find one person in authority to talk to. A cop, a National Guardsman, hell, the fucking mayor. I just want to know what's going on before we make a decision."

Ned inhaled a shaky breath. "All right. I'm sorry. The woman rattled me."

"She rattled me too. And now I think we should get across the bridge and away from this light. We're perfect targets standing here. You with me?"

Joe heard the gurgle of Ned swallowing what sounded like a bucket of spit. "You know I am. Lead on."

Before Ned could change his mind, Joe once again took his hand and led him quickly across the footbridge, hugging the mesh wall, staying as far away from the dead woman as they could get. Not looking directly at her. Trying to ignore her presence completely. Like that was even remotely possible.

A moment later, they found themselves back on the dirt trail, heading uphill this time, climbing the opposite bank of the canyon. The light on the footbridge faded behind them, and Joe was glad to be back in darkness. At least it covered them. It let them slip among the shadows unseen. Amazingly enough, at this particular moment the darkness was almost a friend.

"You all right?"

"I'm okay, Joe. Don't worry about me."

"Still a barnacle?"

Ned gave a sarcastic snort. "Yes, wise guy. I'm still a barnacle."

Moving as casually as he could so as not to worry Ned any more than he already was, Joe slipped the shotgun free from the backpack it was tethered to and replaced it with his walking stick to free up his hands. As he walked along, he kept his thumb on the gun's safety. Ned reached out once and Joe felt the weight of his hand as it touched the gun.

"Good," Ned mumbled. "You're armed." He pulled his hand away from the gun barrel, then returned it to Joe's pocket. Side by side they continued groping their way up the darkened trail. Periodically, Joe could still hear the creak of the rope, twisting in the breeze behind them, its fibers taut from the weight of its gruesome cargo.

Poor woman.

And aloud, beside him in the darkness, Ned muttered, "Poor woman," as if Joe's thoughts had burrowed into his.

Joe tried to concentrate on the trail ahead. It still climbed upward, steeply twisting here and there between the pines. Every once in a while, Joe would switch on the flashlight, just for a moment, so they could get their bearings. As they rounded another bend, Ned softly asked, "Where would we go, Joe? If we leave the city. Where would we go?"

Joe had been thinking about that. "The mountains maybe. Or the desert. Anywhere we can get away from all these crazy people."

"There'll be crazy people there too, won't there?"

"Maybe. But not as many. It'll be easier for us to avoid them. Maybe we can find a secluded cabin somewhere. Break in. Make it our own."

"That would be nice," Ned said, his voice suddenly wistful, as if that idea pleased him very much indeed.

Joe smiled. "It does sound good, doesn't it?"

"Illegal, of course."

Sadly, Joe said, "What once was legal or illegal doesn't seem to matter much anymore."

"No," Ned sighed, "I suppose it doesn't."

Again, Joe sought Ned's hand, claiming it in the dark. "Maybe all that matters now is how we care for the ones we love."

"Maybe that's all that really *ever* mattered," Ned whispered, edging closer.

Joe tilted his head to brush a kiss through Ned's hair and was met with the woolen stocking cap Ned had swiped from the gift shop. He kissed it anyway.

At that moment, gunshots erupted not twenty feet away.

Without thinking, Joe grabbed Ned's arm and yanked him into the underbrush at the side of the trail. He slapped his hand over Ned's mouth while they cowered on the ground, trying not to move because of the brittle pine needles crunching underfoot. They both held their breath and listened while Joe, oh so quietly, released the safety on the shotgun.

"Stop wasting bullets!" a man barked. "You're shooting at nothing!"

"Don't tell me what to do," another snapped. The second speaker sounded young. His voice still cracked as if his journey through puberty had not yet ended. "And there was someone there. I know there was! I heard footsteps. Whispers."

Joe heard the sound of a slap, and after that a muted weeping. He clutched Ned close to him, ignoring the ache in his knees as he knelt in the scrub. Ned's stunted breathing seemed a fluttering fear in the darkness beside him. Joe could feel him trembling. When Ned spoke, his voice was next to soundless and aimed directly into Joe's ear. Yet it was taut with hate. As chilling as any voice Joe had ever heard. Most of all, Joe was astonished by the words coming from a man as gentle as Ned.

"If they hurt you, I'll kill them," Ned seethed in the shadows, his grip on Joe's hand all but cutting off the circulation.

Only then did Joe fully understand. Ned was trembling in fury, not fear. And his fury had nothing to do with his own safety. It was centered solely on Joe's.

They both remained as still as statues, clinging to each other, listening with every ounce of concentration they possessed, prepared to either fly up and lash out to protect themselves, or run like rabbits if that seemed the wiser choice. It didn't take Joe long to realize he felt the same as Ned. He was furious. There was no fear left inside him—only a desperate desire for survival.

And a desperate love for the man at his side.

More than a minute passed before Joe heard the two fools talking again, farther away this time. They were heading down the hill toward the footbridge. Joe could hear their feet scuffing across the dry ground. A tiny avalanche of pebbles scuttled down the trail in front of them. By the way they were cursing the darkness, Joe knew they either didn't have a light with them, or they were afraid to use it.

Sensing it was safe to move on now, Joe tugged Ned out onto the trail, and as quietly as they could, they resumed their trek uphill.

He was astonished to hear Ned softly crying at his side.

"What is it?" Joe asked. "What's wrong?" He didn't let them slacken their pace but continued urging Ned up the hill, hoping to get as far away from the idiots with the guns as they could possibly get. "Why are you crying, Ned? We're away. We're safe."

Ned sniffed and remained silent for a moment. Then he reached out and tucked his hand in Joe's coat pocket again. "Back there, Joe. I suddenly saw you. In my head. You were dead on the trail with a bullet in your heart. I saw it as clear as day. Like it was really real."

Joe slipped his free hand into the same coat pocket and scooped Ned's fingers into his fist. "I'm all right. It was just your imagination."

"I know. But the anger I felt—the anger I feel now—*it's* not imagination. It's still bubbling around inside me. Jesus, Joe, when we were hiding back there in the bushes, I started feeling like all these other crazy fuckers. I wanted to lash out. I wanted to inflict pain. I've never felt such hatred in my life. It—it scared me. It *still* scares me. I don't want to be like that, Joe. I don't want to *be* like they are."

Joe caressed Ned's fingers. He tried to speak softly because they were still moving through utter darkness and could stumble onto people at any time. But he had to comfort Ned too. The hurt in Ned's voice was breaking Joe's heart.

"You'll never be like them. You're the sweetest, gentlest person I know. You only felt that way because you were afraid for me. And I love you for that. But I'm not dead, Ned. I'm not lying on the trail back there with a bullet in my heart. I'm walking right here beside you. And every ounce of love inside me is directed at no one on this planet but you. You're all I care about. And I know you feel the same way about me. And I can't begin to tell you what that means to me."

"Really?" Ned quietly asked.

"Really. And I understand why you got so mad back there. I understand it because I felt the same way. You're not one of these evil pricks running around shooting innocent people you don't even know. You're you, Ned. You're good. And that's why I want to get you out of the city. I want to get you away from all this violence and stash you away somewhere safe where I can claim all that sexy goodness just for me."

"You really think I'm sexy?"

At that, Joe finally laughed. "Don't play innocent with me. You know damn well I think you're sexy. So stop milking me for compliments. Otherwise, I may have to spank you later."

"Ooh," Ned cooed beside him. Then he snorted up some snot and chuckled. Apparently the crying spell was over.

Smiling now, Joe led them on up the trail. Toward the sound of battle in the distance. The air was still growing warmer. The temperature could best be described as cool now instead of cold. The breeze had picked up too, but Joe barely noticed it. His thoughts were centered solely on the battle before them and the man at his side.

He loosened the woolen scarf around his neck and dropped it on the trail behind him. He was burning up wearing it, and if he needed it later, tough. He wasn't about to lug it around. Joe heard the rustle of fabric as Ned removed his scarf too.

"What's happening with the weather?" Ned softly asked.

"I don't know. It's getting warmer."

"Let's hope it stays that way."

A clatter of thunder rippled over their heads, like stones skipping across a lake.

"Stun grenades again," Joe whispered. And suddenly the darkness seemed to open up around them. The ground leveled out. The air turned warmer still, and Joe knew instinctively they had emerged from the shadows beneath the pines. They were at the end of the trail. He could feel the dewy lawn beneath his feet. The smell of old cut grass filled the air. The bocce courts would be just ahead. Tiny still bodies littered the ground, and Joe remembered the birds that had fallen from the sky earlier.

"Watch your step," he ordered. "We're off the trail, and there are dead birds everywhere."

"I know. Poor things." Ned tensed beside him. "I don't hear anyone close, do you?"

"No."

As if he had his own internal GPS mapping out the world around him, Joe reached a hand through the shadows and touched a cool strip of metal as if he knew it would be there all along. It was the children's slide in the tiny playground not three blocks from their apartment building. Sixth Avenue would be up ahead, and along that street to the north, lost now in utter darkness, Mr. Wong's deli would be just around the corner.

"Playground," Ned whispered, figuring it out on his own before Joe had a chance to tell him.

Joe turned to face a shimmer of light on the southern horizon. It was feeble now and came only in flashes. The fires that had been burning downtown were apparently extinguished. The continued eruption of gunfire told him the fighting had not yet stopped, although it seemed more scattered now, less intense.

Joe's thoughts went back to Mr. Wong's deli and the small pile of cold ashes that would be scattered in front of it. The ashes that had once been a human being before he or she was set afire by a laughing mob and pushed from the top of the building in flames. Joe could still hear the screams in his head.

Ned gently pawed at Joe's arm. "I wonder if the deli is still standing. If it is, I suppose there's nothing left inside."

"I suppose not," Joe said.

"Do you think Mr. Wong and Bobby got home all right?"

"I hope so."

Ned stood close. Joe suspected all the memories of what had happened earlier were crashing in on Ned, even as they were crashing in on him. The burning body, the woman on the bridge, the poor young man eaten by lions—all of it. Somehow being back on their home turf brought it all back.

Suddenly Joe longed to see his apartment. To breathe in its familiar smells. Just to know if it was still there. To remember it for what it had always been. A haven when he was alone. Then morphing into a love nest after he was lucky enough to lure Ned into his bed. Maybe they should hide there. But what would be the point? All they could do would be to cower in the darkness and wait for it all to end.

And what if it doesn't *end? What if this nightmare just goes on and on?*

Once again Joe turned his gaze to the southern horizon. To downtown. Toward the battle he could hear raging. To where he was sure he could find the answers to all the questions he wanted to ask.

A blinking red light high in the sky snagged his attention. By the way the light hovered and swooped, Joe knew it was a helicopter. Maybe the same helicopter they had seen as they crossed the freeway—what was it—two days before? Only then did he hear the distant thump of rotors pulsing on the air.

Joe stuffed the flashlight into his pocket. He didn't dare use it.

"Let's run," he whispered, his mind made up. Crouching low, his hand clamped tightly over Ned's, he sprinted as silently as possible across the long sloping lawns of the park with Ned at his side, headed for the sounds in the distance. The gunfire. The stun grenades. The throb of the helicopter hovering over distant rooftops.

They ran like madmen—squarely toward the fighting.

NED INSTINCTIVELY understood by the feel of the air that space had opened up around them again. Then he knew why. They were crossing the overpass on Sixth Avenue that led toward the city center. The sound of gunshots ahead was louder now. *Too* loud. It frightened Ned. His back ached from running doubled over, crouching through the shadows. He was scared and jumpy and out of breath, and if that wasn't bad enough, he was also sweating buckets, even in the cold, and he suddenly had to pee.

The air was thick with the acrid stench of the fires that had burned there earlier. Ned's eyes teared up against the fumes as they raced across the overpass.

Gunfire grew louder.

"It's close now," he said, his voice a terrified whisper. "The fighting. It's close."

Joe squeezed his hand but didn't slow his pace. "I know. Keep your eyes peeled."

Against what? It was so dark Ned could peel his eyeballs like bananas and he still wouldn't be able to see anything. Suddenly he found himself wishing he had a shotgun like the one Joe carried. Then, just as quickly, he was glad he didn't.

In a normal world, it would have been midmorning. Not that the realization made much difference now. The reality of the situation was they were heading into a gunfight blind as bats and probably outnumbered and most assuredly outgunned. On top of all that, they had no idea where, up ahead, the good guys were, or in which direction they were shooting. In Ned's opinion, the most obvious outcome would be for them to stumble into a crossfire and get blown apart by *both* sides.

He was about to grab Joe by the scruff of his neck and drag him to a stop when Joe beat him to the punch, suddenly dropping to his knees and pulling Ned down beside him.

"Cops!" Joe whispered. "Right there!"

Joe was right. Up ahead Ned spotted a twinkling array of red and blue squad-car lights. They were less than a block away, but it might as well have been a hundred miles. The cars were cordoning off one of the side streets. Ned wasn't sure, but he thought he could see policemen leaning over the fenders of the cars, aiming their guns at something in front of them. Only then did Ned hear the voices and cries coming from somewhere around the corner.

"Looters!" Joe hissed.

"How do you know?"

"What else would they be shooting at?"

Ned wasn't having fun. "Crazy people? Armed assholes? Maniacs? Arsonists?"

Joe glowered. "Or looters. Exactly. We need to get to the cops."

"And if the maniacs are shooting *back*? Won't that put us in the line of fire?"

"Hmm," Joe muttered. "You may have a point."

Ned peered around, trying to figure out exactly where they were. Suddenly he knew. The police cars were blocking Broadway, the main drag through downtown. He and Joe were on Sixth Avenue, of course. He had known that all along. But now he could see how far they'd come. One block more would put them squarely in the city's heart. Smack in the middle of the war zone.

They worked their way forward a little more, hugging the edge of a building, then dropped flat again when the scream of turbine engines erupted directly above their heads. Ned's heart shot up into his throat. A blasting wind filled his eyes with dust. Litter swirled through the air. Ned's clothes flapped around him like he was standing in a tornado. A spotlight caught them in its crosshairs, stabbing down from the sky, pinning them to the ground and scaring the hell out of Ned even more.

As quickly as it came, the helicopter passed on. It swooped low along the city street toward the cops, its broad rotors whapping the air, its spotlight shooting off here and there, cleaving the darkness. Ned was left breathless and terrified, but relieved the spotlight was no longer aimed directly at them. He could hear Joe panting in relief as well.

"Holy Christ," Ned gasped. "They could have shot us!"

"Police helicopter," Joe explained, still trying to catch his breath. "They're the good guys."

"Great. And what do you suppose we look like to them? More looters, maybe? Just two more armed assholes?"

Hidden in the darkness, Joe's groping hand sought his. He clamped on to it like a drowning man grabbing a life raft.

"Don't worry," Joe said. "You're safe. I'm here."

Ned dug a pound of imaginary ear wax out of his ear. "I'm sorry. Did you say *safe*? You've dragged us into the middle of World War III. How safe do you think that makes us?"

Joe coughed up an incongruous chuckle. "You sound a little distraught."

The smile in Joe's voice was the last thing Ned expected to hear, and it pissed him off. "Distraught? Really? Gee, I wonder why."

"So now you're saying you don't trust me anymore?"

Ned's anger dissolved like sugar in a cup of coffee. "No," he said quietly, giving in, giving up. "I'm not saying that. I trust you, Joe. I'm sorry. I'm in the middle of a minor nervous breakdown here. Bear with me." He sucked in a deep breath and stroked Joe's hand like he might have stroked a cat. He suddenly expelled enough air to fill a dirigible. "There," he said, "I'm better now."

"You're crazy, you know that?" Scattered around inside the sarcasm, Ned thought he detected a dash of irony in Joe's words, as if he was reluctantly admitting the craziest person present wasn't Ned at all, but himself, and Joe damn well knew it.

Grudgingly, Ned bit back a smile and said, "Thanks."

The gentle moment was lost when a spray of bullets scored the surface of the building they were cowering against. Windows splintered directly above their heads. Shards of glass sprinkled down on top of them. Chips of concrete, like buckshot, zinged about their heads and bounced along the sidewalk at their feet.

"Move!" Joe bellowed. He yanked Ned to his feet and all but shoved him into a vestibule up ahead. They hunkered down in the back corner by a pair of glass doors, as far from the street as they could get. Another spray of gunfire splattered across the building's facade, gouging out chips of rock and sending debris flying everywhere. It was impossible to tell from which direction the bullets came. Or even who was shooting at them, the cops or the wacko fucking civilians.

Ned hooked his fingers in Joe's collar and dragged him close. "Great idea, snotwad! Heading straight into a gunfight! Painting targets on our backs and pissing off all the weirdos just so we can chat with a few cops. That's assuming we stay alive long enough to do it! This was your big plan, Joe? This was the best you could come up with?"

Joe laughed, wiggling out of Ned's grasp. "Wow, your forgiveness didn't last long."

"No," Ned grudgingly sniped, fighting against a grin in spite of himself. "It didn't, did it?"

Out of the darkness, Joe asked, "Where do you think we should go from here?"

Massively uncomforted, Ned snapped, "Vegas?"

Joe faked a pout in his voice. "You're being sarcastic again."

"You're right," Ned said. "I'm sorry. How about Disneyland? It's always nice this time of year. I love Mickey and his big funny ears. Goofy's a hoot too. And best of all, they never shoot at the tourists!"

"Oh be quiet."

Another spray of gunfire sent chips of concrete zipping through the air. A few of them peppered Ned's shoes and he tried to burrow his way deeper into the doorway, like a gopher.

Then a rock the size of a doorknob flew at them. It clipped Ned on the elbow and he howled like a banshee.

"What is it?" Joe cried. "Are you shot?"

Ned rubbed his arm, flexed his fingers, tried not to howl again. "Somebody chucked a rock at me!"

"What?"

"A rock! Somebody's throwing rocks."

"In the middle of a gunfight?"

Still hissing and cursing and tap-dancing around on his knees from the pain in his crazy bone, Ned angrily snatched the flashlight out of Joe's pocket and aimed it onto the street.

"Don't do that!" Joe cried, trying to grab the flashlight out of Ned's hand, but Ned kept it away from him long enough for the flashlight beam to illuminate a little kid, a boy maybe ten years old. He was standing in the middle of the street with a newspaper pouch slung over his shoulder, and by the way it hung heavy on the kid, Ned knew the pouch was filled with rocks. Ammo. He had another rock in his hand, and he was about to let it go right at them.

"Stop that!" Ned bellowed.

The boy was so surprised he dropped the rock. He squinted into the flashlight's glare and had the good grace to look embarrassed at having been caught. If there hadn't been gunfire chipping away at the plaster over their heads, Ned might have actually snickered at the kid's guilty expression.

As it was, he was too mad for his good humor to get much of a foothold. He wrenched himself out of Joe's grasp, and with the pain in his elbow thrumming all the way up to his neck, he hurled himself straight at the kid.

"No!" Joe cried behind him, but Ned didn't slow down.

As he raced across the street, the boy's eyes grew bigger and bigger. The little brat was reaching into his shoulder pouch to grab another rock, when Ned barreled into him, knocking them both to the ground.

Gunfire sprayed the street not two feet away from their heads.

Ned switched off the flashlight, grabbed a fistful of the kid's coat, and dragged him back to the doorway where Joe was screaming, "Are you fucking crazy!"

"He cussed!" the kid yelled, pointing an accusatory finger at Joe while still trying to extricate himself from Ned's clutches. "He said the F-word. I heard him. And you tackled me! That's child abuse!"

Ned growled. "Yeah, well you'd bring out the F-word in anybody, you little shit!" He hurled the boy into the farthest corner of the doorway, narrowly missing Joe when he did. Ned flung himself across the still-struggling boy in an attempt to shelter him from the gunshots that were ricocheting along the street. As an afterthought, he dragged Joe into his protection as well.

The three of them lay tangled together, breathless, pissed off, waiting for the shooters to move on to another target and let them be. When the bullets finally stopping pinging around the doorway they cowered in, Ned allowed himself a sigh of relief. Then he got mad all over again.

He pulled back and glared at the boy. He switched on the flashlight so he could see exactly who it was he was mad at. "Are you crazy?" he screamed. "What are you doing out here in the middle of all this? What's your name? Where are your folks? And why are you chucking rocks at *us*?"

Shown up close in the flashlight's beam, Ned realized he had to alter his assessment of the kid a bit. He looked older than ten. Maybe twelve or so but small for his age. He had fiery red hair and more freckles than any kid should be burdened with. As if that wasn't bad enough, he also had a birthmark, a port-wine stain as big as a silver dollar that spilled down his right cheek. In spite of all that, he was a handsome boy, and at the moment, an angry one. His blue eyes were spitting fire, and he had a tiny splatter of blood on his chin from being struck by a ricocheting shard of concrete or glass. The boy ignored it, so it apparently didn't hurt. Or maybe he was just too mad to let a little thing like pain bother him. His hate-filled eyes swung from Ned to Joe, then back again.

"What's your name?" Ned demanded once more. He was still rubbing his elbow where the little brat had banged him with a rock.

"My name's PJ. What's it to you?" He haughtily ignored the litany of other questions Ned had asked. Instead he took the offensive. *Really* offensive, Ned immediately decided, once the kid began to talk. "What are you guys, perverts?" he growled. "Like little kids, do you? This is kidnapping. I'm a minor. I've got rights!"

Ned wasn't impressed. "Your rights have been temporarily suspended. Where are your folks? Why are you out here all by yourself?"

Oddly, something in Ned's words must have struck a nerve. The boy's blue eyes filled with tears. He craned his head to peer around the doorway. The kid's gaze landed on the massive building standing at the corner of Sixth Avenue and Broadway, right behind where the police cars were parked. The structure was the Shepperton Hotel. Ned had never been inside it. The Shepperton Hotel was a little too expensive for his bank account. Actually it was a little too expensive for *most* people's bank accounts. At least that's what he'd heard.

Ornately gothic, the twenty-story building stood stately and proud, with gargoyles peering over the rooftop. It was so big it filled up an entire city block. At the moment, Ned thought it looked lucky to be standing at all. Tall structures at either side of it—one a department store and the other a bank—had been gutted by fire and reduced to sooty black shells. The damage was visible as the hovering helicopter's spotlight shot across the gutted buildings now and then in their sweep of the city streets below. Ned suddenly understood this was the source of the acrid stench that still hung in the air. The infernos that raged through the buildings at either side of the Shepperton must have been the red glow he and Joe had witnessed on the horizon the last couple of days. Back when they thought all of downtown was on fire.

"Holy cow! What a mess," Joe sputtered, peering over Ned's shoulder and eyeing the destruction.

"Exactly," PJ snarled, trying yet again to squirm out of Ned's clutches. "And my dad's business is there. I need to get to it!"

"Answer my question," Ned insisted, still persistent but a little gentler. He switched on the flashlight again and pointed it down at the ground between them so they could see each other without drawing attention from the street. "What are you doing out here all by yourself?"

The boy huffed in annoyance. A hostile stare too old for the face settled on Ned. "I'm trying to get to him! Don't you understand? You're holding me up. You'll be in big trouble when my dad finds out you attacked me."

Ned frowned. "You were the one throwing rocks at *us*, remember?"

PJ looked momentarily uncomfortable, staring down at his hands before he finally lifted his eyes back up to Ned and Joe. "Okay, fine. I sneaked away from my sitter. I'm too old for a sitter anyway. Dad said he'd be right back but that was two days ago, and I haven't seen him since. I can't even call him 'cause the phones don't work." Again the tears rose in his eyes. "I have to check and make sure he's okay."

It was Joe's turn to frown. "Your sitter's probably freaking out wondering where you are."

PJ didn't look impressed. "Yeah, well, she was freaking out anyway because of the dark. A little more freaking out won't hurt her."

"Tough guy," Ned snarled.

The boy ignored him, making another halfhearted attempt to escape. Both Joe and Ned pushed him back into the recesses of the vestibule, once again impatiently shielding the kid's body with theirs from any stray bullets that might come swooping in.

"Your dad has a shop in the Shepperton?" Joe asked.

"My dad *is* the Shepperton. He owns the hotel. That's my name too. PJ Shepperton. The Third."

Ned bit back a laugh. "And how do you think your dad is going to feel about you running around in the middle of a gunfight chucking rocks, PJ Shepperton the Third?"

"He'd want me with him. I know he would!" PJ narrowed his eyes as if assessing the two men in front of him, seeking a weakness, maybe, seeking a way out of the predicament he was in. "Look. Dad came downtown when the fires started. He was afraid his hotel might burn down." A spark of desperation lit the boy's eyes. "You have to let me go! I need to find out why he hasn't come home. I need to find out if he's okay."

Ned studied the fear in the boy's eyes, then turned to Joe. They shared a glance before Ned directed his gaze at the hotel down the street. "The hotel looks safe enough. Maybe your dad is trapped inside because of all the fighting."

Joe still watched the boy. "Where's your mom?" he asked. "Is she sitting at home wondering where you are too?"

PJ tensed. The wine-stain birthmark on his cheek flared red with anger. "I don't have a mom. I never did. She died a long time ago. All right? Can I go now?"

"No," Ned said. "You're not going anywhere. Stop asking."

The boy sprang up, fighting to reach the sidewalk before they could stop him. Joe grabbed his ankle, Ned grabbed his arm. Pretty soon even PJ knew he was outmuscled.

Furious, he cried, "You can't hold me like this!"

"No," Ned said, suddenly seeing the only solution to the problem and hoping Joe would be willing to see it too. "We can't. But what we can do is try to get you safely to your dad."

He turned to Joe. "Can't we?"

JOE SAW the pleading in Ned's eyes. He saw the stubbornness there too. There was no mistaking it. He shifted his gaze to the boy hunched in the corner between them. The kid was already planning his next getaway attempt. Joe could tell by the way the little monster's eyeballs were skipping around looking for an opening.

He tightened his grip on the boy's ankle, just in case.

At the moment, there were no bullets targeting the building they were cowering against, so Joe leaned around the doorway and peeked up the street. He couldn't see much since the city was still cloaked in darkness, but he could see where the police were by the flashing lights on their squad cars, and he thought he could tell where the looters were by the sound of their gunshots when they fired back at the cops. The helicopter had left. He could no longer hear its thumping rotors or see its lights anywhere.

While Joe couldn't see around the corner on Broadway where the cops were aiming their bullets, he knew what was there. Looters must have targeted the department store that sat directly across the street from the Shepperton. Joe could imagine how the scene must look. With the beams from countless flashlights ricocheting in every direction as the thieves hauled armloads of crap out of the store, then took off running up the street away from the cops to avoid their gunfire. The people shooting back at the cops were probably there to defend the looters. Joe wondered how the bad guys could have gotten so organized when all he had seen before were random, senseless acts of violence perpetrated on innocent people by a bunch of armed morons.

Joe's anger flared. He glanced back at Ned, still cowering in the doorway, then focused his attention on the boy still held captive between them.

Letting PJ go wasn't an option. A stray bullet would find him before he got halfway down the block. Ordering him back home wasn't an option either, since the kid would promise anything to get away from them, and then he would head straight for the hotel anyway.

Joe's eyes found Ned's.

"I guess there's no other way," he said.

"No," Ned answered, clearly relieved that Joe understood. "There isn't."

Joe was aware of a protective fire in Ned's gaze as he stared at the boy. He turned his own eyes to the boy. He forced his voice to take a gentler tone.

"If we try to deliver you to your dad," Joe said, "will you do exactly what we tell you to do along the way?"

PJ blinked in surprise, then let his gaze trail back and forth between the two men in front of him.

"Yes," he said simply. "I promise." Then he spit on his fingers and crossed his heart.

Joe and Ned and PJ shared a glance. For the first time it was almost friendly. While Joe wasn't exactly reassured about what they were about to do, he did feel a little better knowing everybody was on the same page. At least the kid wouldn't be fighting them every step of the way. There was that much to be thankful for. He also knew beyond a shadow of a doubt that Ned was right—getting the kid to his father was the only responsible thing to do.

He turned back to the street and surveyed the situation. Reaching the cops would be impossible. Getting between the cops and the gunmen guarding the looters would be suicidal.

"To get to the hotel, we'll have to go around to the other side of this block," he said, eyeing Ned. "We'll backtrack and get behind the looters and come up on it from the rear." He turned to the boy. "Can we get inside the hotel if we get you there? Your dad must have the place locked up."

PJ pulled a key from beneath his coat. It was hooked to a silver chain around his neck. "This is the key to a security door in the back. Dad gave it to me in case I ever got locked out when he was working and none of the kitchen guys were around to let me in. He didn't like me going through the lobby."

Ned offered up a sarcastic snort. "He probably wouldn't like you joining a gunfight with a bag of rocks either."

For the first time, the kid smiled. "Yeah, my dad's got a million rules that don't make a lick of sense."

WITH GUNSHOTS blasting back and forth on Broadway and bullets zinging everywhere, Ned and PJ hustled back the way they'd come and ducked around the corner. They slipped onto C Street, which ran parallel to Broadway. Here, along trolley tracks that bisected the street, the pavement was puddled with sooty water from the fires, and the stench of wet ashes lay heavy on the air. Fire hoses snaked all over the place, as if the firefighters had simply abandoned them after the fires were extinguished. As it was in Balboa Park, the sodden bodies of birds were scattered about, creating a further nuisance. Ned could feel them squishing underfoot. The street was slippery and a constant hazard to move through in the dark. They trod slowly, trying not to make any noise or stumble over the obstacles in their path.

As it had been for days, the darkness was so thick it made no difference if Ned's eyes were open or closed. He couldn't see a thing either way. Just as he had always trailed along behind Joe, holding on so they wouldn't become separated, now Ned held on to PJ, who was shielded between the two of them. It was PJ who held on to Joe now, and it was like the kid was physically incapable of keeping his mouth shut. No matter how many times Joe shushed him, he jabbered on like a magpie.

"My dad'll prob'ly give you guys a reward. We're rich, you know. He's got other hotels too."

"Be quiet!" Joe hissed.

"Sure," PJ hissed back. Then he rattled on as if he hadn't been interrupted at all. "I go to a private Catholic school. Geez, the nuns are a pain in the patootie. Pain in the patootie. I learned that phrase when one of the nuns said that's what I was."

"Gee, I wonder why," Ned muttered.

Deadpan, PJ said, "Don't know. She didn't say."

"Quiet!" Joe hissed again.

PJ didn't lower his voice at all. He was also making a racket by rattling his bag of rocks like they were worry beads. "Dad's having an affair with the babysitter, but I'm not supposed to know it. She thinks she'll get rich marrying him, but Dad's been through a string of babysitters, and he hasn't married one yet. I'll prob'ly have a sitter when I'm thirty, just so Dad can keep on porking them."

Ned bit back a laugh. "You know more than you should."

"Yeah," PJ replied. "I'm too smart for my own good. The nun told me that too."

At long last, he lowered his voice and whispered back to Ned. "You looked at my birthmark, but you didn't say anything. Adults *always* say something. How come you didn't?"

The answer was at the tip of Ned's tongue before he could even consider what he was about to say. And when the words came, they came freely, without hesitation or fear of hurt. Somehow he knew instinctively that the boy would understand.

"We all have scars we carry around." He fought the urge to lift his fingers to his hair and show PJ what he meant, but it was too dark for the kid to see anything, so he didn't. "Sooner or later, someone will come along and let you see you aren't really scarred after all. It happened to me, PJ. It'll happen to you. Plus, I kind of like your birthmark. It's cool. Like you're a superhero or something."

The boy gave a derisive snort, but Ned could tell he was pondering what he'd said as Joe tugged them on down the street, hugging the side of a trolley car now that had been abandoned on the tracks. Somehow, Ned knew Joe was listening to what was being said as well.

"You got a birthmark too?" PJ asked.

Quietly, Ned answered, "Sort of."

"Look out!" Joe sputtered up ahead, and before Ned could ask what was going on, a gust of wind tore up C Street. It lifted trash and ashes from the rubble at their feet and sent it swirling around their heads, all but blinding them in the process.

Ned could smell sea brine and dead fish on the wind. Clearly the gusts were tearing across the city all the way up from the bay, a mile or more down the hill in the direction they were going.

Ned was astonished to feel the air moving around him at all, lifting his hair, brushing his skin. "Wind! Real wind! I thought the wind had died with the sun."

"It sort of did," PJ mumbled, also sounding awestruck. "At least *that* sort of wind. The air's warmer too," PJ added. "You notice?"

"Yeah," Ned said. "We notice."

"Come on," Joe ordered. "We have to keep moving. I want to get off this street. We're too exposed here."

Ned knew he was right. The gunshots were closer now. He could hear people screaming and cursing and laughing again. It was as if they didn't fear the policemen's guns at all. Whatever insanity had taken over the people in the park, the same madness had clearly taken the downtown looters as well. Human nature sucked, Ned decided on the spot. It simply fucking sucked!

A blast of light crashed down upon the city from one horizon to the other, illuminating everything in a split-second explosion of white. It was so surprising, Ned and Joe and the boy threw themselves to the ground and scrambled into a tight little ball to fend off whatever might be coming.

But nothing did. The blast of light was over as quickly as it came. One second they were blinded by the radiance, the next second they were cowering in suffocating blackness all over again.

"What was *that*?" Ned gasped.

"I don't know," Joe panted. "But that light was everywhere. Not just in one spot. And not just on us. It spanned the city like a flash of lightning. But where was the thunder?"

"There wasn't any," PJ whispered, his face once again lost in darkness.

"What does it mean?" Ned asked, reaching out for Joe's arm, clawing at Joe's coat sleeve. Colored spots still danced before his eyes. He breathed a sigh of relief when Joe took his hand and gave it a squeeze.

"I don't know," Joe said. "I don't *know* what it means."

The boy sounded suddenly frightened. "Come on. I want to get to my dad."

Ned agreed. "Yes. Let's keep moving." He rose to his feet, brushing some of the ashy, muddy muck from the street off his pant legs. Joe and PJ quickly joined him.

Ned had the flashlight now. He risked a quick beam to pinpoint the corner of the block ahead so they would know in which direction to head. That done, he quickly switched the flashlight off. Crouching low, they took off running again. Ned suspected bullets would be equally nasty no matter who was shooting them, so he hoped to avoid the notice of crazies and cops alike. He figured they'd live longer if they did.

"Lead on," Ned whispered to Joe. "Avoid *everybody* if you can."

They chased Joe across the street toward the corner of Broadway and Fifth. As they ran, PJ clutched Joe's coattail, while the fingers of his other hand clamped on to Ned's arm like a steel band.

The next thing Ned knew, they were bunched up together, hugging the building they'd been aiming for. The cold brick wall pressing up against Ned's cheek reeked of ashes and fifty years of exhaust fumes. He had never felt anything so lovely in his life.

PEERING AROUND the corner onto Broadway, Joe could see people now. Looters. They were bustling off down the street, some headed right at them, others veering off the other way. They were ducking low, trying to avoid all the bullets zipping through the air from seemingly every direction at once. The looters' arms were filled with clothes and electronics and other assorted junk that Joe would never have risked his life to acquire. In fact, the whole thing confused him no end. Here they were as a population, all in the same boat, facing extinction maybe, facing the death of the planet. There was no light, no heat, no sun. And certainly no electricity! Why the hell did that one idiot need a new wide-screen TV, stolen or otherwise?

PJ was trying to see past the corner too, so Joe draped an arm around the boy and eased him forward to the edge of the building, just far enough for a glimpse. Two blocks down he could faintly see the sparkling gleam of the red and blue squad-car lights still blinking away. Directly across the street, the Shepperton Hotel stood, with its balustrades and tiers of balconies climbing high in the sky, every inch of it buried now in deep, impenetrable shadow. In intermittent flashes of gunfire, Joe caught glimpses of the hotel. He could see other stuff too. He could see that the crazies had erected a barricade across Broadway with assorted junk—burned-out cars, furniture from looted businesses, and probably stolen stuff from the department store where most of the looting was concentrated.

In a way, Joe decided, the barricade was a good thing. If they were to race across the street toward the hotel on the other side, it would at least prevent the police bullets from targeting them as they ran. All they really had to worry about was the crazy people shooting at everything that moved, whether it wore a police uniform or not.

Joe quietly flicked the safety off on the shotgun he was holding, although he didn't have much faith in the protection it would offer them since he only had three shells. That wouldn't get him very far in a gunfight.

Still, it was all he had.

He whispered to Ned, who was pawing at his shoulder trying to see. The boy was down below, looking out on the street from between his legs. "We're going to make a run for the hotel. Is everybody ready?"

PJ tugged at Joe's pant leg to get his attention.

Joe looked down and saw PJ pointing to the left of the porte cochere at the front of the hotel where the taxis pulled up—back when there *were* taxis—and where the steps led up to the lobby from the outside. The glass front of the hotel had its own barricade in the form of a folded metal grate that had been lowered to seal in the lobby. Maybe a hundred feet to the left, there was a trash can burning. The light it shed lit up a small doorless passageway, just big enough for delivery people to drop stuff off—back when there *were* delivery people.

"See that?" PJ hissed. "If we can get in *there*, we can work our way around back to the door I have a key to. We can't go in the front. They've locked themselves in with the security gate to keep the looters out."

From behind them, a man barked, "Hold it right there. Don't move an inch." Joe heard the unmistakable sound of a gun being cocked.

He whirled around, startled, his pulse suddenly hammering behind his eyes. "Who are you? What do you want?" he hissed, squinting into the dark.

"The boy," the man said, his voice a leering snarl. "I want the boy."

"What do you want with him?" Joe asked, his mind racing, a layer of fear and disgust settling into him like silt. He knew exactly what the man wanted the boy for. He could hear the evil, lurid hunger in his voice.

"You figure it out," the man hissed, his hand groping forward in the dark, brushing Joe's arm in his search for the child. "Give him to me. Hand his tender ass over."

The man's response sent a surge of fury through Joe. Bile rose in his throat. His heart hardened inside his chest.

Without thinking, Joe slapped the man's hand away in disgust. Roughly, he pushed PJ and Ned to the ground behind him. Stepping forward, he raised the shotgun and fired point-blank into the darkness. In the muzzle flash, he caught the momentary glimpse of a wicked, eager face before it exploded into a crimson ball.

Joe didn't wait for the body to fall. Grabbing both PJ and Ned by their coats, he yanked them to their feet and dragged them onto the street. Draping an arm around each one so he wouldn't lose them in the dark, he herded them quickly across Broadway toward the hotel. Bullets zinged past their heads and chipped divots of asphalt out of the street at their feet. Ned switched the flashlight on so they could see where they were going. Its beam bounced around in front of them like a manic strobe light, illuminating abandoned firehoses and dead birds scattered around and more than one human body lying bloodied and lifeless on the street.

"Run," Joe cried. "Don't look down, just run!"

As they stumbled over the opposite curb, Joe watched the flashlight shoot up into the sky when it flew from Ned's hand and clattered to the sidewalk with a tinkle of broken glass. Its light blinked out the moment it struck. Joe's vision was augmented by the feeble orange glow of the fire blazing in a trash can not fifteen feet away.

Still shepherding everyone forward, Joe shoved PJ and Ned toward what, in the dim light, he gathered to be the service entrance PJ had pointed out earlier.

A spray of bullets ricocheted off the hotel steps. Brittle shards of marble from the hotel's facade exploded around them, making them duck. One small chip sliced a burning path across Joe's cheek. He slapped his hand to the pain before pulling Ned and the boy to the ground, where he threw himself over them. Peering out among the hail of bullets, he tried yet again to orient himself to the doorway they were striving to reach.

"Stop right there!" barked a voice to his right. "Where do you think *you're* going?"

Before Joe could respond, PJ spat a curse beside him.

"To my dad, asshole! And you're not gonna stop me!"

A moment later a hailstorm of rocks filled the air, each and every one of them aimed at the head of the man who threatened them. Judging by the screams of pain, more than a few were finding their target. Amazed by the speed and precision with which PJ could chuck his ammo, Joe was tempted to stand back and let the kid take care of the problem all by himself.

But after a few seconds of the man screaming "Ouch!" and "Crap!" and "Shoot that little fucker, Bob!" Joe decided he'd better step in and lend a hand. Especially since there appeared to be more than one bad guy present, although Joe didn't know exactly where he was.

Joe watched another flying rock, this one apparently guided by fate itself, make a beeline through the air and catch the man squarely in the forehead. Stiff as a board, the creep keeled over and crashed to the sidewalk. When he hit, the gun went off and one of his cohorts let out a scream.

"Wow," Joe yelled. "A twofer! Way to go, PJ!" Then he cried more furiously, "Now run! Come *on*."

Joe tried to pull them forward, but PJ and Ned didn't move. It was like their feet were rooted to the street.

Joe turned to see what the holdup was, and only then did he realize he really *could* see. There was light. That's why he had seen PJ's perfectly aimed rock nail the guy in the head. That's why he could see PJ and Ned in front of him now, standing as stiff as statues and ignoring him completely.

There was honest-to-God sunlight spilling down onto the street from somewhere up above!

Joe blinked, trying to understand what was happening. He suddenly realized there was more than light; there was silence too. The gunshots up and down Broadway had abruptly ceased. It was almost as if a collective gasp had fallen over the city.

Joe lowered his eyes to the boy beside him.

PJ stood staring up at the sky, his wine-stain birthmark shimmering red on his cheek. He held an unhurled stone still clenched in his fist. Ned stood beside him, his hand on the boy's shoulder, and he too was staring straight up into the sky.

Not ten feet away, two buddies of the guy lying unconscious on the street were standing dumbstruck beside their friend. They had their heads tilted back, jaws agape, while they gawked at the sky above. One had a pistol hanging limp and forgotten in his hand, his finger through the trigger guard. Lazily, the pistol rocked back and forth. The other, just as dumbfounded by what he was seeing as the first, dropped his rifle at his feet, too astonished to hold on to it another second.

A fourth member of their party—the second half of the twofer—writhed around on the street clutching the bullet hole in his foot after the first asshole's gun misfired when PJ beaned him in the head with a rock.

In Joe's mind, all forward movement of time immediately stopped. The universe hung in limbo. Waiting. In slow motion, Joe watched the still unthrown stone nestled in PJ's fist simply tumble from his fingers. It struck the sidewalk and rolled over the curb into the street.

As if that was his cue, Joe at long last lifted his own eyes to the sky. His jaw went slack, the sting of his torn cheek forgotten. He mindlessly edged closer to PJ and Ned and draped an arm around each of them, as much to protect them as to comfort himself. Together, they stood awestruck and breathless, astonished by what they were seeing.

The sun, approaching noon somewhere on the other side of the endless layers of brimstone it had dumped across the planet, had finally burned its way through. In the uninterrupted blackness that had covered the planet for days on end from one horizon to the other, a hole had at long last opened. Inside the hole, a circle of ocean-blue sky appeared. It hovered there, that splash of perfect azure sky, as if its very beauty had been enough to sear a path through the sooted heavens. From inside the circle, gleaming as white as fire, an arrow-straight beam of sunlight stabbed downward, its edges as crisp as beveled glass.

Joe's throat tightened, and his eyes teared up. He knew beyond all doubt this remarkable beam of light was the most beautiful thing he had ever seen in his life.

"Is it over?" Ned whispered beside him, his voice weak with emotion, his words all but snipped into brittle existence by the chattering of his teeth. They were chattering, Joe realized, not because Ned was cold, but because he was crying. Ned stepped closer, snaking his arm around Joe's waist. His eyes never left the sky. "Joe?" Ned asked again. "Is the darkness over?"

They turned to each other. Joe's heart almost stopped to see the wondrous smile beaming from Ned's tear-soaked face. He opened his mouth to answer, but words wouldn't come. He was too shocked to speak. Seeing Ned's handsome face again in the purity of simple sunlight had stolen the words right out of his head.

Tearing his gaze away, Joe glimpsed the two men left standing who had held them at gunpoint only moments earlier. They were slinking away like frightened dogs, as if the light had somehow exposed them, shaming them for what they had been about to do. One of them dropped a coal-black flag on the ground behind him as he fled.

The man PJ had knocked unconscious with a perfectly aimed rock blinked himself awake. He raised a trembling hand to shield his eyes from the pillar of light and, with a curse, groaned his way to his feet. Cowering, clutching his head, he stumbled off, ignoring the man who was shot in the foot and still writhing around, begging for help. The ringleader disappeared into the crowds who had gathered in the middle of the street. Looters, some of them, their stolen goods lying at their feet where they had dropped them. Others, people who had been hiding in the surrounding buildings, were standing dazed now after wandering out onto the street to glimpse the shaft of sunlight stabbing down from the sky. They too were asking themselves the same question Ned had asked Joe.

Is it over? Is the darkness over?

With PJ still shielded protectively between them, Joe and Ned, their bodies yet rigid with amazement, continued to stare at that stairway of light beaming down from the sky. It was brighter now, the light. Joe had to squint to look at it. As if a curtain had been unfurled, the city too had grown brighter around him. The darkness that had held San Diego captive for so long, slowly relinquished its grip on the city as this remarkable beam of sunshine pushed away the shadows, letting the natural daylight seep back in, filling alleyways, lighting up storefronts, illuminating astonished faces.

Once again, Joe became aware of the growing silence around him. He gazed along Broadway toward the police cars in the distance. He saw cops lowering their weapons and stepping around their vehicles. They pushed their caps to the back of their heads and surveyed the monolith of fiery light streaming down like a laser. Smiles lit faces that had not seen a smile for almost a week. The policemen reached out to each other, draping arms across each other's shoulders, grinning, shaking their heads, holstering their weapons.

Joe whirled at the sound of a male voice crying out, "PJ!"

Before Joe could stop him, the boy wrenched himself free and ran toward the hotel behind them. He ran straight toward the delivery entrance toward which Joe and Ned had been trying to lead him earlier.

There in the doorway stood a man in a rumpled suit, his tie hanging askew at his throat.

"Daddy!" PJ cried, flinging himself into the rumpled man's arms.

Joe watched their reunion with a fresh spate of tears raining down his cheeks.

Beside him, Ned still stared upward at the azure circle of sky peeking through the heavens and the radiant beam of light spilling down from the middle of it. Beyond a shadow of a doubt, Joe knew now that the sun was still up there. It hadn't abandoned them. It still burned, still offered them light and heat, still fed the planet the energy it needed to sustain life. Joe's life. Ned's life. And all the other lives too. Both the good and the bad. Just as it always had.

Just as it always would.

His vision still blurred with tears, Joe stared at the proof of it spilling down.

"It's getting bigger," Ned whispered. "The hole in the sky. The beam of light. They're getting bigger."

Ned was right. Joe watched the city street grow brighter still around him. Shadows receded through doorways, slipped past corners. It was almost as if the city was coming to life again. As if the world was being reborn, the stage lights relit.

Stunned, Joe collapsed backward onto the hotel steps. Sitting there, propping his elbows on his knees and burying his face in his hands, he tried to come to grips with it all. With everything that had happened, everything they had gone through. Ned dropped down beside him and snuggled close, digging his hand once again into Joe's coat pocket.

After a moment, they turned to gaze at each other. Ned was filthy, his clothes a mess. His flaxen hair was so oily and dirty it wasn't flaxen at all anymore. It stuck straight up off his head like he'd been zapped with a Taser. His eyes were bugged out with exhaustion, and he had scratches on his cheek. God knows when he had acquired them. Poor Ned looked like a frazzled, starving coyote that had been gnawing on a porcupine all night.

Joe suspected he didn't look any better. As if to prove him right, Ned plucked a handkerchief from his back pocket and carefully wiped the blood from Joe's cheek where the chip of stone had nicked him.

Ned stuffed the hanky back in his pocket, and they shared a smile. Just as quickly their smiles broadened.

Chuckling softly, Ned scooted closer and rested his head on Joe's shoulder. In return, Joe pressed a kiss to Ned's filthy hair. Like an old friend come to visit, he felt the roughness of Ned's scar against his lips. A surge of desire rushed through him.

Joe closed his eyes. Still smiling, he drew back and tilted his head up to let the heat of the reborn sun warm his face.

Around him he could sense the city—maybe the world—beginning to pull itself together, the cogs of the past aching to mesh again, eager to grind their way back to their old existence.

Suddenly weary of all the thinking, all the metaphysical bullshit, he turned to enjoy the simple sight of Ned watching him. Ned's red-rimmed eyes were tired, but there was happiness shining in them that made Joe's heart stutter back to life with its old purpose, its old excitement.

Joe claimed Ned's hand and held it to his chest.

"Let's go home," he said, losing himself in those bloodshot, weary eyes that he loved so much. And that loved him back. "Just the two of us, Ned. Let's go home."

CHAPTER SIX

THE UNPRECEDENTED solar storm boiled across the surface of the sun for five days, spilling light-killing waste into the solar system. On the sixth morning after the storm began, either by fluke or by the conscious hand of nature, the storm simply ended.

Had it continued, scientists later agreed, or had the coronal mass ejections grown more violent, it might have been a planet-killing event. Even more horrible, perhaps, was what the storm had brought out in the humans most susceptible to it. It was into those with darkness in their hearts already that the storm had cast its deepest shadow. In them, the storm unleashed a curious evil. The inescapable darkness freed and fed that cruelty, and the planet had reeled beneath it.

The returning light reined in the evil. But the memory of it lingered. And that was a good thing.

The real danger would lie in forgetting.

JOE STOOD at the storefront window on the ground floor of the Shepperton Hotel. Behind him all manner of racket and confusion was going on. Nail guns banging. Buzz saws buzzing. Workmen screaming at each other over the noise. Sawdust floated in a beam of sunlight spilling in from outside, which Joe stared at it for the longest time, remembering.

Through the window in front of him, he could see the rush-hour traffic just beginning. Sixth Avenue was clogged with cars and pedestrians. Car horns beeped. Diesel engines roared as a string of city buses trundled past. Christmas music rang out from loudspeakers on decorated streetlights. Santa Claus stood on the corner, ringing his bell for charity, tossing his ho-ho-ho's about like confetti.

Around the corner at the front of the hotel, with its broad sweeping steps climbing up from the street where top-hatted doormen bowed and scraped to the arriving guests, another rush hour was taking place. A horde of writers and publishers were descending on the Shepperton for their annual convention. It had been booked long before the world almost came to an end four months prior, and since the planet had eventually righted itself again, no one saw any reason to cancel the event. After all, why should people let a little thing like the total collapse of society and the near extinction of humanity spoil all their fun?

Joe frowned, not entirely happy with his own cynicism.

He turned away from the bright San Diego morning and cast his gaze inward, quickly regaining his good humor. Slitting his eyes against the dust, he watched the workmen mill about inside the newly leased 500 square feet of retail space on the hotel's ground floor. Mr. Wong had been offered the space for a song. Mr. Shepperton, the owner of the hotel and the doting father of the rock-slinging PJ, thought it the least he could do when he learned that one of the men who saved his son's life during the darkness was now out of a job because a mob of assholes had looted and pillaged the deli that once employed him.

Since the San Diego Police Department had freed him of any culpability concerning the stabbing death of a homeless man, who basically deserved everything he got (even they were smart enough to call the killing a matter of self-defense), Mr. Wong had been looking for a new place to set up shop. When Mr. Shepperton extended his offer, Mr. Wong had accepted with alacrity. He was now happily shouting orders at the workmen in Chinese, which was an exercise in futility if there ever was one, since there wasn't an almond-shaped eye on the premises other than his own and his son Bobby's.

And speaking of Bobby, he was at the moment squatting in a back corner with his new best friend, PJ Shepperton III, the very same rock slinger. They had their heads together, giggling and laughing, digging through an industrial-sized crate of assorted Hostess cupcakes. They had been at it for a while. Snack wrappers sprinkled the floor around them. A blizzard of cake crumbs peppered their clothes and faces, and when they laughed, which was often, their teeth were eerily blacked out with chocolate, which made them laugh even louder.

Funny how from the brink of destruction, life can pull itself together again, Joe thought, watching the boys with a smile and Mr. Wong with an even wider smile.

But the radiance of Joe's *best* smile was reserved for someone else. And there he was now. Ned Bowden. Overseeing the installation of the grill and deep fryers back in the recesses of what would one day become the deli's new kitchen.

Ned's clothes were a mess since he had been working since dawn. His hair was coated with sawdust, and there was a glow in his cheeks that Joe recognized primarily from those moments when he and Ned were engaged in more lively and more *personal* interactions.

Joe patted his heart to stymie a surge of desire that shot through him when Ned looked up to see Joe staring. It pleased him to see the red in Ned's cheek brighten when he did.

Ned turned his back on the workman beside him, and without an ounce of hesitation, wove a path through the bustle to walk straight into Joe's arms.

Beads of sweat sparkled his brow as he gazed up into Joe's face. He hooked a thumb at the racket behind him. "It's getting there."

"So I see." Joe smiled down.

Ned shot him a coy look. "Are you excited about tomorrow?"

Joe pantomimed a shrug as if the question meant very little to him, but on the inside he was jumping up and down with glee. At the same time he was beseeching God every five minutes not to let him screw everything up. He had been suffering those conflicting emotions ever since the general manager of the San Diego Zoo offered him the post of head arborist after learning of everything Joe had done during the darkness to care for the beasts in the zoo's collection when no one else had even *considered* volunteering to help. To show the zoo's appreciation even more, much to Joe's amazement, there had also been a rather sizable monetary gift included. Joe had used that money for a security deposit and first and last month's rent on a spacious one-bedroom apartment for himself and Ned in a far nicer building than the one they had resided in before. As excited as schoolkids on the first day of summer, they had moved in only a week before.

Joe was aching for the two of them to be there now.

"I'm more excited about getting you home and tossing you into bed," he said. "When can you leave?"

Ned's blush deepened, but he didn't look embarrassed; he looked turned on. His erection, which lay pressed to Joe's thigh at the moment, might have had something to do with that.

"I can leave now if you like," Ned said huskily, his fingers beginning to work at the fabric of Joe's shirt, exploring the flesh beneath, mining the heat, obviously aching to rip the thing off.

Without casting a single glance backward, they stepped through the door and out onto the street, where they met another cadre of workmen. They were bustling around two guys in a cherry picker who were pointing and yelling instructions at each other as they lifted Mr. Wong's new street sign into position over the deli's front door.

Joe and Ned hustled out of the way and watched for a minute. Quickly tiring of that, Joe took Ned's hand and led him up the street.

An airliner zoomed low over the city rooftops, lining up for a landing at Lindbergh Field. Its shadow sped down the street in front of them like a phantom, swooping over heads and cars, darkening them as it passed. A moment later, the airliner was gone—sound, shadow, and all.

Ned's eyes stayed on the sky as they walked.

"What are you thinking?" Joe asked, scanning the sky himself. "What's up there that's grabbed your attention?"

Ned gave his head a shake and dragged his eyes back to Joe. They only rested there for a second before they were drawn once again to the crystal sky above.

"There's no endlessly wheeling birds anymore," Ned said. "Remember them?"

"I'll never forget," Joe said, fighting back a shudder, trying not to remember the limp, feathered bodies that had once lain scattered along this very street as far as the eye could see. Or how city cleanup crews had come along with bulldozers to scoop them up.

Still, Ned's gaze never left the sky. "Mostly it's the sun," he said pensively. "That's what I keep staring at. I can't seem to get enough of it, Joe. I keep watching it, wondering if it will slip away again."

Joe lifted his chin, letting his eyes follow where Ned's had gone. As the darkness lifted, it had taken weeks for the full sky to reappear completely—something about the junk in the atmosphere receding at its own pace.

Joe cleared his throat. "Scientists on the news said it is unlikely that what happened will ever happen again."

Ned nodded. "I know. But those are the same scientists who never saw it coming the *first* time it happened."

Joe squeezed Ned's hand as they stood on the street corner, waiting for the light to change so they could cross Broadway and head on up the hill toward home.

"Still, we can't live our lives worrying about it."

Ned gave his head a tiny shake. "Nope. I don't suppose we can."

He resurrected a smile and aimed it in Joe's direction. "Do you still dream about it, Joe? I mean the darkness?"

"No. Do you?"

Ned offered a hesitant shrug, which Joe knew was the same as saying yes. Ned edged closer to Joe. They were walking again, weaving through the foot traffic of other people just like them, bustling home from work. Or doing their Christmas shopping. Or mindlessly roaming the city streets, enjoying the evening.

And quite possibly dreading the darkness to come.

"I dream about the animals," Ned said, the light in his eyes dimming, his attention turning inward. "I hear the dogs howling like they used to do. The big cats roaring. Sometimes I dream about the young man the lions killed. The burning body falling through the sky in front of the old deli. The poor homeless woman lynched on the footbridge. All the bad stuff. I'm sorry those people didn't live long enough to see the world straighten itself out again, or see the lights come back on."

Joe sighed. Ned's sadness hurt him. "I don't like you having dreams like that. You need to find a way to put it all behind you."

At that, Ned let a tiny smile twist his mouth. "I already did. When the dreams come, I slip closer to you on the bed, just close enough to brush your skin, or feel your hairy leg on mine. As soon as I do that, the bad dreams go away."

Joe felt a blush creep up his neck. "Really?"

"Uh-huh."

Without warning, Ned's eyes opened wide. He pulled Joe to a stop. "Listen!"

They were standing beneath the drooping branches of a pepper tree that hung across the sidewalk. In its shade, Joe became aware of a whining sound. He gazed around for the source of the sound, then blinked in surprise, when a hummingbird, its iridescent feathers sparkling puce in the sunlight, suddenly hovered motionless in the air directly before his eyes. It appeared to stare at him, as if tempted to sip the nectar from his gaping mouth. Then with a flick of its wings, it shot off into the air and disappeared.

Joe tried to find it again, but it was lost in the branches overhead. Maybe like them it was on its way home. Eager to settle in for the night, cuddle up to its lover, and put the day's weary labors aside for a while.

That brief moment of beauty cheered Joe up. He took Ned's hand. Together, they continued their slow walk home.

Like the hummingbird, Ned was humming a little song now too. It was horribly off-key, and Joe loved it that way. When he realized Joe was listening to him, Ned grinned and hummed a little louder.

The afternoon sun beating down on their heads was a blessing Joe knew he would never take for granted again.

In that respect, the sun was like the man beside him. Joe would never take Ned for granted either.

"Merry Christmas," Joe said.

"Merry Christmas," Ned softly answered.

JOE'S VELVET skin was damp with sweat, just like his own. Ned slid his tongue over Joe's rib cage and licked a delicious drop of it away. Joe barked a laugh and tried to squirm out from under him.

"That tickles!"

Grinning, Ned lifted his head and rested his chin on Joe's furry chest. He all but purred when Joe cradled the back of his head with his broad, gentle hand. They gazed at each other. Ned could see the contentment in Joe's hazel eyes, and he wondered if Joe could see the same contentment beaming from his own.

Without warning, Ned shivered, remembering Joe's long cock buried inside him. Moving. Probing. Making Ned moan with pleasure. Ned grinned at the brazen hunger still raging inside himself at the memory of Joe fucking him six ways to Sunday not ten minutes earlier.

He buried his face in Joe's stomach and closed his eyes, inhaling the scent of Joe's heated skin, letting it seep through him like a drug. He slid his hands under Joe's back and held him close while Joe's fingers moved gently through his hair. Just as Ned knew it would, Joe's index finger came to rest on Ned's scar. He did not prod it or stroke it, but simply rested his finger there. Protective. Proprietary.

"It'll be dark soon," Ned sighed, his eyes opening to flit toward the window at the side of the bed.

"Don't worry," Joe said. "It's nothing to be afraid of."

"I know. I try not to worry about it. I do."

Ned smiled to camouflage his fears. He pressed a kiss to Joe's belly before lifting his eyes yet again so he could watch Joe's face in the dimming light of dusk.

Joe smiled down at him. His fingertip was moving now, sliding the length of Ned's scar, but gently, back and forth, with infinite care. Joe's other hand rested on Ned's pale shoulder. He stroked there too, gliding his fingers smoothly over Ned's sweat-slick skin, outlining the sharp crease of Ned's shoulder blade. Joe's heartbeat thumped quietly beneath Ned. Or was that his own? He couldn't tell.

"People are nicer now, Joe. Since everything happened. Have you noticed?"

Joe nodded. "I think they're ashamed."

"Ashamed of what they did when the lights went out, you mean?"

"Yes. Ashamed of the animals they became. Let's hope the shame lasts a while."

"Do you think it will?"

"I don't know. People are people. Sometimes they don't seem to learn their lessons very well."

A lazy silence settled over them. In the midst of it, interspersed with the quiet thunder of their hearts and the occasional rustle of bedclothes, darkness filled the room around them. It was like ink being poured into a bowl. Slowly erasing light. Muting sound. Stilling the air.

"Please don't be afraid," Joe said again, clearly sensing Ned's uneasiness with the coming night. "It's only sunset. In a few hours the dawn will break, pushing the shadows away, illuminating you lying there in my arms looking like you've been run over by a truck, your hair sticking out in every direction, a string of drool dribbling off your chin, eye boogers in your eyes, maybe a smear of my come slathered like cream cheese across your nose."

Ned laughed and gave Joe a gentle punch in the gut. He buried his smile in Joe's stomach again. His arms tightened around Joe's waist. As long as they were connected, Ned felt complete. He wondered if Joe felt that way.

Joe's fingertip began moving now. It slid over Ned's scar as if relishing the texture of it. He lifted his head with a grunt and pressed a kiss into Ned's hair. Ned closed his eyes and purred like a cat.

"Ned," Joe whispered.

"Hmm?"

Ned waited a long minute before Joe finally began to speak. Then he lay silent in Joe's arms, listening, held rapt by the gentle timbre of his lover's voice. Joe's words slipped through the growing darkness like the hummingbird that had slipped through the branches of the pepper tree earlier. Fleeting and ethereal but anchored to the world somehow. Blessed by a gentle kindness, Joe's voice was barely loud enough to hear. Still, his words settled over Ned, blocking everything else out.

Blocking everything but the love he felt for the man beneath him.

"As long as you see the sun," Joe whispered, "you'll know you're alive. As long as you hear my breath in the bed beside you at night, you'll know you're safe. As long as you feel my fingers on your skin, you'll know you're loved. That's how the world works for us now. That's how it will always work. As long as we have each other, we'll be happy. I promise."

Ned closed his eyes to capture the words inside his head. He fought to claim his voice from the emotion filling his throat. "Do you need me, Joe? Like I need you?"

"No," Joe said. "I need you more." Joe pulled Ned closer, and his warm lips brushed Ned's ear. His strong hand slid downward to caress Ned's hip, fingers lightly prodding. Beneath him, Ned felt Joe stir, his cock lengthening, hardening, slipping across the heat of Ned's thigh. Ned opened his legs in response, trembling with desire as he hardened too, as his own hunger swelled inside him.

"Make love to me," Ned pleaded, his voice weak, his heart hammering. He slid down in the bed, his warm fingers quickly finding what he sought and gently closing around it.

"It's a little soon, but I'll give it my best shot," Joe breathed, his back arching. He gasped when Joe's mouth enveloped him down below.

Moments later, wrapped together, laughing and eager, they explored each other yet again among the gathering shadows. Only then, in that moment, with their bodies melding together, did Ned finally recognize the truth. In Joe's arms, the coming nightfall didn't frighten him at all.

JOHN INMAN is a Lambda Literary Award finalist and the author of over thirty novels, everything from outrageous comedies to tales of ghosts and monsters and heart-stopping romances. He has been writing fiction since he was old enough to hold a pencil. He and his partner live in beautiful San Diego, California, and together, they share a passion for theater, books, hiking, and biking along the trails and canyons of San Diego or, if the mood strikes, simply kicking back with a beer and a movie.

John's advice for anyone who wishes to be a writer? "Set time aside to write every day and do it. Don't be afraid to share what you've written. Feedback is important. When a rejection slip comes in, just tear it up and try again. Keep mailing stuff out. Keep writing and rewriting and then rewrite one more time. Every minute of the struggle is worth it in the end, so don't give up. Ever. Remember that publishers are a lot like lovers. Sometimes you have to look a long time to find the one that's right for you."

Email: john492@att.net
Facebook: www.facebook.com/john.inman.79
Website: www.johninmanauthor.com

ACTING
UP
JOHN INMAN

It's not easy breaking into show biz. Especially when you aren't exactly loaded with talent. But Malcolm Fox won't let a little thing like that hold him back.

Actually, it isn't the show-business part of his life that bothers him as much as the romantic part—or the lack thereof. At twenty-six, Malcolm has never been in love. He lives in San Diego with his roommate, Beth, another struggling actor, and each of them is just as unsuccessful as the other. While Malcolm toddles off to this audition and that, he ponders the lack of excitement in his life. The lack of purpose. The lack of a man.

Then Beth's brother moves in.

Freshly imported from Missouri of all places, Cory Williams is a towering hunk of muscles and innocence, and Malcolm is gobsmacked by the sexiness of his new roomie from the start. When infatuation enters the picture, Malcolm knows he's *really* in trouble. After all, Cory is *straight*!

At least, that's the general consensus.

www.dreamspinnerpress.com

THE HIKE

JOHN INMAN

Ashley James and Tucker Lee have been friends for years. They are city boys but long for life on the open trail. During a three-hundred-mile hike from the Southern California desert to the mountains around Big Bear Lake, they make some pretty amazing discoveries.

One of those discoveries is love. A love that has been bubbling below the surface for a very long time.

But love isn't all they find. They also stumble upon a war—a war being waged by Mother Nature and fought tooth and claw around an epidemic of microbes and fury.

With every creature in sight turning against them, can they survive this battle and still hold on to each other? Or will the most horrifying virus known to man lay waste to more than just wildlife this time?

Will it destroy Ash and Tucker too?

www.dreamspinnerpress.com

LAUGH
CRY
Repeat

JOHN INMAN

Wyeth Becker is a quiet man. Staid, serious, calm. A librarian. When he meets preschool teacher Deeze Long, he discovers joy for the first time in his life. With joy comes laughter, excitement, and a new way to look at the world through the eyes of the kindest, most loving man he has ever met.

When tragedy strikes and Deeze loses his joy, it is Wyeth who helps him find it again. It is Wyeth, the man who never truly understood happiness, who pays that gift back. Giving all he can of himself to the man who changed his life. Restoring in Deeze what he now so desperately needs.

But the road of their relationship doesn't end there. The joys and sorrows of life are never-ending. As they set out to weather the highs and lows together, Wyeth and Deeze hang on to the one thing that makes all the tears and laughter worthwhile.

Love.

For only through love can life be truly savored at all.

www.dreamspinnerpress.com

Love

WANTED

JOHN INMAN

When it rains, it pours. Not only has Larry Walls been evicted from his apartment, but his hours have also been cut at the department store where he works, leaving him facing homelessness.

Meanwhile, Bo Lansing, a total stranger to Larry, toils at a dead-end job as a fry cook while attending night classes to become a certified chef. When the school closes its doors without warning, leaving Bo in the lurch for thousands of dollars in tuition, his dream of becoming a chef is shattered and his financial troubles spiral.

Desperate for a new beginning, each man answers an ad for live-in help posted by a wealthy recluse, and wonder of wonders, they are both hired! Just as their lives begin to improve, a young Kumeyaay Indian named Jimmy Blackstone joins the workforce at the Stanhope mansion.

When Mr. Stanhope's true reason for hiring the young men is discovered by one of the three, a fourth entity makes its presence known.

Greed.

With all these players vying for position in a game of intrigue orchestrated by one lonely old man and a mischievous ghost, can a simple thing like love ever hope to survive the fray?

www.dreamspinnerpress.com

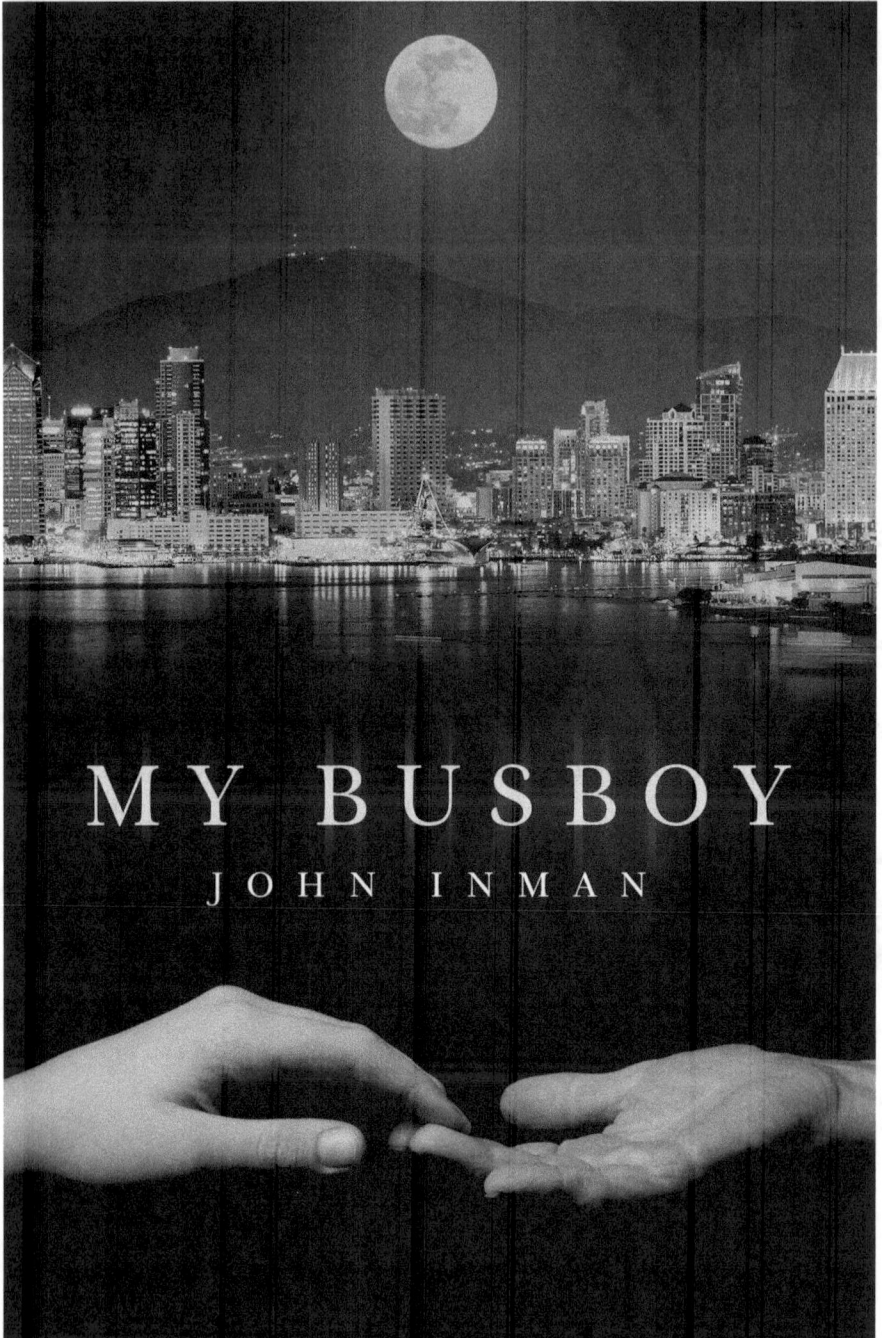

MY BUSBOY

JOHN INMAN

Robert Johnny just turned thirty, and his life is pretty much in the toilet. His writing career is on the skids. His love life is nonexistent. A stalker is driving him crazy. And his cat is a pain in the ass.

Then Robert orders a chimichanga platter at a neighborhood restaurant, and his life changes—just like that.

Dario Martinez isn't having such a great existence either. He needs money for college. His shoes are falling apart. His boyfriend's a dick. And he has a crap job as a busboy.

Then a stranger orders a chimichanga platter, and suddenly life isn't quite as depressing.

But it's the book in the busboy's back pocket that really gets the ball rolling. For both our heroes. That and the black eye and the forgotten bowl of guacamole. Who knew true love could be so easily ignited or that the flames would spread so quickly?

But when Robert's stalker gets dangerous, our two heroes find a lot more to occupy their time than falling in love. Staying alive might become the new game plan.

www.dreamspinnerpress.com

MY DRAGON, MY KNIGHT

John Inman

Danny Sims is in over his head, torn between his abusive lover, Joshua, and Jay Holtsclaw, the bartender up the street, who offers Danny the one thing he never gets at home: understanding.

When Joshua threatens to get rid of Danny's terrier, Danny knows he has to act fast. Afraid of what Joshua will do to the dog and afraid of what Joshua will do to *him* if he tries to leave, Danny does the only thing he can do.

He runs.

But Danny isn't a complete fool. He has enough sense to run into the arms of the man who actually cares for him—the man he's beginning to trust.

Just as their lives together are starting to fall into place, Danny and Jay learn how vengeful Joshua can be.

And how dangerous.

www.dreamspinnerpress.com